Tales from Above and Beyond

Tales from Above and Beyond

SHAYA GOTTLIEB

THE JUDAICA PRESS, INC.

Tales from Above and Beyond
© 2009 SHAYA GOTTLIEB

ISBN: 978-1-60763-017-3

Editor: Toby Cohen
Proofreader: Hadassa Goldsmith
Cover design: Rich Kim
Internal design and layout: Justine Elliott

THE JUDAICA PRESS, INC.
123 Ditmas Avenue / Brooklyn, NY 11218
718-972-6200 / 800-972-6201
info@judaicapress.com
www.judaicapress.com

Manufactured in the United States of America

DEDICATION

With humble gratitude to the One Above,
Who has granted me the priceless gift of words and the
opportunity to publish this volume. May these stories
of the spirit bring us closer to an appreciation of our
holy ancestors and a recognition of their greatness.

CONTENTS

A
COLD CUP
of
COFFEE

*I*n *Koshnitz,* there lived a worthy man by the name of Reb Meilech who was known by the beloved title "Reb Meilich the *Chassid.*" He was a pious, devout Jew, who spent his days and nights learning Torah with great devotion. Yet there were countless others who learned just as intensely. What was so special about Reb Meilech that he was called "the *Chassid*"?

Reb Meilech was orphaned as a young boy and lived alone with his widowed mother. Though they were impoverished, living from hand to mouth, his mother cherished and cared for him as the apple of her eye. As he matured and blossomed into a *talmid chacham,* she attended to all his needs so he could learn undisturbed. Every single day, she cooked him a nourishing meal to give him the strength to continue serving Hashem. Were it not for his mother's admonishments that he eat, Meilech would have fasted for days on end since physical comforts meant little to him. But fulfilling the mitzvah of "*kibud eim*" was another story.

Reb Meilech's mother scrimped and saved to marry him off, and even after his wedding she supported the couple so that her son could continue to learn.

The winds of war and unrest began blowing through Poland and the army was in desperate need of soldiers. Bands of recruiters marched from town to town, dragging away young men to join the army. Once an able-bodied man was drafted into the army, he knew that the best years of his life were over. Even if he survived the dangers of the front lines, he would remain in the army for years on end, far away from his family or any Jewish community.

One day, the news spread through Koshnitz: The soldiers were on their way to draft young men to the army. All able-bodied men quickly scrambled to hide in cellars, attics, outhouse sheds or deep in the woods, until the danger would pass. But Meilech, the *talmid chacham,* was unconcerned. He remained immersed in his learning, as though nothing out of the ordinary was about to occur.

The day that the recruiters from the Polish army arrived in Koshnitz was a routine one for Reb Meilech. He awoke at dawn, immersed in the *mikvah* and hurried to shul to daven with a *minyan*. His mind was occupied with sublime thoughts, and he paid no heed to the people scurrying to hide. People were so agitated and intent on escaping from the danger that no one noticed Meilech's odd lack of concern about being caught on the street.

So there was Meilech going to shul in the predawn, head bent, thoughts a million miles away, when suddenly a loud, raucous shout interrupted his thoughts. "Halt! Stay right there! Don't run if you value your life!" A coarse Polish soldier, gun drawn, grabbed Meilech as if he were a piece of meat and roughly shoved him along. "Come with me! You are about to become a soldier in the Polish army!"

Before Reb Meilech had a chance to digest what was happening, he was roughly thrust into a wagon filled with peasants and one other Jew, who had also not managed to escape in time.

The wagon quickly filled and the horses galloped away, heading to a local army barracks where they would be formed into battalions, trained and sent to a distant camp to serve in the army for twelve years.

The streets were empty of Jews — but there were dozens of Jewish women peeking from behind their shutters who had witnessed the scene. As soon as the recruiters left town with their catch, the women rushed to the elderly widow to tell her the heartbreaking news: Her precious jewel Meilech was among those who had been snatched.

The cries of the young wife, who heard that her husband had been taken, rent the heavens, and Meilech's mother nearly fainted when she heard the news. But she managed to remain coherent as she raced to the home of the Koshnitzer Maggid. Only the Maggid's *tefillos* could save her son. She knew that other avenues of escape would be futile.

Though the widow knew it was highly improper to burst into the Rebbe's study without a prior appointment, her anguish over her son lent desperation to her actions.

"Holy Rebbe!" she cried as she burst into the study, without knocking. "My precious son Meilech has been snatched away to join the Polish army. Rebbe, your precious *chassid* has been taken!"

The Maggid listened to the widow's anguished cries and softly said, "Do not worry. Meilech the *Chassid* will never be a soldier in the Polish army."

"When will I see my precious son again?" sobbed the widow.

"Don't worry," said the Maggid once more. He gestured to the cup of coffee his Rebbitzen had prepared for him. "I will not drink this coffee until Meilich is home, safe and sound."

The widow emerged from the Maggid's study, beaming with joy. She excitedly related the news to the women who stood outside, waiting for the results of her visit. "The Rebbe says my Meilech will return before he drinks his coffee."

The news spread through Koshnitz, and a group of people ran to the outskirts of the city to wait for the return of Meilech the *talmid chacham*. Such was the strength of their *emunas chachamim* in those days.

As the sun slowly rose in her full glory, the *chassidim* could see two figures from afar: Reb Meilech and the other Yid who had been captured were slowly trudging toward the city.

"Rebbe!" the *gabbai* ran into the Maggid's study. "The Rebbe can drink the coffee. Meilech is coming."

"I said that I will not drink the coffee until Meilech is home," the Maggid reiterated, "and he is not here yet."

Another thirty minutes passed, and Meilech was standing at the door to the Maggid's home, weary and exhausted, the other Jew at his side. Immediately, Meilich was surrounded by crowds of excited *chassidim*, demanding to know what had occurred.

When the Maggid saw Meilech, he beamed as he greeted him. "Ah, Meilech!" he said, his holy face shining with joy. "Because of your stubbornness, my coffee became cold!" He drew the young man into his study and closed the door.

The *chassidim* glanced at each other in confusion. What was the Rebbe referring to?

When Reb Meilech had emerged from the Rebbe's study, he related the entire tale:

"As soon as we left the city limits, the horses began galloping at a dizzying pace, and I realized it was impossible to jump off the wagon because that would be tantamount to suicide.

"Suddenly, an elderly man with a long, white beard appeared before me and said, 'What are you waiting for? Jump off the wagon while it is yet dark and no one will notice you. I promise no harm shall befall you.'

"I immediately realized this elderly man had been sent to save me," said Reb Meilech with sincerity. "However, there was another Yid with me, and I refused to leave him at the mercy of his captors. So I said to the elderly Yid, 'I will not leave this wagon unless the other Yid comes with me.'

"Replied the elderly man, 'I do not have responsibility for the other Yid. I was not sent to save him. Come, jump out of the wagon now!'

"'If he cannot come with me, then I will not go!' I replied firmly. The man disappeared and the wagon continued to speed ahead.

"A few minutes later, the old man reappeared once more and said to me in a stern voice, 'Meilich, do you realize what you are doing? Jump off this wagon right now if you value your life. This is the only way you can be saved.'

"I pointed to the other Yid and said to the old man, 'Only with him! Otherwise, I am staying here.' The old man gave up trying to persuade me and disappeared.

"Shortly thereafter, he reappeared a third time trying to persuade me, but I refused to change my mind. All this time, the wagon was carrying me farther away and closer to my doom.

"The fourth time he came, I won the battle!" said Reb Meilech triumphantly. "While the old man watched, I held onto the other Yid and we jumped off the wagon together. We rolled into a ditch and stood up, unharmed. The wagon sped off in the distance, with no one being the wiser. By the time we got our bearings, the old man had disappeared. We quickly ran the four miles back to Koshnitz, and as you can see, arrived safe and sound, *baruch Hashem.*"

Now the *chassidim* realized the meaning of the Rebbe's words, "Because of your stubbornness ..." Were it not for Reb Meilech's insistence on taking the other Yid with him, he could have been home long ago.

"Reb Meilich's self-sacrifice," said the Rebbe, "in refusing to escape without taking his fellow Jew, too, was what earned him the title 'Reb Meilech the *Chassid.*' "

SAVED
by the
MINYAN

*R*eb *Yankel* sat in his wheelchair at Tiferes Avos, the well-known seniors' home, smoking a cigarette. "At my age, cigarette smoke won't kill me," he jokingly told his horrified visitors. "And if Hashem sees fit to take me away, well, I've lived a full life, outlived my wife and two of my children, and I'll go without complaints."

Thus spoke this spry, wrinkled man in his nineties. With his perpetual good humor and wisecracks, Yankel was the favorite of the home care aides and enjoyed entertaining visitors every afternoon. He regaled the neighborhood children with hair-raising tales of his life under the Bolsheviks, when he had been a successful businessman in the fur industry.

Yankel was a treasure-house of stories. He had a tale for every occasion, every listener, every development in current affairs. When local elections were held, Yankel insisted on voting, his loyal visitors pushing him to the polling station in his wheelchair. "We can't ignore what's happening in the world around us," he would tell his eager audience. "*Hakol bishvil Yisrael*. Everything happens because of *Klal Yisrael*. The *Ribono shel Olam* orchestrates events in the world to benefit His chosen nation."

And then he would launch into his favorite tale, the tale of the *minyan*. Though he must have repeated it a thousand times, Yankel never tired of the story because it was the story that gave him life.

"So let me tell you the tale, *kinderlach*," he would wheeze between puffs of his cigarette. "Don't stand so close to my wheelchair. I don't want you to breathe the second-hand smoke. There. That's better. Okay. Listen carefully and I'll begin."

It was in the early 1900s, several years before Lenin's "vision" of Communism had taken hold, before Stalin had spread his net of terror. It was the era of the Bolsheviks, those bloodthirsty rulers who used the pogrom to subdue the terrified citizens.

These were uncertain days for the Jews in the Pale of Settlement, who didn't know what the next day would bring. One day, we could be sitting in our homes with our families, and the next, we could be driven out with only the clothes on our backs — if we were lucky. Entire communities could be expelled — or be cruelly butchered by the Bolsheviks. But the brunt of their wrath was reserved for the businessmen — successful Jews. Woe to the businessman who caught the attention of a jealous official. His end would be bitter, indeed.

At the time, I was a young man, the father of two little children with a wife, who all depended on me for *parnassah*. Thus, with a combination of daring, not to mention a heaping dose of *siyata d'Shmaya*, I invested my entire dowry into the fur industry. Soon I opened a little shop where I sold my furs. I had a small group of employees who refined the raw furs and prepared them to be sold.

Within a short time, *hatzlachah* shone on my endeavors. Business was booming, and before long, I became a wealthy man. But along with my newfound wealth came a fresh set of worries: How long before the Bolsheviks heard of my success? How long before I became their latest victim?

Well, I didn't have the luxury of too much time to spend worrying. I was a busy man and spent many hours in the office, supervising my employees and seeing to my accounts. I always attended a *shiur* at night, though I was often so exhausted that it was difficult to stay awake.

Anyway, the winter season was always busy since the demand for elegant furs rose. I spent many hours in the shop, going early in the morning and not coming home until late at night.

One icy morning, I woke especially early and rushed to daven with the first *minyan*. I was in a great hurry, as a large order was due that afternoon. My customer, a famous Bolshevik, had demanded the furs immediately to trim his wife's suit for a party he was hosting.

As soon as I finished davening, I rushed out of shul down the main street, passing several other *shteiblach* as I made my way to the train station. I had to catch the first train to the business district, where my shop was located.

As I passed a small *shteibel*, a middle-aged, anxious man suddenly flagged me down.

"*Ah tzenter* for *minyan*!" he called.

I tried to pass him, but he blocked my way.

"*Ah tzenter*! Please come join my *minyan*!"

"But I davened already," I protested.

"Oh … but I have *yahrtzeit* for my father! You *must* help me."

"I'm in a very big rush," I said, breaking away. "I have to be in my office in a half hour. I have an important business deadline."

He grabbed hold of me with incredible *chutzpah*. "What can be more important than helping me complete my *minyan*?" he asked.

"Okay, okay, you win," I muttered, following him inside. I was certain there would be eight others waiting and we would begin right away. However, to my utter dismay, there were only four other men inside.

"What is this?" I demanded angrily. "How dare you mislead me! We are only six men! You need another four. I am leaving right away!"

Quick as a wink, he blocked the doorway. "You are going nowhere," he said. "I have *yahrtzeit* for my father and I must have a *minyan*. If you wait here patiently, I will find a *minyan* before long."

"But I have a business deadline," I sputtered. "Please find someone else."

He gave me a long, hard look. "If you had *yahrtzeit* for your father, wouldn't you want me to stay?" he asked.

That clinched it. Instead of focusing on my own impatience, I decided to look at the situation from his point of view. He wasn't being selfish nor taking advantage of me. All he wanted to do was honor his father.

In any case, I reasoned, *Shluchei mitzvah ainan nizokin — those on mitzvah missions are protected from harm.* And in that unstable political climate, I needed all the protection I could get.

So I sat down to wait, drumming my hands impatiently on the table. The other men who were assembled didn't look like businessmen to me. In fact, they appeared to be wanderers, unemployed men with plenty of time to spare. The long wait didn't disturb them. At least they were in a warm building, and there would probably be some cake and *schnapps* after the *minyan*.

While I waited, my "kidnapper" stood outside, trying to lure others into the *shteibel* with threats and pleas. I opened a *gemara* and began to learn a little, willing myself to forget about my deadline and about my numerous responsibilities at the office. "Being nervous won't help anyway," I reasoned, "so I might as well enjoy this breather."

While I sat and learned, three more men trickled inside, and soon we were only missing one man for the *minyan*. Now I decided to help the mystery "*Kaddish* man" and went outside with him, yelling "*ah tzenter!*"

Finally, a tenth straggler was persuaded to join our *minyan*. I stood impatiently as they began to daven, slowly and with great concentration.

Can't they rush a little? I thought, annoyed. Just when I was in a great hurry, they had to daven like they had the rest of the day to spend in shul.

The davening continued at a slow and leisurely pace. Our *minyan* man reveled in every *amein*, in every *Kaddish*, drawing out the words slowly with a special *niggun*.

Finally, nearly two hours after I had been waylaid, the *minyan* was over. The "*Kaddish* man" thanked me warmly and tried to persuade me to partake of the *tikkun:* a meager spread of egg *kichel* and some vodka.

"No, thanks," I answered curtly. "As I told you, I have an important business deadline. Good day."

I raced out of the *shteibel* toward the train station, desperately wishing time could stand still. I had to wait ten minutes for the train, and when it finally came, it was nearly empty. I was surprised; usually, the train to the business district was crowded. What was going on?

During the train ride, I contemplated the scenario I had just witnessed. Here was a group of men who spent nearly two hours doing a chesed for someone — I still didn't know his name — who had *yahrtzeit* for his father. Granted, most of them were unemployed, but still, there were those who may have had other commitments, and giving away so much time was a true mitzvah. And perhaps, I thought to myself, we were the ones who gained most of all.

The train drew up at the business district station, and I quickly disembarked and hurried toward the bustling streets of the district. To my great surprise, the streets were deserted. Now I was positive something had happened. I sprinted the two blocks to my office building, my heart hammering in fear.

There was an ominous air about the gray, somber buildings. The place seemed deserted, but as I scanned the buildings, I saw vague outlines of people behind their curtains, peeking fearfully out. What had happened? Where was the usual traffic? Where were all the businessmen?

I rounded a corner and a chill rose up my spine. An old gentile acquaintance, a former client of mine, came racing toward me, a look of abject terror in his eyes.

"You! You're still alive?" he demanded. "I thought you were dead!"

"W-what happened?" I mouthed, my heart hammering in terror.

"Don't you know? This morning, an hour after opening time, the Bolsheviks surrounded your entire office block. Armed with knives, guns and axes, they stormed through all the offices, killing every Jew they met. They ransacked all the shops and are now drinking vodka, rejoicing at the Jewish blood flowing into the street!"

"W-what about Velvel?" I stammered. Velvel was my able office assistant who frequently filled in for me during an emergency.

"I don't know what happened to your employees," he said, averting his eyes, "but I wouldn't go there if I were you. The Bolsheviks are still lying in wait for the latecomers."

As we spoke, I heard an ominous rumble. A group of drunken Bolsheviks was headed our way. I turned and sped back to the train station, catching the next train home.

My wife greeted me at the door, her eyes brimming with tears.

"Yankel!" she screamed. "You're still alive! *Baruch Hashem!* We've been hearing awful tales! They say the Bolsheviks staged a *pogrom* in town. I have been saying *Tehillim* and davening that you be spared."

"*Chasdei Hashem*, I never got near the office today," I told her, "thanks to a stranger who had *yahrtzeit* for his father." And I related the entire tale.

"You must go thank him for saving your life," said my wife. And she was right.

Despite the danger, I rushed out again to the *shteibel* where I had spent all morning taking part in a *minyan*. When I arrived, there were a few beggars there eating the leftovers from the *tikkun*, but I could find no one from the original *minyan*.

"Where is the man who had *yahrtzeit* today for his father?" I inquired.

"What man?" they asked me. "Who had *yahrtzeit* today?"

"The man who brought the *tikkun*," I said, pointing to the *kichel* they were consuming.

One man shrugged his shoulders. "How would I know?" he asked. "Nobody was here when I came."

Despite numerous inquiries, I was unable to discover who that man was. Then I began to have a suspicion … perhaps the man was none other than Eliyahu Hanavi who had come to save my life.

Anyway, I'm sure you want to know the end of the story. I stayed home for several days, waiting until the Bolsheviks had dispersed. Then came the gruesome task of going to the office building with the police, to assess the casualties. Sadly, many of my employees, including my loyal assistant Velvel, had been butchered, may Hashem avenge their blood. Few managed to escape.

We buried the dead in the Jewish cemetery and mourned their untimely deaths. Then I inventoried the destroyed business, trying to salvage whatever was left, and quietly left the blood-soaked city. I moved away with my family to a small village where I began anew, with painful memories of the past.

And since that day, I never once missed a single *tefillah* with a *minyan* ….

PRIDE BEFORE a FALL

*T*here wasn't a soul in the bustling city of Lipowitz and all the villages beyond who hadn't heard the name Reb Shmuel Batyanski. The wealthy businessman had a nickname, a name uttered reverently, without malice: Reb Shmuel *Matzliach* ("the successful one"). He had golden hands. Everything he touched turned into a success. Reb Shmuel was also blessed with a generous nature, sharing his assets with those less fortunate than he. Small wonder that he was admired and beloved by all the Jews in the Ukraine.

A fiery Chernobyler *chassid*, Reb Shmuel never did anything without consulting his Rebbe, the renowned Reb Mottel. He followed the Rebbe's advice to the letter. This led to a slew of successful business deals, enabling him to purchase vast tracts of land. Soon he owned nearly as much property as the wealthy noblemen of the region. Despite some jealous rumblings about the clever *Zhid*, the nobility dealt kindly with Reb Shmuel who had achieved a reputation as a fair and honest man.

No one had such luck as that merchant of Lipowitz, it seemed. If a local *poritz* decided to sell his abandoned flourmill, he needed only to turn to Reb Shmuel, and within a day, he received his price. Inexplicably, there would shortly be an influx of merchants to the region, necessitating the mill's rejuvenation, and soon Reb Shmuel would own another flourishing business. If a *poritz* gave Reb Shmuel a small estate as a guarantee for a loan, within days the government would need the area to house soldiers — and pay Reb Shmuel a hefty commission. Should the price of timber go down, Reb Shmuel immediately bought a double shipment, and the price would increase tenfold within days!

This remarkable *mazel* overflowed into his private life, too. Reb Shmuel had married well and was blessed with a fine household of sons and daughters who brought him much *nachas*. He owned a huge mansion beside a secluded wood on which he had built a separate house for guests, with a full-time cook to cater to their needs. Impoverished beggars who traveled through the area couldn't bless him enough for his kindness.

On the face of it, it seemed that Reb Shmuel had received the lion's share of success in this world without compromising his virtuousness in the least bit.

However, as is often the case, the test of wealth began to take its toll on Reb Shmuel. He began to believe the world was his for the taking. He no longer davened with a full heart. He no longer asked the One Above to continue showering him and his family with blessings. His *tefillos* became mechanical. Even on the High Holy Days, when all of *Klal Yisrael* beg the *Ribono shel Olam* to have mercy on them in tear-choked voices, his wellspring of tears had dried up.

Success and stupendous wealth made him forget what it meant to be on the receiving end. His visits to consult the Rebbe about his ventures grew less frequent, as he relied on his own clever business acumen. As time went on, he became obsessed with his own self-importance, proud of his clever business decisions and timely contacts. Of course, he remained a *frum* Jew, keeping Shabbos, observing the highest standards of *kashrus* and wearing the traditional frock coat and black *hamburg* of wealthy Jews in those days. And he still fed the poor and hungry with a generous hand. But underneath, in the recesses of his heart, lay arrogance and vanity.

Thoughts of "*kochi v'otzem yadi* (the might and power of my hand)" drummed in his head. He no longer wept when reciting "*Refaenu*," the prayer for health. After all, the most professional doctors would jump to serve his family's needs. "*Bareich Aleinu*"? Well, he was naturally blessed. The yoke of *galus* did not sit heavily on the neck of one who dealt with the noblemen of the area like a peer. "*Yagon va-anacha*"? The classic "*Yiddishe krechz*," the sigh of *tzaros* and financial pressure, was absent from his throat.

But even the wealthiest *chassid* needs a Rebbe. Reb Shmuel still visited the Chernobyler Rebbe every Rosh Chodesh, but they never discussed business matters anymore. He did not even feel it necessary to write a *kvittel,* the traditional slip of paper a *chassid* submits to his Rebbe, outlining his requests and asking for a *yeshuah.*

Why should I bother him? I have everything I need, thought Reb Shmuel.

Ominous storm clouds gathered on the horizon for the Jews of Poland and Russia, which included Galicia and the Ukraine. The cruel Czar Nikolai I was at war with England, France and Turkey. He left to the battlefield with a huge army and high hopes for success, but sadly, the Russians suffered one defeat after the next. His army was completely demoralized.

When the Russians received a blow, they always had to find someone to blame it on. And who were the most convenient scapegoats? The Jews, of course. Czar Nikolai's lackeys began grumbling that the Jews had sold out to the enemy and were in cahoots with them to defeat their Russian overlords. Soon the mutters turned into a roar, and the Jews were charged with spying on Mother Russia.

The evil Czar immediately issued a decree that any Jew living fifty miles from the border of Russia must relocate east, deeper into the motherland. Suddenly, with no warning, impoverished, innocent Jewish families were uprooted from their homes with only the clothes on their backs, forced to seek their fortune elsewhere. No one dared disobey, as the penalty was death. Thousands of families wandered aimlessly through the countryside, penniless and destitute, hoping for mercy from their kindhearted brethren to supply them with a new home and perhaps a source of sustenance.

Now, not all Jews suffered equally under the law. The wily Czar realized he could make good use of certain *Zhid*s, namely the wealthier ones. They would perform a great service for him, acting as "*Padriatchikes*," or suppliers. They would replenish the Czar's army with basic foods, such as flour, sugar and wheat, and supply new uniforms for the soldiers.

These handpicked Jews did not share the suffering of their brethren. In fact, despite the general oppression, they were enjoying peace and prosperity. The Czar treated them well, paying them a respectable wage, recognizing that he needed to stay on their good side to maximize production. He also exempted them from the decree of relocation, allowing them to remain comfortably in their homes. When it suited the Czar's needs, the "spying, lying, thieving" Jews suddenly became upright, honest suppliers for his army. But that didn't make him like them any better ….

Reb Shmuel was one of these chosen "*Padriatchikes*," and soon became a prominent supplier of foodstuffs. He hired additional laborers to keep up with the demand, and his flourmills worked around the clock, baking bread for the insatiable stomachs of the Czar's army.

Despite his hectic new schedule, when Rosh Chodesh Kislev arrived, Reb Shmuel remembered his obligation to his Rebbe, and leaving his numerous responsibilities in the hands of his capable managers, he ordered his personal driver to drive him to Chernobyl immediately.

Many a passerby stared in envy and admiration at the sight of the gilded carriage, drawn by three pairs of strong, perfectly matched horses. In the driver's seat sat a decorated coachman with a tall fur hat, holding the reigns in capable hands. Inside the carriage sat a prince of a man, wrapped in the finest wools and furs. Opposite him sat his devoted bodyguard and personal assistant, Berel.

As they rode toward Chernobyl, Reb Shmuel's mind buzzed with thoughts. A million obligations crowded his brain, vying for supremacy. Carefully, he reviewed his various business responsibilities. The large order of uniforms for the Czar's army was currently under production in one of his many factories. The numerous flourmills were producing vast loaves of bread to be consumed by the Czar's soldiers. He mentally calculated the volume necessary to feed the army and was satisfied. His efficient workers were meeting the demands.

Leaning back against the plump, cushioned seat, he shook his head in amazement and pride at his remarkable abilities and accomplishments. So absorbed was he in his self-importance that not one fleeting thought of where he was going passed through his mind. No thoughts of the great Rebbe, nor of his own spiritual growth.

After several hours' travel over bumpy, unpaved roads, the gilded coach arrived in Chernobyl. It was late afternoon and the sun was low in the sky. Reb Shmuel ordered his coachman to stop at the best inn, where he quickly davened Mincha and refreshed himself with a tall glass of sweet, steaming hot tea, served with some honey cakes. Then he headed straight for the Rebbe. Hopefully, he would have an audience with the Rebbe within the hour and could head back home after Maariv. He wasn't afraid to travel the roads at night. His coachman was armed and his horses strong and steady. Reb Shmuel simply couldn't waste another day away from his hectic business responsibilities.

It was customary for a *chassid* who wished to see his Rebbe to hand the *gabbai* a *kvittel*, which the *gabbai* brought in to the Rebbe. Only then was he allowed to enter the Rebbe's inner sanctum, offering a *pidyon*, a donation to charity. The Rebbe would read the *kvittel*, which listed all the *chassid*'s needs, be it *parnassah, shidduchim* or good health. He then would bless the *chassid* that all would be granted him.

Reb Shmuel, however, had no time nor patience for this procedure. Arrogantly bypassing the *gabbai*, he entered the Rebbe's study. He marched up to the table where the Rebbe sat immersed in a *sefer* and slapped a generous *pidyon* upon the table.

The holy Chernobyler Maggid continued learning for a few moments. Reb Shmuel waited, unconsciously tapping an impatient foot. The Rebbe soon sensed his presence and looked up, perplexed. When he saw it was Reb Shmuel, his forehead creased in displeasure.

"*Shalom aleichem*, Reb Shmuel," the Rebbe said slowly.

"*Aleichem shalom*," Reb Shmuel nodded casually.

"How is your wife and family?" the Rebbe inquired.

"*Chasdei Hashem*, all are fine," Reb Shmuel replied with a smile.

"I see you have not written a *kvittel*," prompted the Rebbe. "Is there nothing you lack? Have you nothing to ask for?"

"Nothing at all, Rebbe," Reb Shmuel answered with frank honesty and self-satisfaction. "I have nothing to complain about and nothing to ask for. I have everything I need."

With these words, Reb Shmuel effectively sealed his fate.

The Rebbe met his *chassid*'s eyes and shook his head, left and right, left and right. "*Oy, Shmulik'l, Shmulik'l*," he said with a loud groan. "I was praying you would say something to avert your fate, but now your arrogance has sealed the Divine Decree." He stood up, and his eyes, glittering like coals, pierced Reb Shmuel's heart. "Your arrogance and self-assuredness have caused you to forget that you are a mere mortal of flesh and blood who exists solely through the kindness of the *Ribono shel Olam*! What is man that he should glorify himself with his meager existence? No man can live on this world without a bit of *tzaar* or pain to help him remember his ultimate purpose. Otherwise, he is no better than an animal. No, it is not good to live without worries, to live a carefree life of ease."

Reb Shmuel listened, pale and trembling, as Rav Mottel elaborated, "The Creator enabled you to live your life without the pain of *parnassah*, without the *pasuk* 'By the sweat of your brow, you shall eat bread.' He blessed you with *nachas* from your children, sparing you the pain of child rearing. What is left to pain you?"

He raised an accusing finger at the cowering Reb Shmuel. "At least …," the Rebbe said, his voice rising, "at least you should have felt the pain of your brothers who are forced to wander without a home. And what of the *Galus HaShechinah*? Why have you not prayed that the Bais Hamikdash be rebuilt?"

Reb Shmuel remained silent, his eyes cast down in shame. There was nothing to say. He had sinned greatly, immersing himself headfirst into his own carefree life without a thought for how others were suffering. Yes, he did his share to feed the poor, but had their pain ever registered with him? No, it had not. Had he davened with all his heart for the Ultimate Redemption? No, he had been comfortable living in *galus*. Tears started in his eyes, and his chest heaved.

The Rebbe watched him and said, his eyes brimming with tears, "I see a terrible decree hovering above your head. You will have to suffer a bitter and painful fate as punishment for your sins."

"Holy Rebbe!" said Reb Shmuel, sobbing, "if this is a Divine Decree then I accept it with grace, however difficult it will be. May it be an atonement for my sins. But please, holy Rebbe, please — may I be allowed to know when the punishment will begin?"

The Maggid replied in a warm, fatherly voice. "Shmuel, my child, know that the *gezeira* will begin soon, at the pinnacle of your career. When you have reached the highest point you could dream of, you will be hurled to the depths of degradation.

"However," continued the Maggid soothingly, "since you have accepted the Divine Decree humbly, without question, and have experienced a spark of *teshuvah*, I will reveal to you that your punishment will not be endless. When you reach the lowest ebb, beyond which one cannot sink, you will slowly be lifted up from the abyss and your *hatzlachah* will begin to shine once more."

Reb Shmuel climbed back into his coach, a changed man. Gone was the haughty manner, the arrogant stride. A broken, shattered man took his seat in the luxurious carriage, seeming to shrink into the plush upholstery and sighing from the depths of his heart, as if in great pain — the pain of a man waiting for the lethal blow to strike ....

His loyal servant Berel, sitting alongside his master, tried in vain to discover the cause of his despondency. Reb Shmuel's behavior was puzzling. What had overcome this normally jovial man? What had occurred to shake his equilibrium and cause him to sigh with such distress? A black storm cloud seemed to have settled upon his features, and he communicated in monosyllables.

Berel tried to recollect what had happened during the few hours they had been in Chernobyl. Had someone insulted Reb Shmuel? Had he received negative tidings about his business? Berel shook his head. There had been no telegram, and Reb Shmuel had barely spoken to a soul after exiting the Rebbe's study. There had been one slight change in schedule. Instead of leaving that night, Reb Shmuel remained at the inn, saying he felt unwell and wanted to rest before heading back home. That had been the only extraordinary event of their trip.

Berel glanced over at his master and noted the red-rimmed

eyes, the disheveled appearance and the preoccupation with staring aimlessly out the window. His reverie was punctuated by heartrending groans.

"Master, you are not well!" he said in concern. "Do you, perhaps, have a fever?"

Reb Shmuel waved him away, as one would brush away an annoying fly. "No, I am fine," he answered abruptly. "Thank you for asking."

"Shall I get a doctor for you?"

"Leave me be," Reb Shmuel commanded sharply.

Berel sighed and turned once more to his own conjectures. Something was definitely wrong. It was not about business, nor was Reb Shmuel ill. Perhaps the Rebbe had chided him about some spiritual matter that needed rectifying? That was it, Berel decided. No doubt the Rebbe had chastised his boss, and Reb Shmuel was simply doing *teshuvah*, trying to mend his character flaw.

The somber party traveled for a couple of hours, reaching the halfway point at midday. There, the coachman made a brief stop to rest the horses and recoup their strength. It was a sunny, mild day, unusual for Kislev, and the two passengers climbed out to stretch their cramped legs and breathe some fresh air.

"A half hour is all they need," said the coachman, gesturing to the horses. "As soon as I get them fed and rubbed down, they'll be ready to go."

Reb Shmuel wandered aimlessly along the village street, sunk in his gloomy thoughts. He visualized his numerous business assets, the fame and glory that had gone to his head. How the mighty have fallen! He sniffed contemptuously at his former self. In a short while, he knew, he would become a homeless beggar, degraded and humiliated, with no trace of his former pride.

"My master," came a solicitous voice at his elbow, "would you like something to drink?"

Concerned as ever, Berel stood holding a golden, jewel-encrusted goblet, Reb Shmuel's favorite *becher* from which he always drank. It was filled with crystal-clear flavored water. Reb Shmuel hurriedly took the goblet, mumbled a quick *brachah* and drank it quickly.

Poor, loyal Berel who serves me so devotedly, he thought in consternation. *Would he even look in my direction if he knew the truth?*

For his part, Berel was stung. Why was Reb Shmuel treating him so callously? Was he angry for some reason?

"Have I hurt you in any way?" Berel asked, tears forming in his eyes.

"*Chas v'shalom!*" Reb Shmuel jumped. "*Chalila!* What makes you think so? I am just preoccupied with something, a great worry I cannot share with anyone. I am sorry," he continued, seeing Berel was about to ask him more questions. "*B'ezras Hashem*, I hope the issue will soon be resolved."

Not another word was spoken of the incident. Somberly, the two men climbed into the gilded carriage and the coachman hitched up the horses. With a crack of the whip, they were on their way.

About a half hour into their journey, Berel gasped. "The goblet!" he cried. "The gold and diamond drinking cup was left behind at the inn. We must turn back!"

"Don't bother," said Reb Shmuel. "The inn is full of customers, and the stable boys usually congregate outside. I am sure someone pocketed the goblet by now."

"But we have to try, to do our *hishtadlus*," Berel argued, gesturing for the coachman to go back. Reb Shmuel was silent. How could he explain to his loyal servant that the goblet had no value in his eyes since, in a short while, it would be lost along with the rest of his fortune? Besides, there was only a slim chance it would be found. Why waste a precious hour going back?

But it was too late. The coachman, apprised of the situation, had backed the horses and turned. Soon they were standing before the inn and Berel quickly dismounted, scanning the area. Reb Shmuel did not join him, sitting impatiently in the carriage.

Incredibly, Berel returned shortly, waving the goblet in triumph. "I found it!" he crowed. "It was right there on the ground, just waiting for us! I don't understand why no one else saw it. You see, it truly was worthwhile to go back for such a valuable item!"

If Berel thought that Reb Shmuel would share his joy, he was sadly mistaken. As he handed the goblet back to his master, Reb Shmuel's face crumpled and his entire body shook with heart-breaking sobs.

"It is the sign I was waiting for," he murmured, recalling the Rebbe's words. "I have reached the peak of my *mazel*. Now it will be downhill all the way ...."

He recalled the Rebbe's words: *"Shmuel, my child, know that the* gezeira *will begin soon, at the pinnacle of your career. When you have reached the highest point you could dream of, you will be hurled to the depths of degradation."*

However, the Maggid had added these comforting words: *"Since you have accepted the Divine Decree humbly, without question, and have experienced a spark of* teshuvah, *I will reveal to you that your punishment will not be endless. When you reach the lowest ebb, beyond which one cannot sink, you will slowly be lifted up from the abyss and your* hatzlachah *will begin to shine once more."*

It took only a short while for disaster to strike. It wasn't a major downfall that destroyed everything at once. The process was painstakingly slow. It started with a telegram, received on the day following their arrival, stating, in concise words:

```
FIRE DESTROYED TREES
FOREST BURNED TO GROUND
```

One of the vast forests from which Reb Shmuel supplied timber to the Czar had been set ablaze, and the lush vegetation was completely charred.

Reb Shmuel took the news badly. He tore out his hair, screaming and crying hysterically. Reb Shmuel, though, was known as a levelheaded businessman who did not usually lose his composure. "What is he so upset about?" his employees and family murmured to each other, confused at his unusual response. "The wealthiest man in the Ukraine can certainly spare the loss of a single forest. He has dozens of forests, besides his numerous sprawling estates, mills and factories."

Little did they dream that Reb Shmuel was not bemoaning the mere loss of his forest. He knew this was only the tip of the iceberg, a sign of greater losses to come.

And indeed, from that day onward, it seemed as if each day brought another loss to Reb Shmuel's vast estate. The loss of the forest cost Reb Shmuel an additional penalty, a hefty fine to the Czar for not supplying the vast amounts of timber he had promised.

Two days later, an unexpected flash flood destroyed a flourmill at the edge of a river. Next, a large and successful tavern owned by Reb Shmuel was vandalized one night, the liquor wasted on the floor and all the glassware smashed. So it continued. The wealthy tycoon, known as "Reb Shmuel *Matzliach*," who had never experienced a major business loss before, was besieged from all sides.

With no profits filling his coffers, the debts began piling up and soon creditors were pounding upon his door. The Czar increased the fine tenfold after Reb Shmuel canceled a flour order. One by one, his employees left him, not having been paid in weeks. Only Berel remained loyal to his master. But it was only a matter of time before he, too, would quit his job ….

The news buzzed through the villages: Reb Shmuel *Matzliach* was now Reb Shmuel the Beggar, without a *kopek* to his name.

The Rebbe's warning had been fulfilled to the last letter. From the heights of wealth and glory, Reb Shmuel had been catapulted to the depths of misery and degradation. But worse was still to come ….

Late one night, Reb Shmuel sat somberly in his palatial home, watching the clock tick the minutes and bemoaning his fate. His magnificent palace that had been commissioned by the finest architects no longer belonged to him. His creditors had brought a lawsuit against him and the local authorities had placed a lien on his mansion, which would be taken away unless he paid his debts within days.

It was a blustery, cold night and Reb Shmuel's family slept peacefully, undisturbed. They knew he was going through some business trouble, but hoped it would soon blow over and Reb Shmuel *Matzliach* would revert to his earlier *mazel*. Only Reb Shmuel knew the truth.

Suddenly, there was a furtive, light knock on the front door. Reb Shmuel grabbed a lantern, frightened. Who could be knocking at this hour?

"*Pani Shmuel, Pani Shmuel!*" came the muffled voice. "Open the door!" Frightened, Reb Shmuel quickly opened the door and a tall, hooded figure slipped inside.

"Wh-who are you?" the former tycoon stammered. He stared with mounting dread at the mysterious figure.

Once safely inside, the stranger slipped off the hood to reveal his face. Reb Shmuel recognized him instantly as Stashek, the local head of the Gendarmes. Stashek was indebted to Reb Shmuel, who, in former days, had arranged for the rascal to receive the prestigious job of Police Chief, with its many benefits. Indeed, Reb Shmuel had never had cause to regret this favor, as Stashek kept him updated about the Czar's latest decrees and dangers facing the community.

Now Stashek had come with a somber mission: to warn Reb Shmuel that his very life was in danger!

"Can I serve you anything?" Reb Shmuel nervously inquired. "A glass of hot tea?"

Stashek waved him away. "No time," he hissed, leaning forward. "They are coming for you tonight."

Reb Shmuel's face whitened. "Who is coming for me?" he said, aghast.

"The Czar's emissaries in Kiev," Stashek explained. "They are under strict orders to arrest you, dead or alive!"

"What are the charges?"

"The charges are severe, indeed. You are accused of spying for the enemy!"

"Me? Spying? But that's absurd! You know how loyally I serve the Czar!"

"No matter. You have powerful enemies in Kiev. Gaspagin Padwil, the Gubernator of Kiev, has been eyeing your powerful estates for some time. He has tried to slander you before the Czar on more than one occasion, but while the Czar needed your services, he turned a deaf ear to Gaspagin Padwil."

"And now that I have lost my fortune, he seized his chance," Reb Shmuel said grimly.

"Last week, he sent a letter to St. Petersburg by special courier with shocking allegations: He claimed the fire that devoured your timber forest was started intentionally — that you received a large sum of money from the enemy to destroy the Czar's stockpiles and undermine morale."

Reb Shmuel listened in horror at the baseless charges. He knew he was helpless to defend himself. He had no fortune, no estates to mortgage, no stashes of bills to bribe greedy officials … were it not for Stashek's loyalty, he wouldn't even have had a chance to escape. His mind worked furiously.

"When are they coming?"

"Later tonight," said Stashek abruptly. "You must leave right now, without telling a soul. Even your family must not know your destination, lest they be tortured into revealing it. And now, I must go. I have already endangered my life."

Before Reb Shmuel could thank him, Stashek lifted the cloak over his head and vanished into the darkness.

Reb Shmuel wasted no time. As soon as the door was shut on Stashek's hooded figure, he slipped into his room and gathered a few personal belongings: one change of clothes, his *tallis* and *tefillin* and his last remaining 100 ruble banknote, a sad reminder of happier days.

His wife stirred in her sleep, and Reb Shmuel contemplated telling her, but decided it was too risky. The czar's emissaries had ways and means of forcing the truth from their victims. No. It was best to simply disappear.

Reb Shmuel stooped to take one more, pain-filled glance at his slumbering children.

I am sorry, my precious children, he thought the tears coursing down his haggard cheeks. *It is not your fault I have sinned, yet you must suffer for my pride and haughtiness. From the heights of wealth and luxury you are cast into the depths of poverty and degradation.*

As he stood over his sleeping daughter, Chanaleh, the youngest of his large family, he suddenly heard a noise outdoors. In a flash, he was at the window, peeking out of the curtain. What he saw made his blood run cold. A group of armed soldiers was marching down the path to his home, preparing to grab their quarry.

There was not a moment to waste. Quick as a wink, Reb Shmuel grabbed his sack and slipped out the back door, fleeing silently toward the security of the nearby woods. As he reached the first copse of trees, he stopped to catch his breath and watched with quickening pulse as the ruthless soldiers surrounded his home, guarding every doorway to prevent his escape.

He clenched his fists in helpless anger as sounds of the armed guards pounding and crashing through his home rent the quiet night. His heart hammered in fear as he heard the wails and cries of his frightened wife and children, and the harsh bawling of the guards ordering him to give himself up.

"*Pani Shmuel*, you are under arrest in the name of the Czar!"

"*Pani Shmuel!* Miserable spy! You can't hide from us! We will hunt you down wherever you are!" These threats were uttered, accompanied by a few choice curse words. Reb Shmuel could no longer wait. In moments they would fan out and search for him. Clutching his sack, he slipped deeper into the forest, which he knew like the back of his hand.

After a half hour, he had cut through the woods to a small, neighboring village where he had several good friends. Despite the late hour, he knocked at the door of the local goldsmith Peretz and explained his predicament.

"You must disguise your identity," Peretz advised him. He grabbed a thick pair of scissors, and in moments, Reb Shmuel, the former *g'vir,* was transformed. His long *payos* were trimmed, his beard was cut off and his hair was matted. Peretz bent down and scooped up a handful of mud, smearing it on Reb Shmuel's cheeks and clothes. Then he stepped back to admire his handiwork.

"Now, even your own family won't recognize you," he said proudly. "You could go home in broad daylight and still be safe. Though I don't recommend it," he quickly added. "The Czar's soldiers will be watching your home for the next few months."

"Where do you suggest I go?" asked Reb Shmuel, with the defeated air of a broken man.

"Anywhere. North, South, East or West, as long as it's far away from here. I would recommend you take a 'journey' of several months, passing as a Polish beggar. Perhaps at the end of the winter, you can write to me and include the name of a contact person who will receive my return letter. I will send you a coded message informing you when it is safe to return. And now, may the Lord be with you."

The two men embraced, and Peretz wished him luck. Then Reb Shmuel vanished into the darkness, a muddy, disheveled figure leaning heavily on his walking stick, wandering sack in hand. Peretz watched him leave, blinking away tears. How the mighty have fallen! Only a short while ago, Reb Shmuel *Matzliach* was the pride and joy of the entire Ukraine. Now, he had a price on his head, and his possessions were not even worth a few *kopek*s.

An involuntary sigh escaped his lips. Peretz murmured the well-known words of *Tehillim*, "*Mashpil gayim adei aretz*," the *Ribono shel Olam* lowers the haughty to the ground ....

After several days on the open roads, Reb Shmuel was a sad sight. A pathetic, stooped figure dressed in filthy clothes, coated with mud and lice, he shuffled his way through the small villages that dotted the countryside. Wherever he went, he aroused the compassion of his kindhearted fellow Jews, and the disgust of others. More than once, he was roughly shoved in the marketplace or shown the back of the shul where the beggars congregated.

Remembering his own open guesthouse, where the poor always found a warm meal and bed, brought tears to Reb Shmuel's eyes. For a while, he had kept a separate guesthouse for these guests, but he had never served them personally nor allowed them to stay in his private home. He hadn't wanted his children to mingle with the common folk and perhaps catch their diseases or become infested with lice. Now he was flooded with shame, realizing that some of these beggars might have once been rich and powerful like him, but had fallen upon hard times.

What I wouldn't give for a little recognition, to be treated like a human being despite my appearance, Reb Shmuel agonized late one night in the crowded *hekdesh* where he lay trying to sleep on a lumpy straw mat shared with two other beggars. The *hekdesh* was a beggar's hostel, which nearly every large town and village maintained for Jewish wanderers to have a place to stay. Needless to say, the accommodations weren't pleasant. But as the saying goes, beggars can't be choosers.

So passed some miserable weeks, as the formerly wealthy and proud *chassid* who couldn't be bothered to write a *kvittel*, suffered the degradation of filth and lice, the misery of hunger, the shame of being treated as a pariah among his fellow Jews. What hurt most of all were the days he spent in larger cities where he had numerous business acquaintances, all who would have been honored to host him — in better days. The way he looked, Reb Shmuel was embarrassed to show his face, afraid someone would recognize him. *Better to remain an anonymous beggar than be kicked out of wealthy homes where people would call me an impostor,* he decided.

Reb Shmuel lived hand-to-mouth, scrounging for a slice of dry bread and a sip of foul water. He traveled from town to town, relying on the kindness of his fellow Jews to keep him from dying of hunger. He survived from day to day usually on a hunk of black bread dipped in water, and if he was really lucky, sometimes a small sliver of herring.

Late at night, his stomach growling, Reb Shmuel would lie on a scratchy straw mat in the local poorhouse and dream of better days. His mind would wander to pleasant memories of his former palatial home, of the plentiful, nourishing meals he had eaten and the soft featherbed that had covered and warmed him on cold nights. The tears would fall, wetting his sleeve as he recalled the dear faces of his wife and children. They surely had no idea what had become of him. He had suddenly disappeared off the face of this earth. Did they miss him? Did they wonder if they would ever see him again?

And what had become of his faithful Berel who had insisted on remaining at his side through thick and thin? Had he, too, been captured? Or had he escaped in time?

Reb Shmuel hoped his wife and children had not been imprisoned or tortured to reveal his hiding place. The agony of not knowing if they were safe pained him most of all. How he wished he could send them a message or secretly correspond with them! But that would put them all in danger.

His only consolation during those difficult, sleepless nights was knowing that anything was better than being imprisoned in the Czar's dungeons, condemned to death. "*Ribono shel Olam*," he would sob, "thank you for keeping me alive to witness Your punishments. I hope my suffering is atonement for my sins."

One day, Reb Shmuel arrived in a large city near the border of Poland with a group of beggars and saw something that made his blood run cold. Hanging on the doorway of the local saloon was a rough sketch of his image, with the following words:

REWARD!
One thousand silver rubles being offered for the capture of Shmuel Batyanski, former tycoon of Lipowitz, wanted for spying against the Czar

With a shudder, Reb Shmuel realized he couldn't stay in this city for even one day. Though his face was now thin and haggard, and his entire figure stooped and emaciated, the former *"Matzliach"* couldn't take a chance.

He turned to the others standing close together on the enclosed porch of the saloon as they sought shelter from the winter storm. "I-I have to go," he stammered.

"What are you rushing for?" asked Zanvil, a coarse beggar. "Do you have an appointment at the barber's, perhaps?" and he began to laugh uproariously.

"Maybe he doesn't like the hustle and bustle of the big city," said another beggar.

"Or maybe …," said Zanvil, staring at Reb Shmuel, "one minute! Your face looks familiar! Are you the man in that drawing?" His claw-like finger pointed to the door.

A cold, icy fear gripped Reb Shmuel's heart. "Of course not!" he denied. "What makes you think so?"

"Well, you are acting mighty suspicious," replied Zanvil, grinning evilly. "In fact, I would wage a thousand rubles that you *are* the man in the poster. And I, for one, could definitely use a thousand rubles." He seized Reb Shmuel's coat. "Come with me! We are going to the police."

As the others watched, horrified, Zanvil dragged Reb Shmuel across the snow-covered road. Reb Shmuel, nearly frozen into a terrified stupor, allowed himself to be dragged off, resigned to his fate.

Suddenly, as if from a deep sleep, he awakened, adrenalin surging through his veins. After suffering so much pain and misery would he allow himself to be turned in by a fellow Jew to be tortured in the Czar's dungeons? With a strength born of desperation, he struck his captor a blow to the face, knocking him to the ground. Then he turned and fled. He did not look back until he had reached the main road out of the city and, panting, saw no one was following him — yet.

All that night, he hurried along the silent roads, not daring to seek shelter, terrified the police were pursuing him. By dawn, he was half-frozen, and knew he must find shelter.

A pale winter sun lit the countryside, and Reb Shmuel saw a small town up ahead. Slowly and cautiously, he made his way into the town, taking care to avoid large groups of people and to remain inconspicuous. Snatches of conversation that he overheard were in Yiddish — and Polish! He realized he must have crossed the border during the night. However, he wasn't sure if he was safe yet from the Czar's men.

Reb Shmuel headed straight to the *hekdesh,* where he sank down upon the first available mattress and tried to rest his weary bones. He felt weak and faint, not having eaten for several days.

Ribono shel Olam! he lamented. *Have I not reached my lowest point? Pursued by the Czar's army, separated from my family, forced to share quarters with other impoverished beggars, with hunger constantly gnawing at my innards, and now I also have to worry about being turned into the police by my own brothers, my fellow Jews.*

Surely, I have reached the nadir of my situation. Can I sink yet lower? Is it not the time yet for my salvation? I beg You, remember Shmuel!

But Reb Shmuel was destined to fall one more rung, to the lowest depths, before being lifted upwards again.

It was Erev Shabbos. Reb Shmuel needed accommodations for the Day of Rest, a place to eat the Shabbos meal and some warm water to wash the filth off his body. As soon as he was somewhat rested, he headed for the *bais medrash,* hoping a kindhearted Jew would take pity on him and invite him for the Shabbos meal. He entered the humble little wooden building, casting fearful glances all around, afraid someone would recognize him.

The custom in that Polish town was as follows: On Friday morning, the poor gathered in the largest *shteibel* in town, where the most *baalebatishe* Jews davened, and waited to be invited for Shabbos. When a wealthy Jew who could afford to feed another mouth or two saw a suitable guest, he would place his hand on the man's shoulder and invite him to come for *"to'ameha,"* a taste of Shabbos. This pre-Shabbos treat included a heaping plate of *farfel* and *tzimmes* with some sizzling potato *kugel* on the side. Then the *baal habayis* took his guest to the *mikvah*, and if the guest was really lucky, he would receive a fresh change of clothes.

However, only the truly wealthy could afford this distinction. The simple laborers only invited poor people on Friday evening, after Kabbalas Shabbos. And sadly, there were some guests who did not get an invitation at all and were forced to remain in the *hekdesh*, eating the standard dry bread for Shabbos.

As Reb Shmuel watched, the *bais medrash* began filling with all types of poor people. With a sinking feeling, he realized that most of them were in far better condition than he was. He had virtually no chance to be invited. Who would want a man who was caked with mud, whose face was scratched, whose every feature expressed defeat? Only a true *baal chesed*, a *machnis orach* par excellence, who could see beyond the external trappings to discover the wounded heart of Reb Shmuel *Matzliach*, once the most admired man in the Ukraine.

Shacharis was over. The *bais medrash* slowly emptied, with most of the working-class headed for their respective occupations. One after another, the important folk rose from the eastern wall and went over to the *"poolish"* (the back rows, where the beggars congregated). They selected their Shabbos guests, and while the others watched enviously, the lucky men followed their *baalebatim* home for the requisite bowl of *tzimmes*.

Reb Shmuel didn't even bother trying to catch the attention

of a *baalebos*. He knew he was the last person anyone would wish to invite. He sat in a corner murmuring some *Tehillim*. He suddenly realized that this Shabbos marked exactly one year since he had escaped Lipowitz with his life. *Look at the changes one year has wrought!* he thought mournfully. In just twelve months, Reb Shmuel's entire appearance and behavior had been transformed. Gone was the arrogance, haughty stride and confident manner of a wealthy, prominent leader. In its place was a hesitant, meek, mud-streaked beggar who shed copious tears over his *Tehillim*. *Ribono shel Olam,* he cried inside, *when will the wheel of fortune turn once more? When will my turn come to be redeemed?*

One of the *baalebatim* had recently moved to town. He was known by the generic term "Reb Moshke," the nickname for every Yid who didn't want to reveal his name. For some reason, Reb Moshke was very reticent about his background. It was rumored that he had escaped from the Ukraine due to business troubles, but whatever they were, they seemed to be a thing of the past. Already, he had achieved a reputation as a warm-hearted *baal chesed* who contributed generously to every cause.

He had arrived nearly a year ago with his wife and four children, as well as a hefty bundle of rubles. With the money, he had invested in a textile business, and *hatzlachah* shone upon his merchandise. Soon he was able to afford to build a large mansion and buy his wife the costliest furs. His children, too, were decked out in the latest fashions and privately tutored.

To Reb Moshke's credit, his success did not go to his head. Despite his newfound status as the wealthiest man in town, he remained humble and unassuming, shrugging off the honors and accolades of his fellow Jews. "Money comes and money goes," he was wont to say. "The true measure of a man is how he behaves in every situation."

Reb Moshke's home had become the address for any Yid in trouble, for he came to the aid of his fellow Jews in a generous fashion. Small wonder that he was the most respected, beloved Jew in the entire town. Every week, his Shabbos table accommodated dozens of guests, and he would send his son to the *hekdesh* on Friday night to find any poor people who had been overlooked. Every single guest, no matter how dirty and disheveled, was given a place at his table, served a warm meal and provided with a bed, all with solicitous concern.

Reb Shmuel knew none of this as he sat hunched over his *Tehillim*, tears making rivulets down his cheeks. He paid no attention as, one after the other, the wealthy folk made their choices, leaving him alone with a few of the more difficult "cases."

Most of the *baalebatim* had already left, and the few remaining guests realized that, in all probability, they would not be invited until after Kabbalas Shabbos. They got up and went together to the *mikvah*, resigned to a quick rinse and then donning their dirty clothes once again, and waiting until nightfall for a taste of *tzimmes*. Reb Shmuel followed them dispiritedly.

The *mikvah* was already crowded, despite the early hour. Reb Shmuel undressed quickly and placed his clothes in an unobtrusive pile, hoping nobody would see how filthy they were. Then he immersed himself in the *mikvah* as quickly as he could, grabbed a towel and rushed to get dressed again.

To his shock and horror, his pile of rags was nowhere to be seen. "Where are my clothes?" he asked frantically, rummaging through the piles.

"Ah, those filthy rags?" the *shammas* asked scornfully, pointing at a smoldering heap in the oven. "I didn't realize they belonged to anyone. I used them to stoke the fire." He snorted.

Reb Shmuel, wrapped in a coarse towel, was shocked beyond belief. Shame made him totter weakly, and two spots of red rose on his stark cheekbones. He didn't even have clothes to put on! Had he truly fallen so low? Were his last few possessions, the tattered clothes he wore, also gone? He fell to the ground in woe.

Suddenly, instead of sinking into despondency, his heart surged with renewed hope. The words of his Rebbe, the famed Maggid of Chernobyl, came back to him with great clarity. First, he had said:

"Shmuel, my child, know that the gezeira will begin soon, at the pinnacle of your career. When you have reached the highest point you could dream of, you will be hurled to the depths of degradation."

And then he had uttered the important words:

"Since you have accepted the Divine Decree humbly, without question, and have experienced a spark of teshuvah, I will reveal to you that your punishment will not be endless. When you reach the lowest ebb, beyond which one cannot sink, you will slowly be lifted up from the abyss, and your hatzlachah will begin to shine once more."

Reb Shmuel remembered when his loyal servant, Berel, had insisted they go back to retrieve his *becher* at the inn, and how he had insisted it was pointless. And how great was Berel's joy when the *becher* was found! And how deep was Reb Shmuel's sadness when he realized that his *mazel* was about to end. At that point, he had cried bitter tears as Berel looked on in shock at the change in his master. Berel had not known what he knew, that a fortunate stroke of luck would herald the pinnacle of his career.

And now, likewise, he had reached the nadir, the lowest ebb. It was impossible to sink any lower than losing the clothes on one's back and not having a replacement.

Reb Shmuel leaped to his feet in tremendous joy and began to clap and sing merrily. Everyone stared, thinking he had — tragically — gone insane.

"Look how he claps as his old rags go up in flames!" they taunted. Reb Shmuel was oblivious. He danced and sang *"Chasdei Hashem ki lo samnu* … (the kindnesses of Hashem are endless …)," still wrapped in the towel belonging to the *kehillah,* without a single garment to his name.

The *shammas,* feeling guilty for his callousness, came to the rescue. He rushed home and brought back a bundle of clean clothes, which he handed the dancing man. "Here, I brought you a fresh set of Shabbos clothes," he said guiltily, "surely in better condition than the rags you were wearing."

Reb Shmuel thanked him heartily and donned the clothes, feeling like a new man. Then, fresh and clean for the first time in months, he headed back to the *bais medrash,* suddenly feeling hungry. *I could use a hot bowl of tzimmes with some farfel on the side,* he thought with a smile.

It was an hour to Kabbalas Shabbos. The shul was slowly filling up with congregants. The remaining poor people waited in the back, hoping to be invited after Maariv.

Soon Reb Moshke, the wealthy textile merchant, arrived, resplendent in his Shabbos clothes. His numerous guests, some of them regulars, the others strangers, were with him. Now he walked over to the *"poolish"* to invite the others, the tough ones, those who didn't know how to behave in public and who frequently made nuisances of themselves. *Nu, they are all the Ribono shel Olam's children,* he mused, walking over to each of them in turn and placing his hands on their shoulders. Their faces lit up as they realized their luck. They had been invited to Reb Moshke's palatial home, where a sumptuous Shabbos meal would be served.

Soon all had been invited, except for one quiet fellow in the corner. Reb Moshke walked over to him and sized him up for a few moments. Strange, the guest did not make the slightest effort to be recognized and continued saying *Tehillim* as if he had no other cares.

Reb Moshke cleared his throat. *"Ahem."*

No response.

"Reb Yid," he tried again, placing his hands on the hunched fellow's shoulders. Startled, Reb Shmuel looked up into the wealthy man's eyes. Something about his gaze was so familiar. Where had he seen that face before?

Reb Moshke looked deep into the man's sunken eyes and at his haggard face, and nearly fainted with shock. Was it really him? Reb Shmuel, the former *g'vir* who had wined and dined with the rich and famous, upon whose every word the gentry and nobility had depended? How had he fallen so low in such a short time?

With supreme effort, he hid his shock and distress, trying to act as if nothing was amiss. *No use making a scene in the crowded Bais Medrash*, he thought.

"Reb Yid," the wealthy *baalebos* said in a gentle voice, "why don't you come to my home as my Shabbos guest?"

Reb Shmuel suddenly recognized his voice.

"Berel!" he shouted, the blood pounding in his ears. "Berel, my former servant, is it really you?"

Before the other guests could fall upon him and beat him for his *chutzpah* in addressing the wealthiest man in town with such a derogatory term, Reb Shmuel fell back, covering his face with his hands. His heart was beating sluggishly and his head was spinning from the shock.

"Leave him be," said Moshke sternly. "What he says is true. I am Berel, his former employee. This was once the wealthiest man in the entire Ukraine, and I was his right-hand man, serving him hand and foot."

"And ... what happened?" one of the guests gasped.

"What happened?" Reb Shmuel looked up with a bitter laugh. "The wheel of fortune turned and I was thrown to the bottom. I escaped with my life — just barely — without even telling my family where I was. And then I wandered from town to town, subsisting on a few crumbs, alone and friendless."

By now, a sizeable crowd had gathered in response to the commotion, and half the *bais medrash* stood around listening.

"What happened after I left, Berel?" Reb Shmuel asked suspiciously. "Did you abscond with my remaining fortune, leaving my wife and children in desperate straits? Is that why you changed your name to Moshke and fled?"

"*Chas v'shalom!*" said Reb Moshke, angry color flying to his face. "I swear by all that is holy that I didn't touch a *kopek* of your money. All I brought with me when I escaped was a small sack of rubles, the bonus you had so generously given me the month before you left town as reward for my efforts."

"And with this money you were able to afford such luxuries?" Reb Shmuel pointed to his luxurious fur coat and hat.

"The *Ribono shel Olam* was good to me," Reb Moshke replied simply. "I invested the money in a textile factory and was *matzliach*."

"*Matzliach!*" Reb Shmuel said bitterly. "I used to be the *matzliach*, the successful one, for whom princes and royalty made time in their appointment books. And now look at me! I am alone and friendless. Even the clothes on my back have been burned. Were it not for the kind *shammas*, I would still be at the *mikvah* with nothing to wear."

"Don't worry, Reb Shmuel," said Berel, clasping his hand. "Your troubles are over! Come to my home, and we will see what we can do as soon as Shabbos is over."

The two men strode out of shul, arm in arm, followed closely by the curious crowd. At Berel's home, after the *seudah* was finished, the two men closeted themselves in his study, while the other guests were directed to the guest rooms.

Reb Shmuel wasted no time. "Where are my wife and children?"

"I tried to save them, but I had to run away the morning after you were arrested," Berel explained apologetically. "As soon as dawn broke, one of your neighbors informed me that you were wanted by the Czar's men, but you had disappeared. I quickly grabbed my sack of savings and escaped with my family, with just the clothes on our backs. Later I heard that the Czar's men were looking for me, too, but I had already crossed the border into Poland."

"Then w-where is my family? Are they still alive?" cried Reb Shmuel fearfully.

"Don't worry," Berel comforted him. "Rest assured, they are safe and sound. The last I heard, they managed to escape to your wife's brother's home in Odessa and are hiding there. I have a contact who provides me with information via telegram."

"*Chasdei Hashem*," said Reb Shmuel, "I sense my troubles are ending. Just as you were the messenger when I lost and found the goblet — remember my tears? — heralding the loss of my fortune, so, too, I hope you will be the vehicle to help me rise to my former position again."

That Shabbos was spent in joyous song and praise to the One Above, as Reb Shmuel and Berel repeated the gripping tale again and again to all the townspeople. After Shabbos, Berel sent a telegram to Odessa, and within days, Reb Shmuel was reunited with his family. Berel gave him a sizeable sum of money, which Reb Shmuel used to buy property. Just as in the good old days, Hashem bestowed a tremendous outpouring of *brachah* upon Reb Shmuel, and within a short time, he was even wealthier than before.

But there was one important difference. Now, Reb Shmuel knew the meaning of hunger and degradation, and he conducted his business dealings with humility. As soon as it was safe, Reb Shmuel secretly traveled to his Rebbe, to Chernobyl, where he was received with open arms.

As Reb Shmuel wept with emotion, the Rebbe comforted him.

"Shmuel, your tears, coming from a broken heart, were accepted in *Shamayim*. All your sins have been forgiven. In *Shamayim*, they do not like haughty people who think the world is theirs and forget that they are but flesh and blood. The higher one goes, the greater is his fall, to remind him of his transient position in this world. However, your suffering is now over. I sense that you are a changed man since you accepted your fate with fortitude. May you be blessed, both in this world and the next."

Reb Shmuel and Reb Berel spent the rest of their lives as beloved, admired hosts in their small Polish town, doing chesed with their fellow Jews and helping anyone in distress. And whenever they met a poor Jew who was down on his luck, they never tired of repeating the miraculous tale, stressing the lesson "Pride comes before a fall."

Truly, Reb Shmuel had learned his lesson well.

LOST
and
FOUND

*R*eb *Yeshaya* Potash was a talented bookkeeper in Volyn. He worked for a wealthy wheat merchant, Chaim, whose business was exporting wheat grown in Poland and the Ukraine to sell in Istanbul.

Reb Yeshaya was a scholarly, learned man, who never missed a *minyan* or his daily *shiur*, no matter how exhausted he was. He gave generous donations to *tzedakah* and paid the cost of the *ner tamid*, the eternal light that burned in the *bais medrash*. A *chassid* of the renowned Rav Pinchas Koritzer, who spent his days and nights laboring in Torah study, Reb Yeshaya was part of the group of illustrious *chassidim* who had undertaken to support him. Once a year, the *gabbai* of the Koritzer Rebbe would come to his home to collect the money.

Thus, Reb Yeshaya lived a contented life with his wife and only son. He was respected and esteemed in his city and well-known in the entire vicinity. He would frequently go on business trips on behalf of his employer, who trusted him implicitly.

One winter, Chaim was offered a lucrative business opportunity in Istanbul, Turkey, but it was impossible for him to travel to Istanbul at that time. He therefore turned to his most devoted and trustworthy employee, Reb Yeshaya, to take his place.

Reb Yeshaya reluctantly agreed, uneasy about undertaking such a perilous mission. He bid good-bye to his wife and four-year-old son, and prepared to depart on the long journey.

His itinerary began with a two-day train trip to Odessa, where he would board a steamship that would take him across the Black Sea to Istanbul. When he arrived at the port in Odessa, Reb Yeshaya sent his wife Rivka a telegram:

```
    DEPARTING QUEEN LOUISE    MONDAY 2:30
  ISTANBUL ONE WEEK    WILL CONTACT UPON ARRIVAL
```

The week came and went. Rivka haunted the local telegraph

office, anxiously waiting for news of her husband's safe arrival. But the days crawled by, with no message from Turkey.

Meanwhile, Reb Yeshaya's boss Chaim was also anxious, and for good reason: He had heard rumors that a large ship had recently sunk off the coast of Odessa. There were no survivors. He prayed that his employee was not on that ill-fated ship, but his heart told him otherwise, for Reb Yeshaya would not let such a long interval go by without contacting him.

When a third week had passed with still no news, Rivka paid the wheat merchant a visit. "Have you heard from my husband?" she asked, nervously gripping her hands together.

"No, not yet," he worriedly replied. "I will try and reach my contacts in Istanbul to see if he arrived. Sometimes the mail service is sporadic and takes a while."

"He promised to send me a telegram!" she sighed.

"Perhaps he was busy and forgot —," Chaim began.

Rivka shook her head. "My husband is very responsible about things like that."

Their conversation was interrupted by the arrival of a messenger boy bearing a telegram from Odessa.

```
GREAT TRAGEDY    QUEEN LOUISE DEPARTING FROM
     ODESSA HAS SUNK    NO SURVIVORS
          NO WORD OF YESHAYA
```

Sweat beaded Chaim's brow as he read the message. He handed it to Rivka with a trembling hand. She read it, gasped and fell over in a faint.

It took a long time to revive her; even when she had come back to her senses, she could not accept her situation. Her husband had drowned in the sea. His remains would never be recovered. She was now, for all intents and purposes, a widow. But, no. There was no *shivah*. She was not a widow, people corrected her. She was an *agunah,* for there was no proof, no witnesses who had seen him drown. Everyone on board the ship, passengers and crew alike, had shared the same fate. Their whereabouts would never be known.

Rivka mourned her husband and the abrupt end of their short life together, and realized she was now a woman alone with a four-year-old child to raise, a boy who would never remember his father.

She had nowhere to go. Her elderly parents had died some years ago, and her siblings lived far away. Was she destined to spend the rest of her life alone? Would she ever be allowed to remarry?

The next few months were the most difficult of her life. Time passed in agonizing slowness. Rivka felt numb, weighed down with pain and sorrow. Her husband's boss, Chaim, still paid Reb Yeshaya's salary to his *agunah,* but she struggled with the daily care of her son and home, and her painful loneliness. Chaim had his own troubles — his wife had taken ill and doctors despaired of her life. After a short but fatal illness, she passed away, leaving Chaim and his two daughters alone.

Before the first *yahrtzeit* of Reb Yeshaya's disappearance had passed, Chaim began making inquiries about a *heter* for the *agunah.* He wished to marry his former employee's wife, who was known for her refined manner and intelligence.

Rivka also was interested in the *shidduch,* which would guarantee her son a life free of hardship and poverty, and would still the loneliness that echoed in every corner of her meager home. She was advised by the local *shadchanim* to go see the Rav of Warsaw and plead with him to find a way to permit her to remarry.

Thus, one bright spring afternoon, Rivka entered the Rav's study, her little boy in tow. With tears streaming down her cheeks, she begged the Rav to give her a *heter* to remarry and ease the pain of her lonely years. The Rav asked her all the relevant details, and sadly shook his head. It was impossible for him to give her a *heter* unless she could bring witnesses that her husband had truly drowned.

"But that is impossible!" she cried. "The ship sank with all on board! No one who saw the tragedy is alive!"

"Well, then, I am truly sorry, but I cannot give you a *heter,*" said the Rav sympathetically.

Rivka returned home, broken and shattered. Chaim, too, was devastated. He sent messengers to other *rabbanim,* hoping someone else could find a *heter,* but all agreed the situation was hopeless. Without a living witness who had seen her husband die, Rivka would remain an *agunah* forever.

Several weeks after the decision, Rav Pinchas Koritzer's *gabbai* brought the annual list of supporters to the Rebbe for approval. Rav Pinchas would quickly scan the names, and if one of the names was unclear or difficult for him to read, the Koritzer knew that that person was no longer among the living, and he would cross off the name.

That year, as usual, Rav Pinchas read the list and crossed off several names, and then presented the list to the *gabbai.* The *gabbai* began his journey to the neighboring cities and towns to collect the pledges. When he arrived in Warsaw, he stopped, as was usual, at Rivka's home.

"Can I speak with your husband?" he inquired.

"My husband?" Rivka asked bitterly. "My husband has been dead for nearly a year now. He disappeared at sea with the other passengers of the *Queen Louise,* leaving me an *agunah.*"

"But that is impossible!" cried the *gabbai,* staring at her in shock.

"Impossible? What are you talking about?" Rivka asked, growing more agitated. "My husband was on the ship that sank, and he has not been heard from since."

"I don't understand it, either, but he is clearly still alive," the *gabbai* declared. "Rav Pinchas Koritzer would never send me to collect a pledge from someone who is no longer among the living! The Rebbe himself checked your husband's name on the list. You can be sure he is alive."

Rivka began to sob uncontrollably. "I don't know what your Rebbe said, but one thing I can assure you. My husband is dead, and I will never see him again!"

The *gabbai*, moved by her sorrow, urged her to visit the Rebbe and discuss the matter. Rivka wasted no time. She sent her young son to stay with a neighbor, packed her bag, and traveled to Koritz. As soon as she arrived, she burst into the *bais medrash* where the Rebbe sat learning serenely.

"Holy Rebbe! My husband was lost at sea!" She covered her face and shook with uncontrollable sobs.

The Rebbe waited for her to compose herself, then calmly asked her for details. He shook his head. "If my eyes clearly read your husband's name, and my hands did not cross it off, you can be assured that he is alive and well and will return soon, *b'ezras Hashem*."

Rivka's eyes softened as hope and gratitude filled her tortured soul. With a prayer in her heart, she returned home. She spent the next few days davening and saying *Tehillim*, beseeching *Hakadosh Baruch Hu* to send her husband back from the depths of the sea.

A few weeks passed. One Monday night after midnight, as Rivka tossed and turned in bed, she thought she heard a noise. Someone was tapping at her door! She tiptoed across the room and opened it a crack. There stood her long-lost husband Reb Yeshaya, pale and haggard, but alive and well! She welcomed him with joyous tears and heartfelt prayers of gratitude.

She quickly set him a place at the table, setting a glass of piping hot tea before him. As she served him nourishing food, he slowly began to relate the miraculous events he had experienced.

"Our ship was filling with water, and chaos and terror reigned. People screamed helplessly. No one knew what to do. I put on my *tallis* and *tefillin* and said *viduy*, certain I would soon be lying at the bottom of the sea. Then I suddenly had an urge to just jump and hope for the best. As the ship rocked back and forth, I leaped into the wild ocean, battling the waves. The tide carried me away from the ship as I furiously tried to stay afloat. But my strength was ebbing and I was swallowing a lot of water. I was about to give up and let the waves wash over me when I spied a barrel filled with oil floating to my left. With my last reserves of energy, I pushed myself toward the barrel and made it. I clung to it for dear life, catching my breath and resting my limbs.

"The next few hours were torturous. I was adrift in the violent, churning sea, holding tightly to a barrel, davening for a miracle. Night fell and still I bobbed about, my body shivering with cold. I dozed on and off, and wakened once to see some dots of light winking along a dark patch ahead of me in the water! I waited a bit until, in the faint light of dawn, I could make out the shoreline of an island. I was saved! I let go of the barrel and began to swim again. I arrived, half-dead, soaked and shivering, and collapsed on shore.

"The inhabitants of the island found me there and had mercy upon me. They changed my clothes, found a doctor to treat my illness and fed me until my strength returned. When I regained consciousness, I discovered that there was no way off the island except on a single ship that stopped there once a year. Unfortunately, the ship had come only a week before and I was forced to remain there for an entire year.

"That year was terrible! I was cut off from those I loved, with no way of contacting my worried family. I was certain you were mourning my death. I spent my early days taking walks to regain my strength. Eventually, I began to harvest coconuts and other island fruit, selling them to the inhabitants and saving the money for my ship's passage.

"Several weeks ago, the ship finally arrived and the good-hearted islanders bid me good-bye. The journey to Odessa took nearly two weeks, and I immediately boarded the first train for Warsaw!"

The joyous couple traveled to Rav Pinchas Koritzer to tell him of the miracle they had experienced. Rav Pinchas told Reb Yeshaya, "In the merit of paying for the *ner tamid,* the eternal light in the *bais medrash,* your life was spared."

The UNLIKELY DOCTOR

*M*any years ago, in ancient Baghdad, there lived a simple, unassuming vegetable seller by the name of Nissim.

Nissim was as pious as he was poor. He spent the better part of each day in the *bais medrash*, and would venture to the marketplace at noon to display his shriveled wares. His vegetables were pinched and meager, and fetched only a few farthings on the market. His customers were those too poor to afford the plump, ripe vegetables displayed in the other stalls at the market.

As a result, Nissim barely made enough to put some stale bread on the table. He never had money left over to enlarge his stall or deal with the better quality vegetables. He often gave away much of his meager stock to those less fortunate than he.

Yet he was happy and content with his lot. Nissim's face was always wreathed in a contented smile.

His wife and children tried to remain cheerful with their fate, but it was difficult to be happy when the stomach was empty and the larder was bare. Nissim comforted them with promises of a blissful Gan Eden promised to those who do the Almighty's will. Yet it was scant comfort to his good wife whose daughters were growing up and had no chance of getting married without a dowry.

The years went by and Nissim's lot remained the same. Yet his gentle acceptance of Hashem's will did not go unnoticed Above. The Heavenly Court convened and decided to reward Nissim on this world for his piety. Even the *Satan* agreed, hoping to test Nissim with the *nisayon* of wealth, which corrupts even the greatest of men ….

One evening, the Sultan was chatting with his astrologer on the roof of his luxurious palace. In those days, sultans and kings were superstitious, placing great emphasis on heavenly signs and constellations. It was not unusual for a monarch to exile an entire kingdom because of a perceived heavenly sign. Thus, an astrologer who could read the stars occupied a position of prominence in Baghdad.

It was a pleasant, balmy autumn evening. The Sultan gazed at the stars, dreamy-eyed. In the meantime, his astrologer surveyed the heavens with cunning, trying to find an opportunity to vent his hatred of Baghdad's Jewish community.

Suddenly, a brilliant flash of light streaked across the sky and disappeared as quickly as it had come. The Sultan was terrified. "What was that?" he asked nervously.

The astrologer was quiet for several moments and then gravely replied, "That is the star of David, your Majesty. It portends destruction for the Jews. Their days of glory are over. They must be driven from your kingdom at once!"

"But the Jews are my loyal subjects," objected the Sultan. "They are peaceful, law-abiding citizens who don't deserve to be driven away."

The astrologer grew solemn. "May the Lord save one who dares ignore the heavenly signs!" he warned. "Woe to those who defy the heavens!"

"But I heard that the Jews are not subjected to the heavenly signs," the Sultan recalled. "Their Lord takes care of them."

"True enough," replied the astrologer, "but that is only applicable when they obey His will. If they stray from the proper path, they lose their heavenly protection and become as vulnerable as the other nations."

"If so," replied the Sultan, "I cannot expel them until you prove two things to me. One, that the Jews are not loyal to the traditions, and two, that their Jewish star's glory has waned."

"How can I prove it to you?" asked the astrologer eagerly.

"You are the wisest man in my kingdom," replied the Sultan. "I leave it to you."

The astrologer thought for a few moments. "I have an idea," he said. "Let us find a Jew in your kingdom who is very pious and also very poor. Let your Majesty order him to find a new profession for which he is unskilled. If he succeeds and becomes rich, and continues to remain faithful to his traditions, then I concede defeat. If he fails or the wealth corrupts him, that will be proof that the Jews deserve to be driven away …."

The Sultan readily agreed to the astrologer's plan.

Early the next morning, the astrologer dressed in ordinary clothes and wandered through the marketplace. He inquired about the poorest man in the market. "You probably mean Nissim, the vegetable seller," he was told. Then he asked others about the most pious man in the community and received the same answer. "You want Nissim, the vegetable seller." The astrologer realized he had found his man. He reported back to the Sultan.

Later that afternoon, Nissim the vegetable seller was summoned to the royal palace by a uniformed guard. Trembling apprehensively, Nissim appeared before the Sultan.

"What is your name and occupation?" asked the Sultan kindly.

"I sell vegetables, your Majesty," Nissim replied.

"Would you like to become a doctor?" the Sultan asked.

"Your Majesty is surely jesting!" trembled Nissim. "I am only a poor vegetable seller and have no training to be a doctor."

"Nevertheless," replied the Sultan, "I command you to become a doctor. You must open your own practice tomorrow and start receiving patients. Report to me in a month."

Pale and shaking, Nissim hurried home and related the afternoon's occurrence to his wife.

"If the Sultan commanded you to become a doctor, what choice do you have?" she asked. "Although I doubt anyone will want to avail themselves of your services …"

The next day at noontime, instead of heading to the marketplace as he had done for the past ten years, Nissim went to several acquaintances and borrowed money. Then he bought a decent suit and rented quarters in the nicest section of Baghdad. He hung up a sign reading "Nissim the Physician." He was officially open for business.

It took a few days before he met his first patient. Nissim received him courteously, listened to his complaints and prescribed a treatment. Wonder of wonders! Within days, the patient was cured.

Word spread quickly. Soon a steady stream of patients trekked to Nissim's door. He listened patiently to their woes, checked their symptoms and prescribed treatments. Some patients were told that they were physically healthy, only consumed with anxiety. They were told to take walks when they found themselves worrying and their ailments would disappear. Patients with stomach ailments were given a diet of vegetables and broth until they healed. Those who were truly ill were given "medicines" consisting of colored water, which miraculously healed them.

Nissim the doctor received a megadose of *siyata d'Shmaya*, and his fame spread far and wide. Although his services were sought by hundreds of patients, he didn't charge a set fee. Each patient paid whatever he could afford. The poor patients simply showered him with blessings, while the richer patients paid generously and bought him expensive gifts.

Yet despite his extraordinary success, Nissim's personality remained unchanged. He was as cheerful and giving as always and never forgot about the poor. Every day he sent a servant to the market to buy fresh vegetables and deposit them at the doors of his former customers, free of charge.

The Heavenly Court was delighted. Nissim had withstood the test.

Thirty days passed, and Nissim remembered that he had an appointment with the Sultan. He promptly closed his office and rode to the palace, requesting an audience with the Sultan.

"His Majesty is very ill," the guards informed him, "and he won't see anyone."

"But I am a physician," Nissim replied, "and I have come to cure him." The guards escorted him into the Sultan's chamber where the Sultan was writhing in agony. While eating his midday meal, he had swallowed a fish bone, and it was slowly choking him. The most experienced doctors tried to dislodge the bone, but they only succeeded in entrapping it farther in the Sultan's throat.

Nissim appeared at the Sultan's bedside. "Your Majesty," he said, "I am Nissim the physician. I have come to heal you."

Hearing those words, the Sultan burst into hearty laughter, upon which a miracle occurred! Due to his hysterical laughter, the fish bone was dislodged and flew out of his throat. Color returned to the Sultan's face as he sat up in bed.

"How can I repay you?" he said gratefully to Nissim. "You have saved my life."

"Your Majesty owes me nothing," replied Nissim humbly. "The Creator of the Universe has seen fit to heal you. I was just His messenger."

The Sultan, who had heard of Nissim's success, then summoned the astrologer and turned to him sternly.

"You have forfeited your life!" he declared. "The falling star you saw was not the star of David, but your own unlucky star. You deserve death for your evil plans!"

The astrologer fell to his knees, begging for mercy. "Please spare me, your Majesty," he pleaded.

"I place your fate in the hands of Nissim the doctor," the Sultan said. "I shall do whatever he decides."

"Your Majesty," said Nissim, "I have seen many sick men, but

I have never seen a man sicker and more consumed with hatred than this astrologer. Yet I believe that he is on his way to being cured. Let his life be spared as long as he promises not to harm another Jew as long as he lives ...."

And so it was.

69

The YESHIVA BACHUR'S KADDISH

*P*inchas *was* the eldest son of Baruch the woodcutter in the village of Demecser. From when he was a child, he had desired nothing more than to study Torah. As he grew older, he soon surpassed the village *melamed* and was ready to move on. He often stayed up late into the night, studying by the light of a meager candle, while everyone else was asleep. Although Baruch was proud of his budding genius, there was little he could do. The tiny village of Demecser was not large enough to support a second *melamed*, let alone a yeshiva. Most of the village boys learned until their bar mitzvah, when they left *cheder* and went to learn a trade. Many were apprenticed to their fathers or uncles, learning to become blacksmiths, weavers or tailors.

But Pinchas was different. He had a burning desire to grow in learning, but his desire had nothing to feed on. Finally, after lengthy consideration, he made his decision. Shortly after his bar mitzvah, the slender lad packed up his belongings to journey to the faraway city of Mishkolz and learn in the famous yeshiva under Rav Shmuel, a renowned *talmid chacham*.

The parting was tearful. Baruch and his wife bid their son good-bye and warned him to be careful. Pinchas climbed into the dilapidated coach with some tradesmen headed in that direction, and was on his way.

The journey took nearly a week of travel on bumpy, dirt roads. Pinchas could barely sleep from excitement. He had no idea where he would stay or how he would eat. He knew only one thing: He was going to yeshiva. These joyous words reverberated over and over in his head.

Finally, they arrived at the edge of Mishkolz. Pinchas paid the driver from the carefully hoarded coins his father had given him, dusted off his threadbare suit and headed toward the great yeshiva.

The young lad was overwhelmed as he stepped into the *bais medrash*. The sound of hundreds of voices learning was like balm to his eager soul. He sought out the Rosh Yeshiva and was directed to an elderly man sitting to one side, immersed in his *gemara*.

"*Shalom aleichem*," said the Rosh Yeshiva Rav Shmuel kindly. "A new *bachur*?"

"I am Pinchas, from Demecser," the *bachur* replied.

"Excellent. We are happy to welcome you. But first, we have to see if you can understand the *gemara* well enough to learn here. Let me ask you several questions."

The Rosh Yeshiva tested the young boy, and to his delight, Pinchas answered perfectly. It seemed as if he had been learning this particular *gemara* all his life. Rav Shmuel was very impressed. Not only was Pinchas a budding genius, his sweetness and refined bearing denoted a worthy *talmid*. He decided to grant the young boy a special scholarship.

Most *bachurim* who did not live in town ate their meals through a system called *"essen teg."* This entailed a complicated schedule whereby every *bachur* ate two meals every day at the home of a different *baalebos* each day of the week. This system had its drawbacks, as not all the townspeople were generous and many did not give the boys adequate food. Therefore, the very best *bachurim* who could not be disturbed from their learning for even one extra moment were given a special stipend with which to buy their own food. They would buy a week's supply at the beginning of the week, and could thus study uninterrupted.

Reb Shmuel wrote a letter for Pinchas, saying he was entitled to the special scholarship. "Take this to Nechemya, the *parnas*," said Rav Shmuel. "And may you be *matzliach*."

"*Amein*," said Pinchas, taking leave of the Rosh Yeshiva. He then walked to the main street and asked for help. Someone directed him to the home of the *parnas*, the most opulent dwelling in town. Pinchas knocked hesitantly at the door and a servant opened it, ushering the timid boy inside.

Nechemya was an arrogant, conceited man, who delighted in throwing his weight around. When he saw the shy *bachur*, he brusquely said, "Nu?"

"I ... the Rosh Yeshiva sent this ...," stammered Pinchas, holding out the Rosh Yeshiva's letter.

Nechemya took one look at the letter and became livid. "So the Rosh Yeshiva is sending me more *shnorrer*s? We have no more money to give you. Go tell Reb Shmuel to put you on the list for '*essen teg*' like the other *bachurim*. We don't need privileged characters over here."

Pinchas slunk out, discouraged and humiliated. He resolved not to breathe of his troubles to a soul. He didn't want to burden the Rosh Yeshiva and hurt his feelings with a report of the *parnas*'s behavior. He simply sat down in the *bais medrash* and began to learn with great fervor.

The first few days passed quickly. Pinchas bought some bread with a few *kreutzer*. However, soon a week passed and his money supply was nearly gone.

One afternoon, Pinchas slowly counted out his last four *kreutzer* — enough to buy day-old stale bread — and walked slowly toward the bakery, wondering what he would do next. As he was about to enter the bakery, he met a frail old woman coming toward him with outstretched palm. "*Tzedakah*. Please. I haven't had anything to eat in two days."

Pinchas felt great pity for the poor woman and gave her his last few coins. He stood near the bakery door gazing sadly at the bread in the window, trying to ignore the rumbling of his stomach.

Suddenly, he heard a woman behind him clearing her throat. He turned and met another elderly widow with a sad expression on her face.

"You are a yeshiva *bachur*, true?" she asked.

Pinchas nodded.

"I noticed that you are hungry," she said. "I want to make a deal with you. I will give you ten *kreutzer*, enough to buy bread for two days. In return, I want you to say *Kaddish* for my husband's *neshamah*. His *yahrtzeit* is tonight."

"Certainly," said Pinchas. "I would gladly learn for his *neshamah* even without the money."

"No, I want you to have a filling meal. It's the least I can do for you. Unfortunately, I …" She sighed. "I have a son, but he … he is … 'imprisoned.' I don't have anyone to say *Kaddish* for my husband. His name is Moshe ben Chaim. And when you say *Kaddish* for him, have in mind all the other souls whose *yahrtzeit*s are tonight."

Pinchas promised to say *Kaddish* and learn *Mishnayos* in his memory. Then he walked into the bakery, bought his fill of bread and prepared to return to yeshiva. The widow was nowhere in sight.

He hurried to the *bais medrash* and arrived just in time for Mincha and Maariv. Pinchas recited *Kaddish* with great *kavanah*, and after davening, sat down to learn *Mishnayos*. The *bais medrash* slowly emptied as the *bachurim* retired to get some rest. Only Pinchas remained, immersed in his *Mishnayos*, his meager supper untouched.

Suddenly, he realized he was not alone. An elderly man was standing by his side.

"I want to thank you for your warm, beautiful *Kaddish*," said the old man. "I haven't heard such a beautiful *Kaddish* in many years. Tell me," he continued, "do you have where to eat on Shabbos?"

Pinchas looked away, shamefaced.

"Such a sweet yeshiva *bachur* with nowhere to eat? I'll help you," said the old man. "I will give you a note for the *parnas*. He will include you in the group of *bachurim* who receive a stipend."

Out of respect for the old man, Pinchas remained silent. Why should he tell this kind person that the *parnas* could not care less, and had even ignored a letter from the Rosh Yeshiva?

He accepted the note and put it in his pocket. Then he continued learning until the first slivers of dawn lit up the horizon.

The next afternoon, hunger pangs hit Pinchas with a vengeance. He was so hungry, weak and exhausted that he couldn't concentrate on his learning. He weighed his options: Should he go to the Rosh Yeshiva and ask to be put on the list of those who ate '*teg*' or should he try his luck with the *parnas* again?

Finally, Pinchas decided to try the *parnas*. After all, he reasoned, what did he have to lose? The worst thing that could happen was that the *parnas* would throw him out, and then he could always go back to Rav Shmuel.

He knocked on Nechemya's door, his heart hammering. It was opened by the same servant who sullenly guided Pinchas into the study. The *parnas* walked into the room, took one look at Pinchas and sneered, "So you came back again? You didn't think I was serious, did you?"

Pinchas placed the note from the old man on the *parnas*'s desk, stammering, "I … have … another letter."

"I don't need your letters!" said the *parnas*, glancing at the piece of paper. Suddenly, he froze.

"Wait a minute," he said. "What is this?!" He snatched up the paper and began to read, his eyes popping. He glared at the trembling boy and leaned forward. "WHO GAVE YOU THIS LETTER?" he bellowed.

Pinchas described the elderly gentleman he had met in the *bais medrash*.

"Just a minute," interrupted Nechemya. "Come over here." He led him to a hallway lined with pictures. "Do you recognize your man?"

Pinchas pointed to one of the pictures. "This was the man."

Nechemya groaned and crumpled in a heap on the floor.

"Someone, help!" cried Pinchas in trepidation. A servant came running, and, at once, the entire household erupted. A doctor was summoned, and he revived the *parnas*.

"What is the meaning of this?" asked the doctor when the entire family had calmed down.

In a weak, shaking voice, the *parnas* explained. "This young boy brought me a letter from my father, who passed away five years ago. Last night ...," he said in a broken voice, "last night was his *yahrtzeit*. And I ... I forgot. I was too busy with my own affairs." With these words, Nechemya began weeping. "But this *bachur* didn't forget. He remembered to say *Kaddish* for all the *neshamos* whose *yahrtzeit*s were today. He saved my father's dignity, and I shall never forget it."

Nechemya signed Pinchas onto the list of *bachurim* and gave him a generous stipend. From that day on, he supported Pinchas and any other needy *bachurim* until the end of his days.

The
AUSTRIAN
SPY

*R*eb *Yisrael* Skoler, an ardent *chassid* of the renowned *tzaddik* Rav Meir Premishlan, was a distinguished *talmid chacham* and *oveid Hashem*. He was known as a generous, kindhearted man who would readily do a favor when asked.

He dealt in fine wines and dried fruits, traveling from Austria to Hungary several times a year to stock up on merchandise. On his return from his travels, Reb Yisrael would visit his Rebbe, leaving an abundance of dried fruit and wine with the *gabbai*. Rav Meir would partake of the delicacies on Shabbos afternoon.

One year, while Reb Yisrael was in Debrecin, Hungary, on business, war broke out between Austria and Hungary and he was caught in the crossfire. Hungarian soldiers with drawn guns surrounded the city. The hapless merchant was trapped with his merchandise, unable to communicate with his family and with no practical means to escape. What does a *chassid* do in such a situation? He went straight to the *bais medrash* and spent his days immersed in Torah and *tefillah*.

Early one morning, on his way from the inn to the *bais medrash*, Reb Yisrael was stopped by a group of soldiers who had set up an army checkpoint in the middle of the street.

"Papers, please!" they demanded roughly. Reb Yisrael paled. He reached into his pocket for his Austrian passport, his heart pounding in fear.

The officer in charge grabbed it out of his hand and sneered.

"Comrades!" he called in Hungarian. "We have caught an Austrian spy!"

They seized him roughly and handcuffed him.

"Please! I am innocent!" cried Reb Yisrael. "I am a simple Austrian citizen, a businessman with dealings in Hungary. Why should you arrest an innocent man?"

His pleas fell on deaf ears. The officers dragged him to military headquarters. There, he was tried by a tribunal of high-ranking officers. As soon as the general and his men saw their prisoner's Austrian documents, they concluded that he must be a dangerous spy. All of Reb Yisrael's pleas that he was innocent and merely caught in the wrong place at the wrong time fell on deaf ears.

As often occurred in wartime, the tribunal hastily passed the death sentence upon the helpless man. Reb Yisrael was locked into a cell to await his death by firing squad. He was trussed like a chicken on the cold earthen floor, unable to move his arms and legs. Yet his mind still worked feverishly, trying to figure out what to do. He realized that escape was impossible; nor was it possible for him to contact anyone back home. He wondered how long it would take his family to find out what had happened to him. Was his wife destined to become an *agunah*? Would his children realize that they were orphans? Who would support and care for them?

Reb Yisrael's eyes filled with tears as he contemplated his fate. There was nothing to do but daven, he realized. Our sages teach us that even when a sharp sword is resting upon one's neck, one must not despair of Hashem's mercy.

He began reciting *Tehillim* from memory, verse by verse, his voice choked with emotion. He davened fervently, begging the *Ribono shel Olam* to spare his life. As the hours went by and the time of his execution drew closer, Reb Yisrael's *tefillos* reached a feverish pitch. He had not eaten or had a sip of water in two days, but his mind was occupied with far more important things. He was preparing for his final journey.

Shabbos morning, the time of his execution, arrived. The door to his cell burst open. Reb Yisrael was roughly grabbed by a couple of soldiers in full army regalia. Somberly, they marched him to an open courtyard.

Reb Yisrael shuffled along, murmuring Shema Yisrael and

preparing to die. He was so absorbed in his thoughts that he barely noticed their arrival at the courtyard. The firing squad stood ready, rifles cocked, waiting for the final order to shoot.

Suddenly, a high-ranking officer astride a white steed rode into the courtyard and stopped before the firing squad.

"What is happening here?" he demanded in a booming voice.

"We are executing an Austrian spy," they replied.

The officer stared at Reb Yisrael and paled.

"Srultche, is that you?" he cried. "You, a spy? Unbelievable."

"I promise that I am not a spy," replied a trembling Reb Yisrael, wondering how the officer could possibly know his name. "I was caught in the city with Austrian papers. That is all the proof they need."

"Preposterous!" replied the officer with anger. "You, Srultche, are not a spy. Why, I know you for years already. There are very few men who are as honest and upright as you are. Soldiers, free him immediately!"

The soldiers hesitated. After all, they had orders to obey.

"We cannot do that, Sir," they said. "The general himself gave the order to kill him."

"Then return him to the dungeon while I speak to the general," replied the officer.

Reb Yisrael was marched back to his gloomy cell where he continued to daven with all his heart. Whoever that officer was, he had surely been sent from Heaven. Reb Yisrael prayed the man would be successful in releasing him.

The hours passed slowly. Suddenly, he heard a racket outside and the sound of heavy shooting. From the frightened screams of the soldiers guarding his cell, he deduced that Debrecin was under attack.

Within a short while, the battle was over. Then Reb Yisrael's ears heard a most welcoming sound: soldiers conversing in

Austrian. The Austrians had reached Debrecin and were taking over the city!

"Praised be *Hakadosh Baruch Hu*," cried Reb Yisrael, overcome with emotion. Had the high-ranking officer not intervened, the only thing the Austrian soldiers would have found was his body.

Soon the sound of footsteps broke the silence in the prison. In minutes, some burly Austrian guards had broken open the door to his cell and freed him.

"What are you doing here?" they asked.

Reb Yisrael explained that he had been arrested on suspicion of being an Austrian spy and was about to face the firing squad.

The soldiers hailed him as a hero. They released him and escorted him back to the inn to find his merchandise. Unfortunately, the Hungarians had been there already and had confiscated the expensive cases of wine and dried fruit.

"Never fear," the Austrian soldiers reassured him. "We will reimburse you for the full value of the merchandise. Tell us how much it was worth." Reb Yisrael named a price and they counted the money into his hands. Then a special contingent of soldiers escorted him across the Hungarian border to safety.

It was a joyous reunion. Reb Yisrael's family had been worried about his safety, but they had no inkling of the real danger he had faced, a hairsbreadth away from the firing squad. As he shared his harrowing tale, his wife and children burst into tears of relief.

Reb Yisrael's wife served him a hot meal and begged him to rest from his exhausting ordeal, but he insisted on doing one thing first.

"I must immediately go to Reb Meir of Premishlan and inform him of the miracles that have occurred to me," he told her.

His wife knew it was futile to argue. That very afternoon, an exhausted Reb Yisrael set out for Premishlan, the hometown of his great Rebbe. As soon as he stepped across the threshold of his Rebbe's home, Rav Meir turned to his *gabbai* and said, "Aryeh, didn't Reb Yisrael's dried fruit taste especially good this Shabbos?"

Reb Yisrael stood, stunned, as he grasped the significance of his Rebbe's words. Reb Meir turned to his *chassid* with a smile.

"If you only knew how my messenger was inconvenienced because of you," Rav Meir hinted. It was then that Reb Yisrael understood: The high-ranking officer had known his name because he was not a human being, after all.

Reb Pinchas
the
G'vir

*Z*anvil was a pauper in the truest sense of the word. He didn't have a rubbed out *kopek* to his name. He, his wife and eight children lived in a miserable shanty at the edge of town. The family subsisted on black bread smeared with garlic and water spiced with lemon during the week. On Shabbos, a handful of dried vegetables and an egg completed the meal.

But Zanvil didn't complain. Though far from the richest man in the *shtetl*, he wasn't the poorest, either. His children had shoes on their feet, patched up with rags to prevent frostbite. Their jackets were similarly patched, and the heavy fur caps on their heads had seen better days.

But Zanvil had no complaints. With a spring in his step and a gleam in his eyes, he continued to eke out his meager living as a blacksmith, shoeing the patient horses in the village and fixing the housewives' gleaming tin pots.

Zanvil's family grew as the years went by, but there was always bread and garlic. His older children took care of the younger ones, patching their clothes, telling them stories and feeding them bits of gruel. Zanvil's good wife, Fayge, was a happy sort, always smiling and humming a tune as she bustled about, children clinging to her skirts.

But as Zanvil's daughters grew old enough to marry, they remained lonely spinsters. In those days, girls who did not have a dowry had no hope of marrying a fine boy. And Zanvil didn't want his daughters to settle for anything less than the best, and so they remained single.

Zanvil was a devoted *chassid* of the holy Koshnitzer Maggid. As the years went by and no worthy suitors appeared, Zanvil began pouring out his troubles to the Maggid.

The Maggid would listen patiently and reply, "Have *bitachon*, Zanvil. The *Ribono shel Olam* won't forsake you. The *yeshuah* will come, *im yirtzeh Hashem*."

When his eldest daughter turned twenty-three (at a time when most girls married in their teens), Zanvil couldn't take it any longer. He harnessed his old horse to its rickety buggy and rode off to Koshnitz to see the Maggid.

"Rebbe!" he burst out as he entered the holy Maggid's chamber.

The Maggid looked up from his *sefer* and regarded Zanvil with his pure and riveting gaze.

"Rebbe! My Pesha just turned twenty-three. What will become of her? My other daughters are twenty-one and nineteen. Even my seventeen-year-old's friends are already married. My wife is crying her eyes out!"

"*Zorg nisht*, don't worry, Zanvil," said the Maggid soothingly. "*Der Eibeshter vet helfen*, Hashem will help."

But Zanvil was not mollified. "When, Rebbe? When will *der Eibeshter* help?" he said, flinging his despairing arms upward.

The Maggid held out his hand. "Zanvil, be patient. Where is your *emunah* and *bitachon*?"

"*Emunah* and *bitachon* can't marry off my daughters!" said Zanvil bitterly.

The Maggid sighed. Zanvil was a fine, if simple man, but the pressure of marrying off his daughters was taking its toll upon his peace of mind.

"Zanvil," he said, "I have a mission for you. I want you to travel to Warsaw and lodge at the home of Reb Pinchas the *G'vir*. Pinchas has an open house for wayfarers. Your mission will be to learn *emunah* and *bitachon* from him. Perhaps the *Ribono shel Olam* will help you be successful and raise a dowry for your daughter."

The Maggid bade Zanvil good-bye, and Zanvil was on his way. He sent a message to his family, saying he would be detained for a couple of weeks. There was enough bread in the house to last for another week or so, and Zanvil hoped to be back before long. The smithy would wait for his return.

Zanvil traveled to Warsaw, arriving toward the end of the second day. He immediately asked for the address of Reb Pinchas the *G'vir*. A kind city dweller showed him the way. Zanvil was amazed by the tall buildings, the cobblestone streets and the elegant carriages. He felt out of place with his tattered clothes and rickety buggy.

He tied his horse in front of Reb Pinchas's spacious home and entered humbly, unsure of the reception he would receive. To his surprise, Reb Pinchas welcomed him graciously, seating him at a comfortable wooden table and plying him with nourishing food. After he had eaten and drunk his fill, he timidly inquired if there was place for him to lodge.

"Of course, Reb Yid," replied Reb Pinchas warmly. "My house is open to you. You can stay as long as you'd like." His host didn't ask the reason for his visit nor how long he intended to remain. Reb Pinchas kept an open house, with guests constantly coming and going, no questions asked. Anyone who popped in was assured of a warm meal and an effusive welcome. Reb Pinchas's good wife was an excellent cook, and she had a staff of maids to help her keep the house running.

Zanvil soon settled into a routine. He kept to himself, didn't bother anyone and spent most of his days learning in a corner of the vast dining room. All the while, he surreptitiously kept an eye on his host, Reb Pinchas, who radiated constant good cheer.

People kept coming and asking Reb Pinchas for a handout. And they were never disappointed. Reb Pinchas seemed to have very deep pockets, always stocked with rubles and full of coins. Anyone who asked for a donation was given handsomely, in a fitting manner.

Whenever Reb Pinchas was asked for a larger sum, he would

excuse himself and go down to the cellar where he kept his well-guarded safe. He always emerged, radiant and content, his pockets refilled with golden coins.

After a day or two, Zanvil's curiosity changed to bitterness. *What did the Maggid want me to learn from Reb Pinchas?* he thought to himself. *What's the big deal to be a baal emunah and bitachon with a safe overflowing with golden coins? If I'd be as rich as him, I would also be brimming with goodwill and cheer. Of course, there are plenty of rich misers, but Reb Pinchas is made of better stuff. He is exceptionally generous and upright. But does that make him a baal emunah and bitachon?*

Zanvil concluded that he had nothing more to learn from Reb Pinchas, except perhaps the art of giving graciously, and resolved to leave that very same day. He hoped Reb Pinchas would give him a generous sum to help with his daughter Pesha's dowry.

That afternoon, he took leave of his host. "You have been very kind," he said, "and I appreciate and admire your hospitality. I plan to leave for my hometown this afternoon."

Reb Pinchas smiled at Zanvil and said, "It was a pleasure to be your host. I noticed you spent most of your time learning Torah, and I respect your character. And now, can I help you with anything?"

Zanvil haltingly explained about his daughters and their non-existent dowry.

"Of course, of course!" said Reb Pinchas. "I'll try to help you, *im yirtzeh Hashem*. But is there anything else you lack? You seemed to be looking for something."

Zanvil marveled at his host's perception. "I'll be honest with you," he said, "and tell you the real reason for my visit."

Zanvil explained the Koshnitzer Maggid's strange command that he learn *emunah* and *bitachon* from Reb Pinchas. "To tell you the truth, I don't understand it. I admire your hospitality, your generosity and your goodwill. But how can you teach me *emunah* and *bitachon*? If I were in your shoes, with a loaded purse full of money, I, too, would be a *baal bitachon*. Having *emunah* and *bitachon* isn't that hard in your circumstances."

Reb Pinchas smiled and sighed softly, sunk in his thoughts. He appeared to be debating whether or not to share something. Finally, his mind was made up.

"Reb Zanvil, I would like to show you something," he said softly. "But first, you must promise not to tell a soul."

Zanvil promised. Burning with curiosity, he followed his host down the cellar stairs to the famous safe where Reb Pinchas kept his money.

The cellar was deep and dark. On one side was a heavy, oak door. Reb Pinchas fiddled with its heavy lock and inserted a key, and Zanvil watched it swing open to reveal a safe as big as a walk-in closet. Reb Pinchas invited Zanvil inside.

Reb Zanvil walked in and looked about him, first along one wall, then the next, and the next, and saw … nothing. The room was stark and empty, except for a rickety table and chair.

"This is my storeroom, Reb Zanvil," said Reb Pinchas. "Here are all my earthly treasures."

Zanvil looked around in bewilderment. "B-but the room is empty!" he protested.

"Not completely," said Reb Pinchas, who walked over to the corner of the room and lifted a heavy, dog-eared account book. "This is the sum total of my 'savings,' " he said. "Bills and demands from my creditors. I own nothing — zero. I have no savings, and never had any. Only my *bitachon* sustains me."

Zanvil was dumbfounded. "Then how … how do you manage to feed so many guests and give such generous donations?"

Reb Pinchas smiled again. "Simple," he said. "I do my share and the *Ribono shel Olam* does His. Whenever someone approaches me for money, I go downstairs to my 'safe,' sit down at the table and daven to the *Ribono shel Olam*. He has never disappointed me yet."

Zanvil was skeptical. Perhaps Reb Pinchas was hiding something.

"You don't believe me, eh?" asked Pinchas. "Well, then, let us go upstairs and you will see for yourself."

No sooner had they gone upstairs than the butler escorted an agent of the large Jewish bakery into Reb Pinchas's study. The man handed him an I.O.U. from the bakery, from whom Reb Pinchas had purchased a quantity of flour and baked goods worth hundreds of rubles. Reb Pinchas assured him he would pay within the hour.

After the messenger had left, Zanvil asked Reb Pinchas, "Why did you promise to pay in an hour? How will you manage it?"

"Have *bitachon,* Reb Zanvil," said Reb Pinchas. "I will now go down to my 'safe' to 'take' some money."

Reb Pinchas returned to the cellar as Zanvil looked on, dumbfounded. What was Reb Pinchas thinking?

After a short interval, Reb Pinchas came back up the stairs, his manner calm and cheerful. As he stepped into the hallway, there was a tentative knocking at the door. Reb Pinchas smiled slightly and tilted his head toward the door. "Come," he said to Zanvil, "let us go see how Hashem will help us."

On the doorstep stood an anxious-looking soldier.

"Can I help you, sir?" asked Reb Pinchas pleasantly.

The soldier cleared his throat and explained. "My battalion is stationed outside Warsaw for another few hours. We are leaving to fight the Cossacks. It will be a long and dangerous war. I don't know if I will survive. My fellow soldiers told me you are an honest and trustworthy man. Therefore, I'd like to entrust my money to you for safekeeping." And the soldier handed him a sack bulging with golden coins.

Zanvil stared in amazement, but Reb Pinchas only smiled pleasantly, as if he had expected it all along.

"You can use the money until I come back," said the soldier. "I trust you and am sure you will repay it when the time comes."

When the soldier had gone, Reb Pinchas took Reb Zanvil's arm and walked with him to the bakery, paying his account in full.

"You see, my friend," explained Reb Pinchas, "how the *Ribono shel Olam* helps those who trust in Him."

Zanvil nodded shamefacedly.

"Now, I am not going to send you away, *chalila*. You can stay as long as you'd like," said his host. "But your mission with me is complete."

"B-but I still don't have any money for my daughter's dowry," protested Zanvil, "or to feed my hungry family."

"Have you already forgotten the lessons of *emunah* and *bitachon* you've learned?" chided Reb Pinchas. "Don't you realize that the *Ribono shel Olam* can give you whatever you need? All you have to do is ask."

Zanvil remained silent, his cheeks burning. Reb Pinchas put a friendly arm around his shoulder. "Now take this," he said, giving Zanvil the remainder of the soldier's money, "and may the *Ribono shel Olam* be with you."

Zanvil took his leave of Reb Pinchas, wringing his hands emotionally. He harnessed his horse to his rickety wagon and was on his way.

As he rode through the woods in the deepening dusk, he heard a terrifying scream. He quickly turned his horse to its source and soon came upon a tragic sight. A miserable horse was pulling a rickety cart on which a poor Jewish family stood, bound together and shivering in fright.

Nearby, a *poritz* sat in his opulent coach, cackling in glee. It was obvious what had happened. Apparently, the poor Jew had fallen behind in his rent and the *poritz* was taking him and his family as hostages. The wails of the frightened children should have pierced a heart of stone, but the *poritz* was unmoved.

"Where are you taking this family?" asked Zanvil cautiously, afraid of antagonizing the *poritz*.

"To the dungeon. Let them rot," spat the *poritz*. "Moshke hasn't paid his rent in over six months. Let him die in jail, together with his family."

Upon hearing these heartless words, Moshke's children began wailing anew. The *poritz* sneered derisively.

"How much do they owe you?" asked Zanvil.

"Two hundred gold coins," replied the *poritz*.

"Will you take one hundred and fifty coins?" asked Zanvil, prepared to bargain.

"No, I'll take the entire sum!" said the *poritz* mockingly. "But from where will you get it, pauper?"

"Right here." Zanvil patted his sack. Without blinking an eye, he handed over all the money Reb Pinchas had given him for his daughter's dowry. The *poritz* pocketed it without a word.

"Very well, you miserable creatures. You can go home now," muttered the *poritz,* disappointed that he could no longer torture them. "Your brother took care of you already."

"The Almighty took care of me," corrected Moshke, struggling to untie his bonds. "My brother was only His messenger."

The *poritz* cracked his whip contemptuously and drove off, leaving a trail of dust in his wake. Zanvil began untying Moshke, his wife and their poor children, who were numb with cold.

"Go home, and may Hashem be with you," said Zanvil.

"How can I ever thank you?" cried Moshke as he embraced his savior. "My family would have perished in the dungeon."

"Don't thank me," replied Zanvil. "Thank the *Ribono shel Olam.* As you told the *poritz*, I am but His messenger."

With a few final words of hope and encouragement, Zanvil and Moshke parted ways. Zanvil's heart swelled with joy. True, he had lost his daughter's dowry, but he had gained a mitzvah whose value was beyond estimation. *Pidyon shevuyim*, redeeming Jewish captives, saving Jewish lives … can any earthly pleasure compare to the everlasting bliss such a mitzvah engenders?

Zanvil rode onward, his nagging worries forgotten. His former anxiety about a dowry for his Pesha vanished into thin air. Gone were the doubts. In their place, a firm *emunah* and *bitachon* resided in his heart. Zanvil had nothing to worry about. His rich Father in Heaven would take care of his daughter and her dowry, and feed his children as well.

When night fell, Zanvil reached the outskirts of a small village, halfway to his home. He saddled his horse near an inn and entered, hoping for a free night's lodging. The owner of the inn, a good-hearted Jew, gladly consented, offering Zanvil a hearty meal and a bed for the night. Zanvil thanked him graciously.

As he ate a plate of warm soup, a rich landowner entered the inn and sat down nearby. The owner served him a hearty meal, replete with wine and spirits.

For some reason, the landowner struck up a conversation with Zanvil and began asking him particulars about his hometown.

"I know your uncle Feivel," said the landowner. "You bear a striking resemblance to him. He lives in my town."

Zanvil perked up his ears curiously.

"Feivel is an honest man," continued the landowner, "and I am sure his nephew can be trusted. I have a brother living near your village. For some time, I have been planning to send him money to tide him over during the dry season. Can you please be so kind and deliver the money for me?"

Zanvil agreed. The landowner handed him a sack filled with gold coins and gave Zanvil directions to his brother's village.

Zanvil left the following morning, stopping first at the village to discharge his errand. But, to his surprise, no one had ever heard the name before. After a fruitless day of searching, he gave up in frustration. But before heading home, he made another detour to the Koshnitzer Maggid and related the entire story.

"The money is yours to keep," said the Maggid with a smile. "It is clear to me that the mysterious landowner was an angel created by your mitzvah of *pidyon shevuyim*. Take the money and marry off your daughters honorably."

With a heart filled with joy and thanksgiving to the *Ribono shel Olam*, Zanvil returned home, where his wife and children anxiously awaited him. As soon as they saw his face wreathed in smiles, they began to sing and dance in joy.

"The *Ribono shel Olam* has saved us," said Zanvil, pointing to the sack of gold coins. "Chaim'l, go fetch Shachna the matchmaker."

Shachna arrived with a list of eligible young men for Pesha, now a young lady with a sizeable dowry. Within a short time, she was happily married, and her sisters soon followed. Zanvil married off his daughters, paid his debts and dispensed charity generously, with a giving heart. And he never forgot the lessons of *emunah* and *bitachon* he learned during his stay at the home of Reb Pinchas the *G'vir*.

LONG LIVE
the CZAR!

*I*t *was* Friday night, shortly before Kabbalas Shabbos. Congregants filled the large shul in the *shtetl* of Bobroisk in Russia, and they sat quietly saying Shir Hashirim and waiting for the *chazzan* to begin.

The candles in the shul burned brightly, casting a rich glow on the worn white tablecloths. Work-weary congregants forgot their exhaustion as they savored the aura of peace that accompanied the arrival of Shabbos. Ah, Shabbos *kodesh*—Hakadosh Baruch Hu's special gift to *Klal Yisrael*!

The congregation, while mainly comprised of tradesmen and day laborers, included a small number of wealthy businessmen who served as supporters of the *kehillah*. These men sat near the aged Rav, whose snow-white beard and stooped shoulders testified to the many years he had been leading his flock. Though he had aged considerably over the past few years, the Rav's magnetic and forceful personality, combined with his sterling *middos* and genuine humility, made him a revered and respected figure in the *shtetl*.

Toward the back of the shul, among the poorest of the townsfolk, sat Leibke the soldier, recently discharged from His Majesty the Czar's army. Leibke had a habit of always wearing his freshly starched soldier's uniform, with the two medals of bravery he had earned during the recent battle with the French. He had spent the best years of his life in the czar's army, having been inducted along with other young cantonists at the age of twelve.

Leibke remembered little of his early years. In the dim recesses of his memory, he recalled his mother, and how she cried when she lit candles on Friday night. His father worked hard all week, but would always learn with Leibke on Shabbos. He had many siblings, but most of them were now married and lived in other cities.

On that sad morning, so many years before, when he had been snatched away by the notorious *"chappers,"* emissaries of Czar Nikolai's army who grabbed young Jewish children off the streets, Leibke's peaceful childhood had come to an end. In one heartrending moment, the carefree, happy child became Czar Nikolai's ward, a nameless soldier living in a crude barrack, deprived of everything dear to him.

Leibke's poor parents knew what awaited their precious son but were powerless to prevent it. They mourned for Leibke as if he had died, for they knew that few, if any, of the cantonist children would return to their families, and fewer still remained Jews.

The story of the cantonists, tender Jewish boys torn away from their families and subject to excruciating tortures, is a tragic epoch of Jewish history. Thousands of young children were kidnapped, marched through the Russian countryside and sent to distant army barracks where they were forced to eat non-kosher food and be baptized. Their *tzitzis* were taken away, their *siddurim* were ripped up, and they were served pork. Any child who tried to resist was beaten nearly to death. Within a short while, most of the children were baptized and indoctrinated to forget their families. Czar Nikolai and Mother Russia became their new parents.

Leibke was one of the stronger boys, who had insisted on keeping kosher and who had refused to be baptized. He had endured unimaginable tortures and suffering; he was whipped and beaten, starved and nearly burned, yet he remained steadfast. Throughout the twenty-five years he served in the Czar's army, Leibke remained a committed Jew, and he said Shema every night.

As Leibke grew into adulthood, he left the children's barracks and joined the regular army. By that time, he had only dim memories of his family, who still mourned their long-lost son. He yearned to escape, yet escape was impossible. The fate of an escaped soldier who was caught—and they all were caught, sooner or later—was execution without a trial.

Thus, the years passed, and Leibke became a hardened soldier. As often happens when people are held captive, Leibke became intensely loyal to his captor, the Czar. He would do anything for Czar Nikolai and the Russian army. He soon became distinguished with his acts of bravery, earning several medallions and decorations on his chest.

Finally, after twenty-five years of army service, Leibke was discharged and allowed to return home to his aged parents. By that time, he was nearly forty, and the reunion was bittersweet. While Leibke's parents were overjoyed to be reunited with their son, who was now a strapping, hardened soldier, they were crushed when they realized that he knew next to nothing about his religion. Slowly, Leibke's father began to teach him Modeh Ani and the Aleph Bais, a little at a time. His mother served him nourishing meals with devotion, trying to make up for all those years he had been deprived.

Leibke's new life was far from easy. He felt like a misfit in the small *shtetl* where he had grown up. Most of his peers were the heads of large families, while he had little hope of finding a *shidduch* at his age. In addition, Leibke talked, walked and acted like a soldier, behavior that was scorned in his village. His open allegiance to Czar Nikolai was not looked kindly upon, either. Some felt that Leibke was a walking tragedy. Others, including the Rav of the *shtetl*, realized that Leibke was a walking *kiddush Hashem*, a living example of the resilience of *Klal Yisrael* during those difficult times.

On that Friday night, as the congregants recited Shir Hashirim, Leibke sat among them, painstakingly pronouncing every syllable of the unfamiliar *tefillah*.

The peace and serenity of the shul was abruptly shattered as the door opened, and a smartly dressed gentleman strode in. The young man was dressed in a short frock and high Homburg hat, and sported a trimmed, fashionable beard. The congregants gawked at the newcomer, wondering who he was.

They did not have to wonder long. The stranger strode to the *bimah* with an assured air of confidence, banged for silence and announced, "I am Dr. Hirschman, the new rabbi of this congregation, appointed by His Majesty, Czar Nikolai."

A collective gasp rose from the congregants. They had heard rumors that the Czar had decided to replace the revered *rabbanim* in their communities with university-educated, progressive individuals, who would lead the communities into a new era of enlightenment. There were tales of the new rabbis in neighboring communities being escorted by soldiers, forcing the venerable *rabbanim* from their positions and taking over. But no one had dreamed how soon this would occur in their own little *shtetl*.

"Since when is a doctor a rabbi?" asked Leibke, to no one in particular. "And since when did the Czar begin to choose our Rabbis for us?"

"Czar Nikolai's goal is to wipe out every vestige of religion from Russian Jewry," replied Tuvia the furrier, who was well-versed in world affairs. "He is using every method he can think of to accomplish this."

"And this new rabbi—he is an emissary of the Czar?" Leibke persisted.

His listeners snickered. "Of course. He certainly was not elected by us."

"If so, he must know the entire history of the Czar's extended family," remarked Leibke.

A burst of laughter was the only response from his fellow congregants.

It was the custom in those days for every single soldier, and for anyone in the Czar's employ, to diligently study the entire family history of the Czar, his parents, aunts and uncles, and any cousins. The genealogies of the Czar's family, going back several generations, were the most important "studies" the soldiers were required to know. Woe to any soldier who was remiss in his obligations and neglected to memorize the Czar's obscure relatives on his great-aunt's side. The soldier would be brutally beaten and barely escape with his life.

"I'm sure the good doctor doesn't know the Czar's family tree half as well as you do, Leibke," replied Tuvia. Leibke smiled and nodded, proud of himself.

Several noisy moments passed in this manner, while Doctor Hirschman waited for the hubbub to die down. Then he restated his mission: "His Majesty, the Czar, has commanded me to lead this congregation." Doctor Hirschman then marched over to the seat of the venerable Rav, and waited for the Rav to rise and abdicate his seat.

The aged Rav did not move, nor bat an eyelash. The doctor waited, his eyes glinting with determination, while the entire congregation sat uneasily, watching the confrontation unfold.

One minute passed, then another. The Rav and his rival faced each other, neither side giving an inch. The venerable Rav realized that giving up his seat to an ignoramus who was not fit to lead the community would be a true disgrace to the Torah. The aura of hatred and revenge that emanated from the young upstart was palpable.

Finally, after several minutes, the new rabbi slunk away and found an empty seat on the *mizrach* wall, where he sat down quietly. The *chazzan* began to recite Mizmor L'David and

Kabbalas Shabbos began. The congregation chanted the Lecha Dodi with a sweetness and tranquility that belied the anxiety they were experiencing. They were sure that this new rabbi boded no good for the community.

After Maariv was over, the congregation flocked to their venerable Rav to wish him a good Shabbos. There were only a few cool nods in the direction of Dr. Hirschman, who sat quietly, seething. Slowly, the congregants trickled out of the shul, and soon the cavernous building was empty. The sound of sweet *zemiros* began to waft out of the cottage windows, as the inhabitants of Bobroisk sat around their Shabbos tables and honored the holy day.

That night, the new rabbi could not fall asleep. He tossed and turned, fuming at his failure to wrest control and considering his next course of action. Should he arrive in shul the next morning with an armed bodyguard and force the Rav to abdicate his position? While his move would ensure that he got the seat, it would show the congregation that he lacked the power to handle the battle for authority on his own.

I must deal with this crisis on my own, decided Doctor Hirschman. After a little while, he hit upon the perfect plan.

Though he had fallen asleep long past midnight, Doctor Hirschman made sure to awake before dawn the next morning. He dressed quickly and made his way to the shul, whose doors had just been unlocked by the *shammas*. As the *shammas* was busy straightening up the women's section, the new rabbi walked over to the Rav's empty seat and sat down resolutely, determined not to budge.

One by one, the congregants trickled into shul and found themselves staring in shock at Dr. Hirschman sitting in their beloved Rav's seat. They trembled with rage and helplessness at the audacity of the upstart. Several of the more vocal congregants argued quietly. Should they oust the new rabbi with force? No, it was far too dangerous. One word from the doctor to the appropriate authorities, and those who ousted him would be exiled to Siberia.

After hushed deliberations, the congregants decided not to intervene. "Let us wait to see how the Rav will handle this" was the consensus.

The new rabbi gloated at their discomfort as he sat there smirking. His plan had succeeded!

Soon the shul was nearly full, and Shacharis was about to begin. A hush fell over the congregants as the aged Rav entered the shul and began slowly walking to his seat. All waited with bated breath to see what would occur.

The Rav stood at his place for several moments, waiting for the doctor to rise. When it became clear that Dr. Hirschman had no intention of rising—in fact, he was gloating over the Rav's discomfiture—the humble, aged *talmid chacham* turned away. As he passed the *mizrach* row, the entire group of distinguished *baalebatim* stood up, wordlessly begging the Rav to take their seat, cringing at this disgrace to the Torah. Yet the Rav refused to take anyone's *makom kavua*. He simply walked down the rows to the back of the shul and sat down in the last row, near the tailors and the peddlers of Bobroisk.

The congregants seethed with fury. To witness their Rav being humiliated in such a manner and watch Dr. Hirschman sneering at them with triumph in his eyes? Could there be a greater humiliation? Yet they were all afraid to speak up and publicly throw the new rabbi out of the shul.

The davening began, but it was a strained and uncomfortable Shacharis. The good people of Bobroisk were disturbed and pained beyond words. The whispering, which began at the end of Shacharis, continued through *kriyas haTorah* and showed no signs of abating. In vain did the *gabbai* bang on the *bimah*, repeatedly calling for silence. The congregants were too perturbed and upset to comply.

The loyal *gabbai* made sure to call up the elderly Rav for *shlishi* and left the *aliyah* of *shishi* for Dr. Hirschman. When he arose for his *aliyah*, he glared at the congregation, and fixed the *gabbai* with a steely glare that sent shudders down his spine. "I am the official rabbi here," said Dr. Hirschman in a voice that brooked no argument, "and I will be given the *aliyah* of *shlishi* from now on."

The *gabbai* nearly had a heart attack when he heard the veiled threat hidden in the new doctor's words. As Dr. Hirschman said the *brachos*, the congregation booed him loudly. The resulting furor was noisy and disturbing, shocking the elderly congregants.

"To the best of my knowledge, this has never happened before," whispered Reb Pesach, the *talmid chacham* who served as a water carrier in his spare time.

"Shocking," murmured Tuvia the goldsmith.

However, the most shocking part of that unusual Shabbos morning *tefillah* was yet to come.

It was a universally accepted custom in Russia in those days to utter the *tefillah* "Hanosen Teshuah Lamelachim," pledging allegiance and loyalty to the Czar, right before reciting "Av Harachamim" after *kriyas haTorah*. Heaven protect the congregation who forgot to say this *tefillah*! The Czar, who was well aware of this custom, did not take kindly to those congregations that neglected to praise and bless him during their Shabbos davening. There were spies in the shuls, loyal to the Czar, who would report such an indiscretion with glee.

The congregation of Bobroisk scrupulously observed this custom without fail. Yet on this eventful day, when the entire shul was in turmoil, the *chazzan* forgot to say the *tefillah*, and no one even noticed. No one, that is, except for Leibke, the former cantonist.

Leibke still harbored deep feelings of loyalty for Czar Nikolai, whom he regarded as a father. Thus, as soon as the *chazzan* began saying Ashrei before Mussaf, Leibke flew into a fury that shocked the entire congregation. Screaming and bellowing like a madman, he raced up the aisles, knocking over *sefarim* in his eagerness to get to the front of the shul. He ran toward Dr. Hirschman, who was complacently sitting in his seat, very proud of himself, and began to roar. "Traitor! Coward! You deserve to be exiled to Siberia! How dare you slight the honor of His Majesty, the Czar? How dare you forget to say the *tefillah* in his honor? I gave my entire life away for the Czar, and you forget to honor him? How dare you?" Then, in a fury, Leibke let loose two resounding slaps on the cheeks of the distinguished rabbi.

Dr. Hirschman gasped in fear and shock, and the entire congregation gasped along with him. No one could believe that Leibke had actually had the temerity to slap the new rabbi. Dr. Hirschman, whose beard was neatly trimmed and shaven on his cheeks, now sported two fiery red marks on his face.

Leibke continued to rant and rave. He did not calm down until Dr. Hirschman jumped out of his seat and ran from the shul, humiliated.

After Leibke's outburst, it was impossible to maintain any sense of decorum at all. The rest of the *tefillah* passed amid a raging tumult, which did not abate that entire Shabbos day.

Bright and early the next morning, Dr. Hirschman lodged a formal complaint with the office of the Police Commissar of Bobroisk, detailing how he had been publicly humiliated in shul on his first Shabbos as the new rabbi. He demanded an immediate appointment with the Police Commissar, Patrick, but the Commissar was unwilling to discuss the matter at such an early hour. Finally, at the urging of his deputy, the Commissar rolled out of bed, put on his morning robe and agreed to meet Dr. Hirschman in his sitting room.

"So, what is it you want?" asked Patrick, still yawning.

Dr. Hirschman snorted derisively at the ridiculous official, who clearly did not appreciate the importance of this meeting.

"Honored Commissar, I have come before you on a matter of great importance," began Dr. Hirschman in a fiery voice. "There is a young upstart in the Jewish community who has undermined the authority of His Majesty, Czar Nikolai, by publicly humiliating one of his loyal servants."

With great gusto, Dr. Hirschman described how Leibke, an ignorant soldier, had slapped him in front of the entire congregation. He demanded that Leibke be exiled to Siberia without delay.

But the Commissar was in no hurry to pass judgment. "First, we will hear from Leibke himself," he said. "Sergei, go and summon Leibke the soldier," he commanded.

In the half hour it took for Sergei to find Leibke, who was learning in a corner of the Bais Medrash, Dr. Hirschman had decided to accept the Commissar's offers of a steaming cup of coffee and an expensive Turkish cigar. By the time Leibke arrived, the doctor was in an expansive mood.

"Here I am, honored Commissar," said Leibke humbly. "The Commissar wished to talk to me?"

"Yes, I did," said Patrick. "This gentleman here," and he pointed at Dr. Hirschman, "says you slapped him in public yesterday. This is a grave and serious charge indeed. Do you have anything to say in your defense?"

In reply, Leibke delivered another ringing slap to Dr.

Hirschman's face. "Yes! I am slapping him, not for my own honor, but to uphold the honor of His Majesty, Czar Nikolai," he explained to the shocked Commissar. "This new 'rabbi' had the audacity to scorn the honor of the Czar by forgetting to remind the congregation to say the special prayer we say on our Sabbath, praising the Czar and blessing him with long life."

"Hmmm ...," said Patrick, turning to Dr. Hirschman. "Is this true?"

"Um ... yes ...," began the doctor, "but, on the other hand, it is not my responsibility to remind the congregation to say it. After all, I am a new rabbi, and I'm not so aware of the customs in Bobroisk. In addition, my seat is in the front of the synagogue, far away from where the Torah is read, and thus I cannot hear exactly what the congregation is praying, and if they did or did not say a particular prayer."

The irony of the doctor's explanation was not lost on Patrick. In a voice laden with sarcasm, he retorted, "Is that so? You are sitting too far away to hear whether your congregation is sufficiently honoring the Czar? If so, I have the perfect solution. You will no longer be allowed to sit in the front row during prayers. Your seat will be right in the center of the synagogue, near the platform where their Torah scroll is read. Thus, you will be able to follow along, and give the Czar his due honor."

As the flabbergasted doctor digested these words, Patrick turned to Leibke. "And you, Leibke, who stood up and defended the honor of the Czar, I say to you: Bravo! You deserve a medal of honor! I will mention your loyal behavior in my monthly report to my superiors in St. Petersburg. If only Bobroisk had more patriots like you!"

From that day onward, Dr. Hirschman was forced to sit in the middle of the shul, right next to the *bimah*, while the venerable Rav returned to his seat of honor on the *mizrach* wall.

Patrick, the friendly Commissar, personally visited the shul each week to make sure his decree was being upheld. And the Jews of Bobroisk breathed a collective sigh of relief.

The CLEVER MERCHANT

everal hundred years ago, a wealthy spice merchant lay dying in an inn in the city of Lublin.

The merchant had left his hometown several months before for India to stock up on spices. After completing his business, he had traveled back through the Far East, the Middle East and the Near East, selling his wares. By the time he arrived back in his native Poland, he was some 25,000 rubles richer, his stock almost completely sold. With feelings of relief, he eagerly set out upon the last leg of his journey toward Lodz, where his wife and infant son were anxiously awaiting him.

He reached as far as Lublin when he became ill. His fever soared and he writhed in agony, mumbling gibberish and crying out in pain. The local doctors who were quickly summoned to the inn threw up their hands in exasperation.

"It must be some rare infection he contracted in India," the senior doctor of Lublin declared. "He's not likely to live much longer. Just make sure he's comfortable and give him fluids. If anything changes, call me." And he stalked out of the room.

Some of what the doctor had said penetrated the senses of the deathly ill merchant's feverish brain, and he fell into deep despair. After such a long and exhausting journey, was he to die in an inn in Lublin, alone and unknown? Where would he be buried? Who would eulogize him? It was not unusual for a traveler to simply disappear, with no one ever discovering his fate. How would his young wife know of his passing?

These thoughts tormented him, giving him no peace. Slowly, he grew weaker. The concerned innkeeper offered to write to the sick man's family, informing them of his condition.

The merchant gave the innkeeper his address, hoping a letter would arrive before he left this world. In those days, it took weeks before a letter reached its destination and there was no guarantee it would arrive. Mail service was notoriously unreliable.

While the spice merchant lay ill, his purse was hidden under his mattress where he hoped it was safe from prying eyes. He was certain nobody would remove it as long as he was still alive. But as soon as he left this world and was buried, the 25,000 rubles were free for the taking.

He grew weaker every day. His heart was broken with the pain of a man who was dying without his loved ones nearby. He constantly thought of his poor wife and young son who would be left alone and penniless. He suspected that the innkeeper, who tended to him so devotedly, had a money-hungry heart and was just waiting for him to die.

The merchant racked his feverish brain, trying to think of a way to keep the money safe. Should he hide it under the floorboards and send his wife a note telling her where to find it? In his feeble state, the sick man barely had strength to move. And how would his wife have access to the hidden treasure? Besides, he could not leave his bed, and his lucid moments were becoming fewer and shorter. And anyway, the innkeeper was a clever, wily man and would not rest until he found the money.

One evening, the sick man received a visitor. It was the Rav of the *shtetl* who had heard that a deathly ill man was counting his final days at the inn. The Rav sat next to the pitifully ill man and tried to give him *chizuk*.

"Do not despair," said the Rav. "*The Ribono shel Olam* can always send the *malach* Refael to heal you."

"One may not rely on miracles," croaked the sick man. "I know my days are numbered. I accept Hashem's will in peace. Only one thing bothers me. I have 25,000 rubles hidden under my mattress. That will be enough to support my family in peace. But how can I guarantee that my wife will receive them?"

The Rav thought for a few moments. Then he whispered some instructions in the sick man's ear. The Rav procured a quill and paper and helped the spice merchant write his will.

A few days later, it was all over. The ailing merchant returned his soul to his Maker. He was buried in the cemetery in Lublin, escorted to his final rest by strangers. The innkeeper immediately removed the money from its hiding place and discovered the will. He read it quickly and chuckled, rubbing his hands in glee.

Two days later, the bereaved widow arrived. She had set out immediately on receiving the first letter and had heard the sad news as she entered Lublin. She hurried to the inn where her husband had spent his final weeks. The innkeeper greeted her with sympathy and handed her the will.

The distraught woman opened the folded paper and read in a quavering voice:

"I hereby decree that my entire fortune of 25,000 rubles shall go to the innkeeper who selflessly cared for me during my illness. However, there is one provision: He must give my wife as much money as he desires."

"What?" said the widow. "My husband left you the entire sum? How can that be?" She began to weep bitterly, but the innkeeper was firm.

"I am sorry," he said, trying to sound sympathetic, "but the will clearly says that I get the money. All I have to do is be generous and give you a gift."

The woman had heard enough. "I'm going straight to the Rav," she announced. She left the inn, her heartrending sobs drawing a crowd of curious onlookers. The *gabbai* allowed her to enter the Rav's study immediately. The wise Rav listened to her story and summoned the innkeeper. He arrived, looking smug and satisfied, arms folded over his broad chest.

The Rav minced no words. "How much do you want to give the widow?"

"Twenty-five rubles," said the innkeeper firmly. "Not a penny more."

"Have mercy on me and my tender infant!" cried the woman. "My husband sacrificed his life for these earnings. How can you be so cruel?"

The innkeeper merely shrugged. "A deal is a deal," he said. He opened the purse and counted out twenty-five rubles, holding them out to the woman.

"Not so fast," said the Rav, taking the twenty-five rubles in one hand and the bulging purse in the other. "The sack belongs to the wife of the spice merchant and the twenty-five rubles belong to you."

"What!" bellowed the innkeeper. "Look at the will! It clearly says that I get the money and I give the *almanah* as much as I want."

"That's right," said the Rav. "You must give the *almanah* as much as *you* desire. You were ready to give up twenty-five rubles, which means that you wanted to keep 24,975 rubles for yourself. Therefore, the 24,975 rubles that you desired belong to the wife of the deceased."

The innkeeper threw the twenty-five rubles on the ground and stomped back to his inn, defeated. The relieved widow thanked the Rav for being the messenger to fulfill her husband's last wishes.

The
SULTAN'S
CHALLENGE

any years ago, in a distant land, lived a mighty Sultan. His Majesty was a kind and benevolent ruler who treated all his subjects, especially the Jews, with sensitivity and understanding. In fact, he greatly admired the Rav of the capital city, Rav Kalman, and would often meet with him to discuss matters of state. Rav Kalman was an exceptionally wise, astute and humble man, and the Sultan counted him as one of his closest advisors.

All would have been fine were it not for the ferocious hatred of the Grand Vizier, the Sultan's second-in-command, who despised the Jews, and especially their rabbi, for usurping the Sultan's attention. Time and again, he would denigrate Rav Kalman to the Sultan in the hope of antagonizing him. Yet the Sultan continued to hold the Rabbi in high esteem.

One afternoon, as the Sultan sat on a gilded chair enjoying the fresh air on his veranda, the Grand Vizier casually asked him, "Why does His Majesty admire the Jewish rabbi?"

"How could I not?" replied the Sultan. "He is so clever, sharp and astute, yet so humble and modest. And his loyalty to me is beyond question."

"Your Majesty, it is all a charade!" exclaimed the Vizier. "In his heart, he despises the Sultan. He considers himself more important and distinguished. He laughs at the Sultan's edicts and does not take them seriously."

"I don't believe such nonsense!" said the Sultan in sharp rebuke. "I think you are simply jealous!"

"I?" said the Vizier indignantly. "Heaven forbid, Your Majesty! I am merely concerned with Your Majesty's honor and glory."

"But what does the Jew have to do with that?" wondered the Sultan.

"Aha! I was just getting to that," said the Vizier, rubbing his hands together eagerly. "I can prove to Your Majesty that it is all a facade. The Jewish rabbi doesn't care about the Sultan at all! In fact, he frequently denigrates Your Majesty in the privacy of his home!"

The Sultan's face darkened in anger. "These are severe accusations," he thundered. "Are you prepared to prove them? If what you say is true, I know how to punish traitors. But if your words are false and slanderous, you will pay for them with your head!"

The Vizier blanched, but he quickly composed himself and smoothly replied, "Very well. A head for a head. Either the Rabbi's head or mine."

"Fair enough," agreed the monarch. "We shall see if you can prove your serious accusations. Accusing someone of treason is not to be done lightly."

There was an uneasy silence as the Sultan stood up and began pacing to and fro, obviously perturbed.

The Vizier watched him, his mind working furiously. At last, he spoke. "Your Majesty," he said warily, "I have a plan. As Your Majesty is aware, tomorrow night is the first night of Passover, a Jewish holiday. The Jews will be celebrating their *Seder*, a special ceremony where they eat their Jew cakes and drink four cups of wine. The wine they use for their *Seder* is so important to the Jews that they would sell the shirt off their backs to buy some. In fact, their desire to drink the four cups of wine is even more important than their desire to obey the Sultan!"

"So what do you propose?" asked the Sultan skeptically.

"Let Your Majesty declare an edict forbidding all the Jews in your kingdom to drink wine for the next week. The Jews will be dreadfully upset because not drinking wine at the *Seder* is unthinkable." The Vizier uttered a short, harsh laugh. "Then Your Majesty will have ample opportunity to see how these Jews snub their noses at the Sultan."

"But how will you prove to me that they are, indeed, drinking wine?" asked the Sultan, suddenly interested.

"I propose a novel and daring idea, Your Majesty," said the Vizier, warming up to his diabolical plan. "Every year, before the *Seder*, Rav Kalman visits the local Jewish poorhouse and invites many homeless, impoverished people to be guests at his *Seder*. You and I shall don ragged clothing and join these beggars. We will surely be invited along with the others and will be able to observe the *Seder* and see for ourselves!"

"Bravo!" said the Sultan enthusiastically, looking forward to the adventure. "A brilliant plan!"

The Vizier allowed himself a small, smug smile. Finally, he would have his revenge.

The next afternoon, Erev Pesach, the Sultan summoned Rav Kalman, his loyal advisor. Although the Rav was busy selling the townspeople's *chometz*, he dared not ignore the Sultan's summons and hurried to the palace.

As Rav Kalman stood before the Sultan, he waited to hear what His Majesty wanted advice about. *Did he, perhaps, wish to acquire some property and need an emissary to arrange the sale? Was there a discrepancy in his accounts? On second thought, His Majesty was looking pensive and serious. This could only mean trouble.* The Rav shuddered with foreboding.

"Tonight is your *Seder*, is that correct?" the Sultan began sharply without his customary warm greeting.

"Yes, it is, Your Majesty," Rav Kalman replied cautiously.

"And at this *Seder* you drink a lot of wine?"

"Yes, we are commanded to drink four cups of wine," Rav Kalman affirmed. He wondered where this was heading.

"Commanded? Who commanded you to drink the wine?" the Sultan hissed, his eyes narrowing.

"The Lord, Master of the Universe."

"Indeed." The Sultan scowled down at the Rabbi. "Do you value the edicts of your Lord above my edicts?" he challenged.

Rav Kalman looked up in surprise. "We are loyal subjects of Your Majesty," he reassured the Sultan. "In fact, the Lord has commanded us to honor and cherish our rulers. We pray for Your Majesty's welfare every single day."

"That is not enough!" said the Sultan angrily. "I want proof that the Jewish community is loyal to my commands. Therefore, I forbid you to drink wine for the next week. Anyone caught drinking wine at the *Seder*, or during the rest of the week, will forfeit his head."

"Your Majesty," said the shocked Rav, tears welling up in his eyes, "what have we done to deserve this? Have we not always been loyal to your commands?"

"Quiet!" barked the Sultan. "Not another word. Now be off!"

Summarily dismissed, the Rav went home with a heavy heart, puzzled and worried. He immediately summoned the leaders of the community to a meeting where he informed them of the Sultan's new decree. After a stormy discussion, it was clear that no one knew what to do. It was too dangerous to disobey the Sultan's edict. The entire community could be expelled, or worse. Yet ... to have a *Seder* without wine was unthinkable!

The meeting came to a close and the bitter edict was announced in the village square, accompanied by wailing and weeping as the distressed Jews heard of the terrible decree.

That night, the first night of Pesach, as the Jewish community gathered in the *bais medrash*, the Rav compassionately addressed the congregants.

"My dear fellow Jews," he began gently. "You have heard the

Sultan's edict forbidding us to drink wine during the next week. To our great distress, we must celebrate our *Seders* without wine."

Bitter sighs echoed through the *bais medrash*.

"Let me advise you, brothers and sisters, about our course of action," said Rav Kalman. "As we set our *Seder* table, we should prepare the goblets, but leave them empty. Then each time we must drink a cup of wine according to the *Haggadah*, let us lift our goblets and say, 'Master of the Universe! You know that we want to fulfill Your *mitzvos* with our entire hearts. Yet the Sultan has forbidden us to drink wine during the *Seder* on pain of death. Since Your holy Torah forbids us to risk our lives to fulfill a mitzvah, except during times of *shmad*, and risk to life supersedes the *mitzvos*, please forgive us for not drinking wine, and please accept this empty goblet just as You would have accepted our *borei p'ri hagafen*.'"

After Maariv, as everyone made his way home, Rav Kalman hurried down a narrow lane to the poorhouse to invite some fellow Jews who had nowhere to go for the *Seder*. He saw many poor people rushing around, preparing to leave to the various homes where they had been invited for the Yom Tov meal.

Most of the regulars were local beggars, tragic victims of circumstance. The poorhouse, run by the *kehillah*, offered free food and lodging to any Jew, no matter how strange or unconventional. Since the people there were not scrutinized carefully, no one noticed two odd-looking strangers arriving that evening, nor did anyone mark the presence of two guards hidden behind some bushes, protecting the Sultan from a distance.

The Sultan was dressed in old, cast-off clothes, with his head covered by a tattered cap. His Vizier was dressed even more shabbily, with patches on his wardrobe. The two of them eagerly looked forward to their adventure, especially the Vizier who was itching with excitement, so sure was he that the Rabbi would disobey the

Sultan's warning. They stood waiting with a few other people who had also not yet received invitations, watching the bustling last-minute preparations of the others. Finally, the door opened and there stood Rav Kalman.

"Welcome, guests!" he said warmly. "I invite one and all to join me at my home for the *Seder*. Of course, we may not drink wine due to the Sultan's edict, but all will partake of a delicious meal."

The two guests looked at each other strangely, but no one took notice. Everyone without a prior invitation eagerly followed Rav Kalman to his simple home where an elaborate *Seder* table had been prepared. True to the Sultan's edict, not a drop of wine was to be seen.

The *Seder* began. The Rav raised his empty goblet and called out "*Kadesh.*" Then he uttered the *tefillah* that he had instructed his congregants to say:

"Master of the Universe! You know that we want to fulfill Your *mitzvos* with our entire hearts. Yet the Sultan has forbidden us to drink wine during the *Seder* on pain of death. Since Your holy Torah forbids us to risk our lives to fulfill a mitzvah, except during times of *shmad*, and risk to life supersedes the *mitzvos*, please forgive us for not drinking wine, and please accept this empty goblet just as You would have accepted our *borei p'ri hagafen.*"

One by one, the guests repeated the Rav's *tefillah*. The *Seder* continued with more fervor and *d'veikus* than usual. After the Rav, resplendent in his white *kittel*, recited "*Ha Lachma Anya,*" his young children asked the *Mah Nishtanah* and were rewarded with a handful of nuts. Then the Rav repeated the four questions and began the *Haggadah*.

The guests were drawn into the gripping tale of the Exodus from Egypt replete with *Midrashim* and stories, recited by the Rav with drama and excitement. All who sat at the table were touched and moved by the saga.

However, the two unknown guests were acting rather strangely. The one wearing a tattered cap kept smiling and nodding eagerly, looking very pleased. The other sat morosely, an angry scowl on his face. Luckily, no one paid them much attention as all were riveted on the Rav's *Seder*.

After *Maggid*, the Rav lifted his empty goblet of wine to recite the blessing of "*Ga'al Yisrael*" and again repeated the *tefillah*. Then he washed his hands in a beautiful silver cup, brought to the table by his eldest son. The others got up to wash their hands at the washing-barrel in an adjoining room.

The *matzah* was distributed, two *k'zaysim* for each guest. The two strangers looked ill at ease with the flat pancake-like *matzah*, but the one in the cap gestured to his friend to take some and not draw attention to himself. By that time, the shenanigans of these two strangers had begun drawing attention, and the other guests began whispering to each other. "Who are these strangers? Why, they don't even act Jewish!"

With great discomfort, the two mysterious guests managed to swallow the *matzah*. But when it was time for the *maror,* they were more reluctant. Realizing they would look peculiar if they didn't participate, they each took a bite, immediately gasping and choking at the sharp taste.

"Are you all right, my honored guests?" asked the Rav, wondering who these strangers were.

"Certainly, certainly," came the reply from one of them. All at once, the Rav looked them over sharply. The stranger had definitely spoken in an odd, nasal drawl, like someone making an effort to disguise his real voice. A strange idea occurred to him. Could it be that these guests were hiding their identities? But he said nothing, and the *Seder* continued.

Shulchan Oraich. The hungry guests had been sated with the *matzos,* but still eagerly looked forward to the sumptuous meal.

The Rebbitzen did not disappoint them. Though the hour was late, each guest was served a dish of tasty carp, washed down with a sweet fruit juice. Then they dined on a steaming bowl of soup, followed by chicken and roasted potatoes. A delicious compote rounded out the tasty meal.

After bentching, the Rav prepared to "drink" the third cup of wine again. He lifted his empty goblet and recited the *tefillah*. As he began to say *Hallel*, one of the strange guests, who had been growing progressively more nervous, suddenly fell into a dead faint!

"Help! The guest has fainted!" the guests began to shout hysterically. The Rav rushed over to the guest and began to douse him with water. At this, the first stranger rose and waved him away.

"Let him faint," he declared in the powerful, booming voice the Rav knew so well. "He is marked for death, anyway. As we agreed, a head for a head."

Before the shocked eyes of the crowd, the first guest, who had regained consciousness, fell to his knees and began to plead for his life.

"Your Majesty, please spare me! I don't want to die!"

A collective gasp went through the onlookers at these words. The Sultan slowly removed his tattered cap and nodded his head at the guests around the table. "Yes," he said with dignity and humor, "it is I, your Sultan! I had decided to come visit you in person to make sure my decree was fulfilled."

Casting a disdainful glance at the Vizier cowering on the ground, he said, "This evil, jealous man dared to falsely accuse your beloved Rabbi who is, as always, my devoted subject. Now I have seen with my own eyes how carefully you protect my honor and obey my edicts. And this miserable liar, who dared to malign Rav Kalman, will pay with his life. As he himself said, 'a head for a head.'"

The assembled guests stared in shocked silence at the miraculous scene unfolding before their eyes. The only sounds were the whimpering pleas of the Vizier, begging the Sultan to spare his life.

"Silence, fool!" snapped the Sultan. He made a motion toward the window. "You deserve to die as you plotted for the Rabbi. Guards! Take him away!"

At the sound of the Sultan's raised voice, his two guards, who had been hiding in the Rav's garden, stormed in and dragged away the Vizier.

But the Sultan was not finished. Turning to the Rav, he said, "My dear subjects, I hereby decree that the edict against drinking wine on your holiday is null and void. It was simply my intention to test you and see how devoted you are to me. You have passed the test and I want to reward you. The entire Jewish community is exempt from paying taxes for the next two years."

And with these words, His Majesty left the Rav's house and returned to his palace. The next morning the Vizier was executed. When the Sultan's new edict was known, the entire Jewish populace rejoiced with their double miracle. That year's Pesach was the most joyous Yom Tov Rav Kalman and his community ever celebrated.

A
TALE
of
TWO COWS

*R*eb *Uri* of Stralisk was a great *talmid chacham*, but he was desperately poor. Nowadays, the image of poverty conjures up one who cannot afford to buy his children new outfits for Yom Tov or pay the rent on time. But in those days, poor meant subsisting on a meager round of cheese, a stale loaf of bread and some dried herring for Shabbos. Poor meant not owning an overcoat or a pair of warm boots. Poor meant a scratchy straw pallet for a bed and a rickety table with four mismatched chairs for furniture. Poor meant always feeling hungry and slightly chilled in the winter. But for Reb Uri, poor still meant being happy, truly happy, with his lot.

Luckily, Reb Uri's wife Chana shared his lofty ideals and vision. For her, poverty was merely a technicality, a so-called state of being. She didn't envy the "rich" women in the tiny hamlet of Stralisk who had more than enough food and plenty of warm clothes for the cold season, which lasted six months a year. Reb Uri's wife was content to subsist on the meager salary her husband received from the *shammas*, who gave all the Torah scholars a small stipend.

Both Reb Uri and Chana's parents lived far away, and Chana was too devoted a mother to leave her children at the neighbors while she tried her hand at some sort of business. "I'd rather stay home and raise my children, and struggle," she stoically said whenever Yente the milliner or Zlata the seamstress would offer her work. In addition, Chana was not a natural businesswoman. She felt more comfortable sitting with a well-worn *Tehillim* than haggling with customers in the marketplace. So it seemed that Reb Uri's family was destined to be forever hungry.

"So be it," Reb Uri would say, smiling in genuine happiness. For how could hunger and cold affect him? He sat in the *bais medrash* most of the week, coming home only for Shabbos. His children, all daughters, helped their mother mend whatever usable discards the neighbors gave them.

Life continued, for better or for worse. One bright winter morning, Chana gave birth to a son, the first boy in the family, and the entire family rejoiced. Eight days later, the tender newborn was to be brought into the *bris* of Avraham Avinu. But there was not a drop of food in the house with which to serve the guests.

"That should not bother you," Reb Uri told his wife gently. "The *Ribono shel Olam* knows exactly how much food we need. If He wills it, we will have a meal."

Reb Uri's good wife bit her lip and tried to look cheerful. The sleeping newborn lay in a rickety cradle that looked like the slightest wind would blow it over, and the table was completely bare. The new mother hadn't had a nourishing meal in a long time. Their situation was truly desperate, but Reb Uri didn't lose his trust in the One Above.

Earlier that week, he had hung a small notice in the *bais medrash* informing one and all that he, Uri of Stralisk, was making a *bris milah* for his son on the second day of the week, *Parshas Shemos, im yirtzeh Hashem*.

In response to the notice, the important men of the community hastened to Reb Uri's home to share in his *simcha*. Everyone admired Reb Uri, the reticent *tzaddik* who sat and learned, completely cut off from the world and its cares.

Up until now, no one had known the extent of his poverty, though they presumed that he was far from wealthy. Imagine their horror when they arrived at the flimsy hut and found a bare table, four rickety chairs and nothing else at all! The one-room shanty was barely large enough to accommodate the standing-room-only crowd. The tiny infant cried while the *mohel* prepared his equipment, and his mother wept with him in shame that there was nothing to serve the worthy guests.

The leaders of the community looked at each other in

amazement. Was it possible to live under such circumstances? Reb Uri, oblivious to their confusion, smiled as he prepared the steadiest chair for the *sandek,* the Rav of Stralisk. The two community leaders huddled into a corner and began whispering. Within a few moments, some among the crowd had slipped away, returning shortly with different foods. One person brought a basket of rolls; another, a small barrel of herring. A third brought two jugs of beer, while a fourth provided a freshly baked *kugel.* Almost every one of the guests left and came back with some delicacy, which they placed upon the table, now groaning with foodstuffs. Reb Uri's next-door neighbors crammed into his home, and the *simcha* began.

When the tender newborn was circumcised and named, the guests partook of the hearty meal. Reb Uri's wife glowed with joy as she sat in a corner holding the newborn and listening to the *talmidei chachamim* exchanging words of Torah over their meal.

When the last bits of food had been cleared away and the guests began to disperse, the *parnas* of the *kehillah,* Reb Nachman, approached Reb Uri hesitantly.

"*Ahem … er …* Reb Uri, may I ask you a question?"

"Certainly," said Reb Uri effusively.

Reb Nachman glanced about to make sure no one was listening and asked, "On what do you live?"

Reb Uri continued smiling. "I have two *kihen* (cows) and they sustain our family," he said.

Reb Nachman nodded, wished Reb Uri a hearty *mazel tov* and left. As soon as he reached his palatial home, he summoned the maid and gave her new instructions regarding the purchase of milk. No longer was she to buy fresh milk in the marketplace.

"Under no circumstances are you to buy milk from Reb Chaim's stall," he commanded. "I want you to go to the home of Reb Uri —"

"Reb who?" asked the maid. "I never heard that name before."

"Reb Uri. He lives at the edge of town in a rickety hovel. You can't miss it. He owns two cows and his wife sells fresh milk. I want you to start buying milk there from now on."

"But what if his cows are old and tired, and the milk is not so rich?" asked the maid.

"It doesn't matter," said Reb Nachman. "I want to support Reb Uri who is very poor. If that means the milk will be of poorer quality, so be it." And the matter was settled.

Early the next morning, the maid dutifully wended her way through the village streets, seeking Reb Uri's home. She came upon three women hanging out their wash and asked if they knew of his whereabouts.

"Home? You call that a home?" laughed Zlata. "Reb Uri's wife and children live in a miserable shanty on the edge of the village. And Reb Uri himself lives in the *bais medrash*. His entire life is Torah."

"Chana just had a baby boy, poor thing, and there is nothing to eat in the house," offered Yenta helpfully.

"*Nebach*, I heard that all the guests brought something, and they had a hearty meal, the first in a long time," said Baila.

Finally, the maid arrived at Reb Uri's dilapidated home, fenced in by a tiny yard. There was not a cow, or even a baby calf, in sight. She hesitantly knocked on the door.

A young girl in tattered clothes with a pitifully pinched face opened it. "Yes? Can I help you?" she asked respectfully.

"Uh, I'd like to buy milk," stammered the maid.

"We don't have any milk to sell," said the young girl.

"Don't you own two cows?" she asked.

"Cows?" the girl smiled bitterly. "I haven't tasted milk since last year Chanukah when we went to visit my Bubbe in another town."

The maid thanked her for her trouble and left for the market-place, where she bought milk at Reb Chaim's stall. That afternoon when Reb Nachman arrived home, he immediately questioned the maid about her errand.

"Did you buy milk from Reb Uri today?" he asked.

"Reb Uri? You should see that miserable hovel. Milk? Their daughter said she hadn't tasted milk since last Chanukah. They have no cows. They have no goats. They have nothing!"

Reb Nachman was shocked. He immediately turned back toward the *bais medrash* where Reb Uri was sitting blissfully and learning without a care in the world.

Why would Reb Uri lie to me? thought Reb Nachman. *He is known as an exceptionally honest man.*

Reb Nachman was perplexed. He went slowly to the *bais medrash*, and approached the *talmid chacham* warily, not wanting to disturb him. "Excuse me, Reb Uri," he began. "I sent my maid to buy milk at your home and your daughter said you don't own any *kihen*."

Reb Uri smiled. "I didn't mean the *kihen* you were thinking of, Reb Nachman. I meant the two *ki-hen* in the *pasuk*, '**Ki** vo yismach libaynu, **ki** v'shaim kadsho vatachnu (For our heart will rejoice in Him, for we trusted in His holy Name).' I own two *ki-hen* — trust in *Hakadosh Baruch Hu* — Who provides for all my needs."

Reb Nachman stood, mouth agape, at Reb Uri's simple faith. "From now on, you will own two real '*kihen*' as well," he said. "I will buy two cows in the marketplace and have them sent to your home. And may the *Ribono shel Olam* repay you for your righteousness."

With JUST One WORD

During the sheva brachos of Rav Chaim Brisker in Smargan (Rav Chaim was a son-in-law of the Smarganer Rebbe, Rav Refael Shapiro), the local inhabitants told the Bais Halevi (Rav Chaim's illustrious father, Rav Yoshe Ber, the Brisker Rav) about a local miser who had not contributed a penny toward the community's fund. It was winter, and the *askanim* were gathering funds to buy timber to heat the homes of the poor. Rav Yoshe Ber promised to see what he could do.

The Brisker Rav sat next to the miser at *sheva brachos* and began discussing the sorcerers in Egypt. The miser was particularly intrigued about their "*kishuf*" (magic) and wanted to know how it was possible for them to duplicate some of the plagues.

"Well, I, too, can produce *mofsim* (miracles)," smiled the Bais Halevi. "I will fill an earthen vessel with water, ashes and oil. Then we will place four bank notes at the four corners of the table, and when I utter one word, the money will be in the vessel."

The miser was intrigued. "Prove it to me," he said.

"On one condition," replied Rav Yoshe Ber. "If I am successful, you must promise to donate one hundred gulden to a *d'var mitzvah*. And if I fail, I will donate the money."

The miser agreed and watched the Brisker Rav prepare the potion. He placed the clay vessel in the middle of the table. Then the miser withdrew four twenty-five-ruble bank notes and placed them at the edges of the table. All the *rabbanim* and *roshei yeshiva* watched with bated breath.

The Brisker Rav uttered one word. "Chaim'ke!"

Immediately, the *chassan* Rav Chaim approached, took the bank notes and put them into the vessel. Rav Yoshe Ber removed them, wiped them off and gave them to the *gabbai tzedakah*.

"What is this all about?" asked the astounded miser.

"I did exactly what I promised," said the Bais Halevi. "With one word, the bank notes were in the water."

"But where was the *mofes*?" asked the miser.

"The *mofes* is that you just donated a hundred gulden to the community fund," replied the Brisker Rav meaningfully.

The miser understood, and he hung his head in shame.

When VINEGAR Becomes WINE

eibel the wine merchant was a *y'rei Shamayim* and a *baal bitachon*. He was also a devoted *chassid* of the holy Ropshitzer Rebbe. Though he lived in a small village, he often traveled to Ropshitz to spend Shabbos with the Rebbe. If Leibel was able to settle his affairs and be with the Rebbe on Shabbos *Mevarchim*, then his joy knew no bounds.

He would often say, "Is there a greater joy than to be in the proximity of the holy *tzaddik hador*? As our *chachamim* say, '*Kol rinah viy'shuah b'ahalei tzaddikim.*' This can be understood to mean that the song of *tefillah*, and the *Shechinah* that radiates from the tents of *tzaddikim*, are already a *yeshuah*, a salvation."

Leibel always brought a few barrels of wine along with him and offered them to the *talmidei chachamim* who were part of the Rebbe's court.

One Sunday, on a Rosh Chodesh, Leibel prepared to depart from the Rebbe's court where he had just spent a lofty Shabbos. He placed a few jugs of wine on the table in the *bais medrash* in honor of the Yom Tov *seudah*. At that moment, the Rebbe walked into the *bais medrash*, and his face lit up when he saw the wine. "Let this be a *kapparah* for you," he told Leibel happily.

Everyone became frightened. What was the holy Rebbe talking about?

"When a gentile wants to drink some wine, he goes into a tavern," said the Rebbe. "However, a Yid's desires are more lofty. A Yid's desire is to pour wine upon the holy altar in the Bais Hamikdash. Due to our grave sins, the Bais Hamikdash has been destroyed. Our *Chazal* give us advice, 'One who wants to pour wine upon the altar should pour it down the throats of *talmidei chachamim*.'" Having concluded his enigmatic remarks, the Rebbe retired to his chamber.

Leibel rushed home, filled with foreboding. What could

the Rebbe have meant? He approached his doorway apprehensively, his heart thudding. He knocked on the door and waited nervously.

His wife opened the door with her usual smile. "I'm glad you're back, Leibel. The baby just took his first step."

"And?" asked Leibel sharply.

"Why, aren't you pleased?" she replied, surprised. "*Baruch Hashem* our Yankele is walking."

"*Baruch Hashem*," echoed Leibel. "It's just that, I was wondering ..."

"What's bothering you, Leibel?"

"Is everything okay at home?" he asked, in reply.

"Why do you ask?"

Leibel hesitantly repeated the Rebbe's words.

"Don't worry so much, Leibel," she reassured him. "Where's your *bitachon*?"

Leibel knew she was right. Still, he was somewhat anxious, but as the week wore on and everything continued as usual, his fears abated.

On Thursday morning, Leibel davened Shacharis, went home to eat breakfast and went down to his wine cellar to check on his barrels of wine. As he was opening the door to the cellar with his key, he heard a Jewish boy shouting and crying for mercy on the street.

Leibel dropped his key and rushed to the child who was surrounded by street urchins, taunting him mercilessly. Leibel chased the urchins away and escorted the child to *cheder*. When he returned home, he was horrified to find the cellar door wide open, and Ivan, his peasant neighbor, ensconced inside, guzzling wine from the barrels.

"*Gevald!* You are making my wine *treif*!" yelled Leibel, chasing him out. Ivan, who was already drunk, guffawed and said, "Well, if it's not kosher for you Jews, it will be kosher for my church."

Leibel's heart sank. He pushed Ivan out the door and began spilling the barrels into the sewage drain. The drunken peasant stretched out on the ground and began lapping up the running wine. When he had drunk his fill, he got up on his tottering legs and tried to stagger home. Unfortunately, the drunken peasant lost his balance and fell into the slippery wine puddle, breaking his hipbone. "Ouch! Ow!" he screamed in pain as onlookers dragged him away. Leibel heard him shout, "That Jew made me fall! He purposely tripped me because I drank his wine!"

In Eastern European villages in the 1800s, the gentile was always right. No matter how obvious it was what had occurred, the judge was not interested in the truth. Sure enough, the village magistrate, himself a devout Christian, listened sympathetically to Ivan's tale and meted out the punishment: Leibel was required to pay Ivan the sum of four hundred ducats.

"From where shall I get this fantastic sum?" cried Leibel to the judge. "This drunk made my entire wine *treif* and I had to pour it down the drain. And now I have to pay him!"

When the judge heard that the Jew had poured out the wine because a non-Jew touched it, he saw red. "The nerve of you Jews!" he yelled. "How dare you insult the good Christians in our town!"

Leibel stood cowering in fear, wondering what would happen next.

"Because you insulted us, you have to pay the village another four hundred ducats!" said the judge. "You have three months to pay the entire sum of eight hundred ducats. Otherwise, you forfeit your life."

Leibel left the courtroom, pale and trembling. Now he understood what the Ropshitzer Rebbe had been talking about. How would he raise such a fantastic sum in such a short amount of time? His wine barrels were depleted and his savings were gone, and he didn't even have enough food for his family.

Leibel staggered to his wine cellar and took a good look at the empty storeroom. Suddenly, he remembered the back storage room, where there were several barrels of old wine half buried in the ground. They had been lying there since the days when Leibel was a child and helped his father, Berish the wine merchant. Leibel was a descendant of many generations of wine dealers. The barrels could have been lying there for over a century.

Leibel opened the cluttered storeroom and began prying the dusty barrels out of the earth. After an hour of backbreaking labor, he got out the first barrel. He carefully opened it and saw that it resembled wine.

His hopes soaring, Leibel rushed to his friend Reb Simcha the philanthropist and offered to sell him the barrel for ten coins. Reb Simcha good-naturedly gave him the coins, opened the barrel and poured himself a glass. He made a *borei p'ri hagafen* and began to drink.

As soon as he took the first sip, Reb Simcha made a face and spat it out, soiling his elegant clothes. "This wine is as sour as vinegar!" sputtered Simcha. "Give me back my ten coins. You have caused me to make a *brachah l'vatalah*!"

His spirits sagging, Leibel took back the barrel and trudged to his cellar. *What next?* He replaced the barrel and went home.

His good wife was sitting in their bare kitchen, crying bitterly. "We have nothing to eat in the house," she sobbed. "The children haven't had a decent meal in days."

"We must have *bitachon*," Leibel comforted her. "The One Who gives life will also give us food."

"But you owe eight hundred ducats," said his wife.

Leibel sighed. "I will go to the Rebbe," he said.

Leibel hired a wagon and traveled to Ropshitz, where he poured out his heart to his Rebbe and repeated the whole sorry tale.

"The whole story began when you ran to do a mitzvah — to save a Jewish child from the gentiles. Our *chachamim* say, '*Shluchei mitzvah einan nizokin* (those on mitzvah missions are protected from harm).' Go home and have *bitachon*. The *Ribono shel Olam* will help."

Leibel traveled home with a load off his chest. What a wonderful feeling to have *bitachon* in *Hakadosh Baruch Hu* and trust in His messengers, the *tzaddikim* on this earth!

When he arrived home, his wife was waiting to hear what the Rebbe said. Though the Rebbe's words calmed her, she wasn't appeased. So Leibel explained, "What do we mortals know about the *Ribono shel Olam*'s ways? Everything that happens is for the best. We must have *bitachon*."

A month passed, then a second. The *tzarah* intensified. Leibel's children soon had that hungry look in their eyes, and their faces were pinched from lack of nourishing food. Soon Leibel's wife couldn't take it anymore. She traveled to the Rebbe and began to cry. "There is nothing to eat in our house. Within a few weeks, the gentiles will kill Leibel because he doesn't have the money."

"Don't worry," the Rebbe calmed her. "Leibel was a *shliach mitzvah*. No harm will come to him."

The weeks passed by. Leibel decided to purchase a lottery ticket. The prize was one thousand ducats, enough to pay the judge and have some left over for bread. Two days before Leibel was to appear before the judge, the winnings were announced. Leibel was not the grand winner. He did not even win a small prize. What's more, Leibel now owed his neighbor the ten ducats he had borrowed to buy the lottery ticket.

But Leibel bore it stoically. He said to his lamenting wife, "Our sages say, 'Even if a sharp sword rests on your neck, do not give up hope.' The *Ribono shel Olam* does not need an additional minute. His salvation can come in the blink of an eye."

The day of reckoning arrived. "Say *viduy*, Leibel," said his wife in a broken voice.

"I was a *shliach mitzvah*," he replied. "Nothing will happen to me."

Suddenly, there was a fierce knock on the door. "They have arrived!" wailed his wife.

But it was not the village magistrate. It was the *poritz* of the neighboring town who was riding by in his elegant wagon.

"Are you Leibel the wine seller?" he asked in a gruff voice.

Leibel nodded mutely.

"How many barrels do you have?"

Leibel began to stammer and stutter.

"Show me your wine cellar," the *poritz* ordered. Leibel escorted him to the cellar, and the *poritz*'s entire retinue entered the narrow room.

The *poritz* glanced at the empty barrels littering the room. Suddenly, he walked to the storeroom and said to his servants, "Dig out these barrels!"

His servants got to work and dug the barrels out of the ground. The prince unscrewed the first barrel and tasted the wine.

"Ah, delicious!" he said, smacking his lips. "I have never tasted such good wine before. How much do you want for this wine?"

Leibel knew the wine was sour and was about to say so, when he suddenly stopped himself. After all, if the *poritz* liked the wine, who was he to argue?

"One hundred ducats per barrel," he said.

"Bring in the gold!" ordered the *poritz*.

His servants loaded a total of one hundred barrels onto the wagon and rode away, leaving Leibel with the sum of ten thousand ducats! Leibel had enough money to pay the magistrate, restock his wine cellar, feed his family and become a wealthy man. He never heard from that *poritz* again.

Why did the *poritz* visit Leibel on that day? Some say he had become a minister and was hosting a party for the nobility. Others say the king had paid him a visit and he needed wine. But Leibel knew it was much simpler than that. If the *Ribono shel Olam* wants to save someone, He has His messengers, and even sour vinegar can become wine fit for a king.

A MARRIAGE Made in HEAVEN

*R*ivka *was* a young mother of two, living in the idyllic *shtetl* of Kashau, busily raising her little ones. Her predicament (though common nowadays) was so rare then as to be almost an oddity.

Rivka was divorced. It had not been, as she was wont to say, a marriage made in heaven. When she finally had the courage to leave Berel, he disappeared before the *get* arrangements were finalized. After five bitter years, Rivka's persistent great-uncle tracked down the delinquent husband and forced him to free Rivka from her lonely existence.

The years went by. The children, a boy and a girl, matured, surrounded by doting grandparents, devoted aunts and uncles, and the rock-solid security of the *shtetl*. In addition to caring for her children and seeing her son off to *cheder* (there was no school for girls), Rivka was an experienced seamstress who outfitted the young women of the *shtetl* with the finest clothes.

Rivka's exquisite dresses were well constructed and made to last a long time. She was in great demand, especially when someone was making a *simcha*. Her nest egg doubled and then quadrupled, and as the neighborhood *yentas* liked to say, she was almost as rich as Reb Pesach, the wealthiest *baalebos* in town.

Yet wealth and happiness don't necessarily go hand in hand, and as Rivka's children grew, she began to keenly feel the loneliness. She felt especially lonely during the Yamim Tovim, and also in the long, cold winter nights when she was shut in her home, sewing the hours away.

On Pesach and Sukkos, Rivka always took her children to stay at her parents. Her children only had dim recollections of their father whom they hadn't seen in years. So they were content with their life. Yet Rivka wanted more for them. She wanted to marry someone who could help her make a good home for them, keeping the Yamim Tovim in their own happy abode; someone who would care for her offspring with the same love and devotion that she did; someone relatively young, preferably, a *talmid chacham*. Or if he was a businessman, he needed to be successful, not just a *schlepper*. In short, Rivka was searching for a match that was, to say the least, hard to find. And the *shadchanim* told her so. "Rivka, you're walking around with your head in the clouds," they warned her. "If you turn up your nose at everyone we propose, you'll be single for a long, long time."

Rivka simply replied, "If I managed to raise my children without a husband until now, why would I sacrifice for second-best?"

Her overprotective mother echoed the sentiment. "My Rivka isn't going to marry a *shlemazel*, not if I live to see the day," she would say with righteous indignation.

Rivka had a married sister, Pessel, who lived in Ihel, a prominent city in Hungary, where Reb Zorach Green, a respected *baalebos* and *baal tzedakah*, and his wife, Ettel, lived as well. Reb Zorach and his wife were blessed with ten children, the oldest barely bar mitzvah, the youngest a toddler. Then tragedy struck.

Ettel contracted typhus, in those days a deadly disease, and before the family could bring her to the hospital, it was too late. Ettel had left this world, her ten orphans alone with no mother to raise them.

Reb Zorach almost collapsed from shock and heartbreak. His ten little ones had lost their mother, and he was robbed of his young wife who had been a shining model of chesed and loving-kindness. The pain was almost too bitter to bear.

The good women of Ihel rallied around the family, cooking them meals, washing their laundry and seeing that the children were cared for. The younger ones were farmed out to neighbors, and a housekeeper was hired to look after the older children. Life continued as normal, or as normal as it could be after the sunshine had gone out of their lives.

Pessel went out of her way to ease the Green family's burden. She cooked their cholent for Shabbos and mended the children's socks, for which Reb Zorach was eternally grateful.

And then came the dream.

It happened one humid summer night. Rivka had gone to bed early but found she couldn't fall asleep because of the oppressive heat. She tossed and turned, finally falling into a troubled sleep.

In her dreams the image of her grandfather, Reb Moshe, appeared, looking just as she remembered him. Her Zaidy smiled at her and relayed a careful message. "Rivka, I have been given permission to visit you down below to give you an important message. You have a *zivug* (match) waiting for you. His name is Reb Zorach Green from Ihel." And with those words, her Zaidy disappeared.

Rivka awoke, bathed in sweat, her heart pounding. Reb Zorach Green from Ihel? But as far as she knew, he had a wife, the righteous Ettel, may she live and be well. Rivka dimly remembered the Green family from her visits to her sister Pessel in Ihel.

"Well, dreams are ninety percent nonsense," Rivka firmly decided, and then went back to sleep. When she woke up in the morning, she had forgotten about the dream.

However, the dream repeated itself the next night. Her grandfather appeared again, urging her to travel to Ihel and fulfill his bidding.

Rivka woke in shock. Shivering, she realized this was no laughing matter. She got out of bed, quickly put on her dressing gown and ran next door to her aunt Gittel's house. At her frantic knocks, Gittel opened the door, aghast. "Rivka! What happened? Are the children okay?"

"Everything's fine," said Rivka. "I just had the strangest dream." And she repeated the entire tale.

Gittel burst into laughter. "For a silly dream you became so hysterical, waking me in the middle of the night? What's the matter with you? Forget about it!" and she shepherded Rivka back to her home and sleeping children.

However, when the same dream repeated itself for the third night in a row, Rivka knew it was time to act. She packed up her children, hired a wagon driver and went to visit her sister Pessel in Ihel. Perhaps she could shed some light upon the story.

The trip was uneventful, and the excited children could barely sit still. "Are we there yet?" asked eight-year-old Chanale. Ten-year-old Yankel was more pragmatic. "Don't ask so many questions," he said. "It won't make us arrive faster."

Finally, the horse and buggy reached Ihel. Pessel, who had not known about the visit, was beside herself with joy. She eagerly welcomed her sister and the children who were soon comfortably ensconced in her sturdy home, eating pumpernickel bread with herring.

"So what's new, Pessel?" asked Rivka between bites.

"Everything's okay, *baruch Hashem*. My neighbor Yente just had her twelfth child, a boy. And Leike from down the block had twins two weeks ago. Everyone is taking turns sending her suppers."

"Your Yossel told me you are cooking supper tonight for a family. Yente's, I assume?" asked Rivka innocently.

"Oh, no. I'm cooking for the Greens. We have a rotating chart; every night another neighbor cooks them supper."

"The Greens? You don't mean Ettel Green, do you?" said Rivka uneasily. "From what I remember, she is an excellent *baalebuste*."

Pessel's eyes filled with tears. "Ettel passed away five months ago," she said. "Typhus."

"Oh, no," cried Rivka. "Poor family. How are they managing?"

Pessel sighed. "As well as can be expected. What they need

is a mother, not a housekeeper or neighbor to do the laundry. But Reb Zorach can't seem to find a *shidduch*, and certainly not someone distinguished enough to take his late wife's place. One second," said Pessel, and stopped short. "I just had this idea —," she looked at Rivka carefully.

"I know what you're going to say," said Rivka. "You're going to propose a *shidduch*. And you're not the first one."

Pessel sat, dumbstruck, as Rivka related the unbelievable tale of the dreams.

"And that's why I came to visit you," concluded Rivka.

Rivka remained in Ihel, and within a few weeks, was engaged to Reb Zorach. In an act of selfless devotion, she pledged to raise Reb Zorach's ten children in addition to her own. The family of twelve weathered many a crisis until things settled down and the children accepted their new mother with love and trust.

All because of a silly dream.

The
MAN
in the
TRASH

erish was a wealthy, arrogant man who thought he knew it all. He didn't mind dispensing charity, but the recipient of his generosity had to meet his qualifications. All the paupers of Zychlin knew his conditions. He even boasted about them in public, especially when a beggar accosted him.

"You know my rules," he would say with a self-satisfied smirk. "I only give charity to those who have given up all hope and have nothing to look forward to."

While the indigent of Zychlin were truly a sorry sight, they did have an ounce of pride left in them. None was ready to say they had given up all hope of a *yeshuah*. So Berish's pockets remained sealed. As his wealth increased, his arrogance grew, and he strutted across town like a peacock showing off his feathers.

One fine afternoon, Berish was strolling home from the neighborhood tavern, where he liked to have a glass of *schnapps* now and then, when he chanced upon a sorry sight. A beggar, for that was the only thing he could be, wan and haggard, was sitting upon a pile of refuse that emitted a malodorous stench. Holding his nostrils against the pervasive odor, Berish approached, his curiosity piqued. Surely, this was a man who met his qualifications. A man who could sit on a garbage heap, despondent, dressed in filthy rags, was a man who had given up hope.

"*Shalom aleichem*," said Berish expansively, making sure not to get too close. "And how can I help you?"

"I beg your pardon?" replied the pauper.

"I said, how can I help you? I'm Berish the *g'vir*, and I have this policy, uh, to help those who have given up all hope. You look like you fit the bill," he said, laughing at his witticism.

"You're mistaken," replied the pauper in a smooth, even voice, not abandoning his perch. "I have not abandoned my trust and *bitachon* in the Almighty. I live with the hope of a better future."

Berish couldn't contain his indignation. "But look at you!" he sputtered. "Sitting on the garbage heap like a piece of garbage!" The minute these words were out of his mouth, he regretted them, but it was too late. To his surprise, the beggar was not affronted in the least. With a pleasant smile, he explained.

"David Hamelech says in *Tehillim*, '*May-ashpos yarim evyon* (Hashem lifts the pauper from the garbage heap).' As long as I am alive, I shall never cease to hope. The only person who has no more hope is a dead man. So your charity is wasted, Mr. Rich Man."

Berish was outraged. His pompous dignity was affronted. "If so," he shot back, "I shall do exactly as you say. I'll give my charity to the dead."

He strode back home, gathered a tidy sum and summoned his workers to the cemetery, where they dug a small hole. The arrogant Berish deposited his money, cynically calling it "a gift for the dead." And then he promptly forgot about the matter.

Years passed. The wheel of fortune spun again, downward this time. Slowly but surely, Berish lost one business deal after another. As his creditors began to hound him, he had to pawn his silver pieces and expensive furnishings until he was left with the bare walls of his home. Soon, that, too, had to go. The once proud and arrogant Berish was reduced to a mere pauper, every vestige of his former glory gone, reduced to dust. In a remarkably short time, he was forced to go from door to door begging for food to keep body and soul together.

As he went upon his pathetic rounds, gathering scorn and abuse from those he had once shunned, his state of mind went from bad to worse. For a time, he even entertained thoughts of hopelessness.

Of what value is my life, he thought, *a miserable beggar with nothing to call my own?* He remembered the days of his glory and wealth when he thought the world belonged to him, the days when he refused to give anyone a donation unless they had given up hope.

Suddenly, he recalled the beggar who sat upon the garbage heap, with his strange words. "I have not given up hope. He lifts the poor from the garbage heap."

And then Berish remembered what he had done in his arrogance and foolhardiness. He recalled the money he buried in the graveyard, money that held the key to his last vestiges of self-respect. With the coins he had buried, he could buy some bread to last him for several weeks. And then what? The first flickering of hope stirred within his desperate soul.

Under cover of darkness, Berish stole away to the graveyard where he strained to recall the exact spot where he had buried the money. After he got his bearings in the dark, deserted field, he scurried amongst the tombstones until he found what he was looking for. With his bare hands, he began to dig with the determination of a desperate man. The wind howled through the field and he shivered in his meager garb. But nothing could stop him now. Another few moments and the money would be his.

Suddenly, a voice rang through the stillness of the night. "Stop! Thief!"

He looked up, startled. A night watchman was walking toward him, grimly determined to do his duty.

"Why are you digging in the graveyard?" he demanded gruffly. "Don't you have the decency to let these bones rest in peace?"

Stammering and frightened, Berish replied, "I have come to collect my money."

The watchman guffawed. "And you really expect me to believe that, huh? Money in a cemetery? What do the dead need it for?"

And before Berish could protest, the watchman hauled him away to spend the night in the local jail. Berish was trussed like a chicken on the hard, dry earth, nursing his wounded pride and the last vestiges of hope. He passed a restless night. Visions of his former pride and glory, his unmitigated arrogance, gave Berish no peace. In a voice choked with tears, Berish admitted his sins and decided to change his ways. He davened with the fervor of a man who has given up hope, whose only recourse is the *Ribono shel Olam*, the *Chonen Dal*, champion of the poor.

As the first slivers of dawn crept into his prison cell, Berish drifted into uneasy slumber. Within a short time, he was awakened by harsh knocks on his door. The warden thrust a slice of bread through a crack and informed Berish that he would stand trial that very afternoon.

It was late evening by the time Berish was brought before the judge. His stomach was rumbling with the now-familiar pangs of hunger, and anxiety gave him no rest.

As he was ushered into a large spare chamber, he was surprised to find the judge looking at him sympathetically with a calm and cheerful expression. His hopes soared briefly and then were dashed again. Did he have a fighting chance? Did it matter in the end?

"Order in the court," the judge commanded. "Let the prosecution present its case."

The watchman of the cemetery described his horror when he noticed a pauper scrounging in the graveyard, apparently digging up bones. "And he had the nerve to say he was looking for money!"

The atmosphere in the courtroom changed. The policemen glared at Berish angrily. Only the judge remained unperturbed.

"Now let the plaintiff present his story."

In a broken voice, Berish described his former wealth, his arrogance and glory. He described the man he had met sitting on the garbage heap who had taught him the lesson that as long as there is life there is hope.

"And then," said Berish, "I did a foolish thing. I went to the cemetery, dug a hole and deposited a sizeable sum inside. You see what happened." He pointed to his tattered clothes. "I lost all my money.

My pride went down the drain. And suddenly, I remembered the money, and I went to the graveyard to retrieve it."

The judge looked at him with interest, smiling broadly. At first, Berish thought he was mocking him. But, no! There was something familiar about his features.

"Don't you remember me?" asked the judge.

Berish stared at him, and through the dark recesses of his memory, the face came back to him. How could he have forgotten?

"You — you're the one who sat on that pile of garbage!" he said, shocked. "You're the one who taught me the lesson!"

"The very same," said the judge. "It's a long story and I'll tell it to you some day. Suffice it to say that my wheel of fortune took an upward turn and slowly, I was raised from the garbage heap, achieving a respectable position, until I became a judge."

The judge patted Berish on the shoulder and said kindly, "I recognize you, too, and I believe your tale. You have learned your lesson well. Now go to the graveyard and retrieve your money. And may you enjoy much success."

Berish found his money intact, a much larger sum than he had remembered. He invested most of it in a new business venture and became quite wealthy. But now, he dispensed charity with an open hand and achieved a reputation as a truly kind, humble man, thanks to an old friend on a garbage heap.

For the
SAKE
of a
BROOM

ack at the turn of the century, Yerushalayim was not the bustling, vibrant city it is today. Yerushalayim of old was a simple *yishuv,* centered mainly in the Old City and several newer neighborhoods. The *yishuv* of Meah Shearim, founded by a group of *askanim* outside the Old City walls, was inhabited by pious men and women who lived in tiny, spotless homes, serving their Creator with joy.

In the small, close-knit community, neighbors were more than just neighbors; indeed, they were like one family. They shared one another's *simchos* and cried with each other's sorrows.

As recounted in *The Heavenly City,* an account of Yerushalayim in those days, one of the well-known inhabitants of Meah Shearim was Bubbe Malka. Malka, a descendant of a long chain of *rabbanim* and Torah leaders, had originally come from Pinsk with her widowed mother to escape the turbulence and pogroms in Poland. With the help of the famed *askan* Rav Shlomo Eliach, and other communal figures who knew the family from Pinsk, Malka and her mother moved into a small apartment and became part of the neighborhood. The pious child thrived in the pure, spiritual environment and became known as the *"Tehillim* sayer" who never missed a day at the *Kosel.* Malka would trek to the *Kosel* each morning and daven for those who needed a *refuah, parnassah* or *yeshuah* of any sort.

Malka loved the tall, stone buildings of Meah Shearim that gave the community its character. They stood like sentinels, guarding the inhabitants from unseen dangers that lurked beyond the walls. After she finished her davening and *Tehillim,* Malka would spend the rest of her day helping others in the *yishuv,* bringing food for one bedridden neighbor, cleaning house for another and visiting the old women who counted on her for companionship.

"Malka has a pure *neshamah,"* the women of Meah Shearim would praise her. Whenever she went to the market to buy fruits and vegetables, she bought for her neighbors as well, telling them it had been on sale at a bargain price. For her, doing *mitzvos* was the greatest bargain.

The years went by. Malka became of age and married a young yeshiva *bachur,* settling into her new apartment in Meah Shearim. She merited to raise ten children and see them married, with grandchildren and great-grandchildren, all in the same Meah Shearim community where she had grown up. At every milestone in her life, she would go to the *Kosel* or the local Yeshuos Yaakov Shul to daven for *brachos* and *yeshuos.* When she sat in the women's section of the shul and davened to her Father in Heaven, it was as if a heavy load was lifted off her chest.

Life wasn't easy in those days. The advent of the first World War brought famine and poverty, but that was tolerable in comparison to the pogroms. In 1929, violent Arab hordes descended upon Meah Shearim in a terrible pogrom, maiming and killing many defenseless Jews. Most of the residents of the *yishuv* barely escaped with their lives. The English army patrols, who had turned a blind eye to the Arab rampages, relocated the citizens of Meah Shearim to the relative safety of the Shaarei Chesed neighborhood. Malka, by then an elderly widow, moved to Shaarei Chesed with her daughter and son-in-law.

Though she now lived in a new neighborhood, Malka never severed her ties to Meah Shearim, her beloved first home in the Land of Israel. Malka seized every opportunity to visit Meah Shearim and daven in the Yeshuos Yaakov Shul. She would daven there every Shabbos, Yom Tov, Erev Rosh Chodesh and fast day, and often during the week as well. In addition, she chose to do her grocery shopping at the small store in Meah Shearim, shunning the open air Machaneh Yehuda market with its plethora of choices.

"Mamma, why do you travel so far with your basket?" her daughter would plead. "Why do you insist on shopping in Meah

Shearim when there are so many markets nearby?"

But Malka was undeterred. "The fruits are cheaper and better in Meah Shearim," she would say. "Besides, I am used to it."

But these were mere excuses. The real reason was that Malka derived spiritual satisfaction from visiting her old neighborhood, the *yishuv* where she had grown up. Every Thursday morning, the elderly woman would plod from Shaarei Chesed to Meah Shearim, an empty shopping basket on one arm, wearing heavy wooden slippers to shield her feet from the unpaved roads across the city. She would return home that afternoon bathed in a peaceful glow, having davened at the Yeshuos Yaakov Shul and having met her old neighbors in the market.

Her daughter, who tried to stop her, would often arrive at Malka's house Thursday and find she had already left. Invariably, the dutiful daughter would follow her mother to the distant market and help her carry her purchases back home.

One week when Malka's daughter arrived at her home a little later than usual, she saw her mother's basket filled with food already resting on the ground, but her mother was not home! She waited a few moments and then decided to retrace her mother's steps to Meah Shearim. How surprised was she when she saw her mother wearily plodding home, holding a broom!

"Mamma, where have you been?" asked the concerned daughter. "I saw your basket on the ground, but I couldn't imagine where you went."

"Look what happens when one gets old," sighed her mother. "My mind doesn't work anymore like it used to. I have a neighbor who has a few little children and can't go out much. I promised her I would buy her a broom, and I forgot. So I had no choice but to go back and get it."

"Mama, you are killing yourself!" her daughter said in exasperation as she helped her mother sit down. "You are breathing so heavily and your feet are swollen. Why do you punish yourself so, to go back again for a broom? You could have asked me to pick it up for you."

Malka merely smiled as she explained. "Tatteh, may he rest in peace, used to say that a haughty person is compared to an idolater. Why? Because 'idols have feet but do not walk.' So, too, is the person who is too proud to pick up his feet and do a favor for another Yid. Do you want your elderly mother to transgress the prohibition of *avodah zarah*, Heaven forbid?"

Before her daughter could reply, Malka continued. "Now, my dear daughter, take this broom and bring it to my neighbor who is waiting for it. You, too, will have a portion of the mitzvah. But don't tell her I went a second time for it because she will be hurt."

That was Malka, the "*Tehillim* sayer" from Meah Shearim.

The
PORITZ
and the
TAILOR

Velvel the Schneider, they called him, and usually added a wry "*nebach*." For though Velvel was a skilled tailor, he took his time to create a quality garment, so his contracts were few and far between. Most people went to the high-class tailors in town who, because they had many assistants, could have a suit ready in a week. Velvel, who could not afford an assistant, would labor for days on his customers' orders, not sleeping more than a few hours a night, and all his hard work left him exhausted.

Velvel had one consolation, one source of comfort that kept him from drowning in despair. A close *chassid* of the Apter Rebbe, he often visited him, pouring out his heart to the Rebbe and asking for a *brachah* for *parnassah*.

"Rebbe!" Velvel would cry. "My family members have not tasted meat in several months. Rebbe, please give us a *brachah* for *parnassah*."

The Rebbe would smile encouragingly, saying, "Don't despair, Velvel. The *yeshuah* is near. Better days will come."

The months and years went by with Velvel always on the brink of poverty, never quite making enough money to pay off his debts.

But one day, Velvel burst into the Rebbe's study, his face aglow. "Holy Rebbe!" he cried. "*Baruch Hashem*, I am saved!"

"What has happened?" asked the Rebbe.

Velvel explained. "Several weeks ago, the *poritz* of our village sold his palace to another *poritz*. The new *poritz* inquired about a suitable tailor, and one of his servants told him about me. Last week, he summoned me to his ornate palace and sent his coach to pick me up. I quaked in my boots as I was escorted into his exquisite chambers and told to take a seat.

" 'Don't be afraid,' the *poritz* told me kindly. 'I want to do business with you. I have heard that you are a professional tailor who takes pride in the quality of your work. I have just moved to the area and my wardrobe is in urgent need of an update. Can I hire you as my personal tailor?'

"At first, I was too shocked to speak. Finally, I found my tongue. 'But, of course,' I said. 'I would be honored to work for you.'

"We agreed on a list of clothes I was to sew and a tentative timetable. Then we parted. I went straight to the cloth merchants, purchased the finest fabrics and immediately got to work."

The Rebbe listened intently, deep in thought. "What is the name of the *poritz*?" he finally asked.

"Franz Marcus," replied Velvel. "He claims he has a royal pedigree, dating back to the Anglo-Saxon kings."

The Rebbe was not impressed. "I have a feeling that your *poritz* is a Yid," he said. "Try to find out where he comes from."

Velvel went back to the village and made some discreet inquiries. After several days of research, he discovered that the *poritz* was, indeed, an apostate who tried mightily to conceal his Jewish origins.

"Franz Marcus is really Efraim Fishel from Vienna," said Velvel to the Apter Rebbe. "I just confirmed it. Does the Rebbe want me to refuse the job? If so, I am ready to do the Rebbe's bidding," said Velvel with great trepidation.

"You can continue working for the *poritz*," said the Rebbe, and as Velvel breathed a sigh of relief, he added, "with one condition. You must refrain from sewing anything that contains *shaatnez*. Once a Yid, always a Yid. Though he considers himself far removed from Judaism, you may not be the cause of his violating the prohibition of *shaatnez*."

Velvel promised to be careful, and the Rebbe blessed him with *hatzlachah*. Then the lucky tailor went home to start his new job.

All went well, at first. Velvel took his time, but the results were perfect. The *poritz* was extremely satisfied with the quality and attention to detail on each of his new garments. He usually ordered his robes or suits several weeks before they were actually needed so Velvel was able to work at a leisurely pace. Franz Marcus paid handsomely for his services. Now Velvel's family had meat on the table every Shabbos, and chicken once a week. His elder daughters began to dream of getting married, and his wife even allowed herself to smile once in a while. Life looked good.

Several months after Velvel began his new career, the *poritz* summoned him and ordered a special set of robes to be sewn from a beautiful fabric.

"These robes will be worn at an inaugural ball hosted by my friend in a neighboring village," explained the *poritz*. "The ball will be attended by the elite of society and everyone will be dressed with magnificence. I want you to start on this set of clothes immediately, for they will be the most elegant you have ever sewn."

Velvel listened intently as the *poritz* described the style he had in mind. Then Franz Marcus drew a bolt of fabric from a cupboard and handed it to Velvel. "This time, I have purchased the fabric myself because I wanted it to be just perfect," he said.

Velvel took the bolt of fabric and felt it carefully, rubbing it between his fingers. He peered closely at the woven threads of the fine material. His many years of experience working with all types of fabrics had taught him about various textures and threads. His heart began to hammer. He knew this fabric was undoubtedly *shaatnez*.

"Why are you hesitating?" demanded the *poritz*. "Don't you trust my taste?"

"I … Your Excellency … I have seen a bolt of exquisite fabric at the factory," Velvel began, his voice a confused stammer. "The fabric I had in mind is far superior to this one."

Franz Marcus flew into a rage. "Are you implying that I don't have good taste?" he demanded. "What nerve! I don't know what you have in mind, but this is exactly what I wanted," he ordered.

"I bought ten yards of this fabric, enough for whatever I have in mind. Now take it home and get to work."

"Y-yes, Your Excellency," said Velvel, the taste of fear in his mouth.

He parted from the *poritz* and hurried home to check the fabric. As he had suspected, the beautiful, soft wool was woven through with glittering, golden threads of linen! It was definitely *shaatnez*. Velvel rushed to the Apter Rebbe.

"Rebbe, what shall I do?" cried Velvel. "I am finished! He will punish me severely."

"Never fear, Velvel," the Rebbe calmed him. "When the *poritz* asks why you won't complete the suit, tell him the Apter Rebbe forbids you to do so. Then the *poritz* will come running to me and I will take care of him."

One week passed. Velvel passed the days in a state of nervous tension, waiting for the axe to fall.

The *poritz* called for him at the beginning of the second week. Velvel was shaking like a leaf as he was ushered into the room.

"Nu, let me see the pattern," said the *poritz*. "I hope you have cut out the pieces already and are ready to start sewing."

"Actually ...," said Velvel, his face white like a sheet, "actually, I have not begun."

"What?" exploded the *poritz*. "I need this suit in a week for the grand ball. How will it be ready if you haven't started yet? What's wrong with you!"

"I'm s-sorry," stammered Velvel. "I wanted to start, but I just couldn't."

"And why not?" asked the *poritz* in a dangerous voice.

"Because my Rebbe, the *tzaddik* of Apt, forbade me to." Velvel caught his breath and added in a small voice, "The Rebbe says that since the *poritz* was born a Jew, Your Excellency may not wear clothes made of *shaatnez*, linen and wool combined." He was about to explain further but saw the *poritz* understood exactly what he was talking about. And he wasn't liking it one bit.

Franz Marcus ranted and raved, waving his fists in the air. "So your Rebbe doesn't let me wear *shaatnez*? What nerve! Who does he think he is? I'll teach him a thing or two!" He snatched his hat, called his servant to harness his coach and rode off toward the Rebbe's modest home.

The Apter Rebbe was in his study, immersed in his *sefarim*, when the clatter of hooves broke the silence. The door burst open and the *poritz* stormed in.

"C-can I help you?" gaped the *gabbai*.

"I will see the Rabbi — now!" the *poritz* glared.

The *gabbai* entered the study, pale and trembling, the *poritz* at his heels. Franz Marcus's face was fiery red, and he gnashed his teeth with indignation. The Rebbe merely smiled serenely and welcomed his visitor.

"*Shalom aleichem*," said the Rebbe. "How can I help you?"

The *poritz* advanced, waving a threatening fist. But as he gazed into the Rebbe's holy eyes, the hand came down and the color receded. He breathed more calmly, but when he began to speak, he still sounded angry.

"What nerve do you have mixing into my personal business? I asked my tailor to sew me a set of clothes and he told me you forbade him to use the fabric because it is *shaatnez*. What nonsense! I converted to Christianity twenty years ago and your laws no longer apply to me. Besides, what business is it of yours?"

"Our sages teach us," explained the Rebbe, "that a Jew who sins remains a Jew forever. Unlike a Protestant who becomes a Catholic, or a Christian who becomes a Muslim and gives up his previous faith, a Jew always remains a member of the Jewish nation, even if he becomes an apostate. One cannot tear one's connection to our Father in Heaven, no matter how many sins one commits.

No matter how far he has strayed, Hashem constantly awaits his return."

The *poritz* listened intently. The Apter Rebbe continued, "Thus, I forbade Velvel to sew you a garment with *shaatnez* because, after all is said and done, you are still a Yid."

The nobleman stared silently at the Rebbe for a few minutes. Then, all of a sudden, something broke in him, and his shoulders began to heave as his wrenching sobs split the silence. The Rebbe's heartfelt words had pierced the layer of grime surrounding Efraim Fishel's heart! He remained with the Rebbe for some time and then quietly left the Rebbe's home. Several weeks later, the village of Apt buzzed with the news: Franz Marcus had sold his estate and had quietly departed for a distant location. Rumor had it that he had purchased a more lucrative property in the north.

Few knew the real reason for his departure: Franz Marcus had become Efraim Fishel once more, a genuine *baal teshuvah*. Thanks to the Apter Rebbe's insistence on protecting an estranged Jew from *shaatnez*, a lost soul was returned to his roots.

The
DRAFT
BOARD

*n impoverished* villager burst into the home of the *"Shoresh v'Yesod Ha'avodah,"* Rav Avraham of Slonim, crying desperate tears.

"Rebbe, please save my son!" he sobbed.

"Is he ill?" asked the Rebbe, concerned.

"Not at all," replied the villager. "In fact, he is healthy and strong, and that is precisely my problem. My son has been commanded to appear before the draft board and will very likely be drafted into the army."

The Rebbe sighed as he heard the bitter news. Being drafted into the army was a dangerous ordeal that lasted a long time and robbed young men of their most productive years. It was nearly impossible to daven, keep *kashrus*, observe Shabbos and adhere to the *mitzvos* in the iron discipline of the Polish army barracks.

Rav Avraham comforted the distraught man and gave him the following instructions.

"Tell your son that during the final nights until he is to appear before the draft, he should remain awake the entire night and say *Tehillim, pasuk* after *pasuk,* with great *kavanah* and concentration. In this merit, Hashem will save him."

The grateful father thanked the Rebbe and rushed home to relay the good news to his son and the rest of his anxious family.

True to his instructions, the *bachur* faithfully remained awake for the next week, saying the entire *Tehillim* with *kavanah* and desperate tears through the night until dawn. This was in the month of Teves, during a frosty winter with heavy snow and rainfall. All through the night, as the *bachur* swayed over his *Tehillim*, the wind howled up and down the alleys of his village, sending shivers down his spine. While his family lay cozy and secure under their blankets, he shivered from frost. Yet the desperate *bachur* persevered, trusting in the power of *tefillah.*

One especially stormy night, as the youth was huddled over

his *Tehillim*, there was a sharp knock on the door. The *bachur* shivered in fear. Who could be knocking on such a wild and stormy night?

At first he hesitated, wondering whether to wake his sleeping parents. Soon the desperate knocking grew louder. With a pounding heart, the *bachur* opened the door and stood face-to-face with three burly sergeants from the Polish army. They were soaking wet and nearly frozen to the bone, their faces blue with cold. Their teeth chattered as they begged for mercy.

"Please let us stay with you for the night," they cried. "We have trudged through the entire town and every single home was dark. Yours was the only cottage with a light in the window. If you don't take us inside, we will freeze."

The *bachur* wavered until the second sergeant spoke up. "Please let us indoors!" he cried. "It is a matter of life and death. Another few minutes and we will become chunks of ice." As if to underscore his plea, a wild gust of wind tore through the ice-covered street. Though he was afraid of spending the night with these rough soldiers, the *bachur* had no choice and let them in.

He ushered them into the small cottage and served them warm tea and some biscuits. The *bachur*'s parents, who had awakened, set about trying to make their guests comfortable. When the three soldiers were somewhat revived and some color had returned to their sallow cheeks, they related their harrowing tale.

"We were on our way to our barracks, some distance away, when we took a wrong turn in the ice-covered forest. Due to the terrible gale and winds, we couldn't see in front of us and lost track of the rest of our group. We wandered alone stumbling through the snow, holding onto each other for support until we reached the village. We felt that we could not go on another moment and would surely perish in the snow, when suddenly we saw a light shining from your home. We decided to take a chance and knock on the door, hoping for your mercy."

The *bachur* replied, "But, of course. Our Torah commands us to be generous and merciful to friends and strangers alike. You are welcome to stay the night." The grateful guests spread out on sacks of straw and soon were fast asleep. However, the *bachur* continued saying *Tehillim* with fervor. The soldiers woke up from his chanting and looked at him in puzzlement.

"What are you mumbling?" one of them asked. "Don't you Jews ever sleep?"

The *bachur* apologized and considered whether to relate the true story. Finally, he decided to be honest and explained that he faced the threat of being drafted into the army. He was following the advice of his Rebbe and praying to be rescued from the draft.

The guests listened soberly, asked some questions and then dropped off to sleep. The *bachur* continued saying *Tehillim* until dawn.

In the morning, as the first shafts of sunlight began to penetrate into the cottage, the three overnight guests thanked their hosts and set off to join the rest of their troop. Before they left, they wrote down the *bachur*'s name and address for their records.

A few tense days passed. Finally, toward the end of the week, the *bachur* received his notice to appear before the draft board. With trepidation, father and son set off for the army base at the edge of town. Three gruff-looking sergeants and an army doctor were waiting to examine him and declare him fit for the army.

The *bachur* waited his turn, fully expecting to be pronounced fit and sent right off to the nearest army barracks.

The doctor manipulated him roughly, tested his reflexes and proclaimed, "Healthy as an ox. He would make a good soldier for His Majesty's army!"

The *bachur*'s heart sank as he realized his fate was sealed. "*Hakadosh Baruch Hu*, I accept Your judgment," he whispered.

Suddenly, he felt the sergeants' eyes on him. He looked up and had the shock of his life: The three soldiers sitting there were the very guests who had stayed at his home that stormy night. Since the doctor was present, they were unable to show any recognition.

"What's the status with this boy?" asked the first sergeant.

"An exemplary specimen of good health!" said the doctor.

"No. I don't agree," said the sergeant. "He appears weak and scrawny. We don't need such undernourished scarecrows in our army. Send him away!" And before the astonished doctor's eyes, the sergeant filled out an exemption form, handed it to the *bachur* and sent him on his way.

With praise and thanks on their lips, the youth and his father made their way back home. Now they understood the power of the Rebbe's advice, advice that applies all year-round and especially during the month of Elul — "*Tefillah* saves one from evil decrees."

Déjà vu

*R*eb *Chaim* was a distinguished merchant living in the city of Lomza. He dealt in furs, buying and selling the precious commodity on the open market. Twice or three times a year, he traveled to nearby Lodz where he met with several of his trusty suppliers and restocked his inventory. Usually these trips took only a day or two, and Chaim dozed off in his carriage. However, on one occasion he had to remain in Lodz for several days and booked a room at a local inn, the Shining Star.

Feitel, the innkeeper of the Shining Star, was a coarse, boorish man with a booming voice. He had an unsavory reputation in the city for "pocketing" the items of his guests during their stay. Reb Chaim, of course, knew nothing of this. Thus, he felt quite comfortable leaving his money pouch with a sizeable amount of cash and his gold watch hidden securely under his pillow.

On the morning of his departure, Reb Chaim packed his bags and headed for the train station. He walked over to the ticket booth and reached his hand into his pocket, but it came out empty. Then he realized that he had left his money pouch and watch under the pillow in the room at the inn.

Reb Chaim grabbed his bags and raced back to the inn, out of breath. He banged on the door and Feitel greeted him with a curious sneer.

"Yes, can I help you? Did you miss your train?"

"No, but I just realized that I left my money pouch and watch in my room."

"No problem," said Feitel coldly. "I haven't been in there yet. Let me open the door for you." Feitel led Reb Chaim to his now-vacated room, opened the door and waited as Reb Chaim headed for the bed. He reached under the pillow and nearly fainted with fright. The watch and money pouch were gone!

Reb Chaim's trained eye glanced about the room. He realized

that the curtains had been moved a fraction of an inch and one of the bureau drawers was slightly open. Then he knew. The room had already been searched. The pouch and watch were in Feitel's possession, no doubt.

"No success?" smirked Feitel.

"No. The money pouch and watch are gone. Strange. I was certain I left them under my pillow."

"Impossible. No one was in this room since you left a short while ago. I repeat: no one. Not a soul. You probably dropped them at the train station. A few street urchins are spending your money right now at the tavern."

Chaim realized immediately that he was dealing with a seasoned thief. Shrewdly keeping his cool, he "agreed" with Feitel.

"You're right," he said. "I probably lost them at the station. What a pity. I'll go there right now and try to look for them."

Feitel bid his former guest good-bye, barely concealing his glee. So he wasn't suspected! He thought he would have to hide the money and watch until the suspicion passed.

Reb Chaim walked toward the train station and then made an abrupt u-turn and hurried to the home of Rav Elya Chaim Meisels, the famous Lodzer Rav. The Rav was sitting in his study, absorbed in a *sefer*, when Chaim knocked at the door. Rav Elya Chaim greeted him with a warm smile.

"*Shalom aleichem*. From where do you come, dear brother?"

"From Lomza."

Rav Elya Chaim welcomed him enthusiastically and they conversed for several minutes. Then Chaim mentioned the purpose of his visit.

"I lost my money pouch and gold watch today."

The Rav raised his eyebrows. "Where?"

"At Feitel's inn. The Shining Star."

The Rav nodded in comprehension. He knew Feitel well. He

was a mean character with quite a reputation. In fact, Feitel was currently involved in a *din Torah* with another charlatan and neither side was willing to compromise one iota.

"Hmmm … getting the money out of him won't be an easy affair, but we'll try to do our best. Give me the *simanim*, the identifying marks of your money pouch and watch. In the meantime, go to the *bais medrash* and wait until I call you."

Reb Chaim thanked the Rav and hurried to the *bais medrash* where he soon forgot all his worries and began to learn with devotion.

Meanwhile, Rav Elya Chaim told his assistant to summon Feitel regarding his pending *din Torah*. Feitel hurried to the Rav, eager for the opportunity to clarify certain points.

The Rav drew Feitel into a discussion about the upcoming *melavah malkah* at the home of Berish the merchant. It was safe territory and would not put Feitel on his guard. Suddenly, the Rav asked, "Can I have a pinch of snuff, Feitel?"

Feitel proudly withdrew his silver tobacco case and handed it to the Rav.

The Rav held it for a few moments, took several pinches of snuff and sneezed. *Achoo! Achoo!* Then he walked around the room, deep in thought.

"I just remembered something important," said Rav Elya Chaim. "Wait here for a few moments. I'll be back soon." And he walked out of the room, still holding the tobacco case.

Feitel sat patiently, reviewing the upcoming *din Torah* in his mind. From time to time, he thought of the bonanza he had managed to steal from Chaim, the wealthy merchant. His mind raced with thoughts of how he would spend the money.

The instant Rav Elya Chaim left the room, he summoned his assistant and handed him the tobacco case.

"Take this and go to the home of Feitel, owner of the Shining

Star. Tell his wife that you have come to pick up the pouch and watch from his safe. Show her the tobacco case as proof that Feitel sent you."

The assistant hurried off to do the Rav's bidding. Fifteen minutes later he was back, grinning broadly and holding the pouch and watch in his hand.

"She was suspicious at first, but when she saw the tobacco case, she immediately went to get the items," said the assistant. The Rav thanked him and locked Chaim's belongings securely in a desk drawer. Then he walked back into his study, holding the tobacco case.

Feitel looked up, startled. The Rav had been gone for a long time, but it didn't really matter. He had used his time well to concoct another defense for his *din Torah*.

"I'm sorry it took so long, Feitel," said the Rav, returning the tobacco case. "By the way, your snuff is excellent. First quality."

"Thank you," replied Feitel.

"So what else is new?"

The Rav schmoozed with Feitel for another few minutes and then remembered that he was in a hurry for an appointment.

A few minutes later, a grateful Reb Chaim received his watch and pouch, all its contents intact. He warmly thanked the Rav and headed for the train station.

Feitel left for home, baffled at the Rav's summons. What had been the purpose of the visit? Simply to discuss shul politics?

When he arrived home, he soon found out what the Rav was up to. His wife greeted him by saying, "I gave the purse and watch to the Rav's assistant like you wanted."

"What?" exploded Feitel. When he heard the whole story, he was consumed with rage and fury. He would teach Rav Elya Chaim a lesson or two.

A few weeks passed. The story of Feitel's downfall somehow

leaked to the townspeople (perhaps the Rav's assistant unwisely mentioned it to one or two people) and Feitel became the laughingstock of town. The Rav's cleverness and wisdom were widely discussed and admired.

Feitel's business suffered. His inn was empty for days on end, hosting only the occasional traveler who had not yet heard of his reputation. Most of his regulars switched over to the guesthouse at the other side of town.

Feitel's anger intensified until he was ready to explode.

And then he had a brainstorm. He would get even with the Rav and with his competitor, Yankel, owner of the guesthouse, at the same time.

Feitel recruited Mottel, one of his cronies, into his scheme, offering him a "pretty penny" for his cooperation. Mottel dressed up as a wealthy merchant, and paid for a room in Yankel's guesthouse for two days' stay.

When the two days were up, Mottel returned the key to Yankel and set out on his way. A half hour later he returned, claiming he had left his pouch in his room.

Yankel opened the door and Mottel began to search for his pouch. "It's gone!" he yelled. "Gone! I've been robbed! You thief!"

Yankel became terrified. He had not had a chance to enter Mottel's room and was sure no one had entered, either. The story was eerily similar to what had happened at Feitel's inn, yet he knew he was innocent.

Mottel would have none of it. "You thief! Give me back my money! How dare you?"

None of Yankel's assurances calmed him. "I'm going to the Rav!" declared Mottel as he stormed off toward the home of Rav Elya Chaim.

The Rav accepted his irate visitor and listened to Mottel's tale with a sense of déjà vu. Something was fishy. It was the identical story, but the characters were different. And Yankel had an excellent reputation.

"Wait a few moments," said the Rav. "I'll look into the matter."

The Rav summoned Yankel and met with him quietly in a back room. Once he was convinced of Yankel's innocence, he walked into his study and announced, "I have good news, Reb Mottel. We have found your pouch! Just give me the *simanim* and I will return it."

Mottel became confused. This was definitely not what he expected. He started to stammer and stutter.

"Uh ... um ... I ... uh ..."

"Out with it!" said the Rav. "Tell me the entire story!"

"It wasn't me, honestly!" said Mottel. "Feitel made me do it. He paid me ten rubles and told me to pretend Yankel had stolen my pouch. He wanted to get even with the Rav ...."

Rav Elya Chaim's wisdom and cleverness saved the day.

Do CLOTHES Make the MAN?

oshe was a wealthy landowner whose business travels brought him all over Europe. As a consequence of his financial success and his dealings with the rich and famous, he had become arrogant and proud. To him, money and social prestige meant everything.

When his only daughter Mirel came of age, Moshe began earnestly scouting the thriving yeshivos across Poland looking for the perfect *chassan* for his daughter. Of course, the young man in question would have to be top quality in every respect — a real *ben Torah* with excellent *middos*.

He sent emissaries from one yeshiva to the next who met with the Roshei Yeshiva and put forward Moshe's request: Give me the very best *bachur* in your yeshiva. At each stop, the Roshei Yeshiva hemmed and hawed, unsure of what Moshe was referring to. Did he really want the best learner or simply the best-dressed young man? They were rarely the same *bachur*.

Finally, the *shliach* struck gold at the grand yeshiva of Rimanov. The minute he met with the Rosh Yeshiva and stated his request, Benzion Shein's name came up. The eighteen-year-old youth was described in glowing terms as a possible candidate for the next *gadol hador*.

The messenger was so overcome by the glowing descriptions that he neglected to meet with the *bachur* in question, something that he was later to rue. The tempting thought of the thousands of gold coins promised to him upon fulfillment of the mission beckoned. And so he hurried back to Moshe's hometown to tell his employer that he had found "the right *bachur*" for his daughter Mirel.

Moshe, who was in the middle of a complex business deal at the time, was ecstatic. He trusted the messenger's glowing description, and since he was especially busy with his travels, the *tena'im* was conducted from afar. (In those days, a long-distance *shidduch* was quite a common occurrence.)

To celebrate the occasion, Moshe hosted a lavish party for his influential friends where he boasted about the *chassan* he had never met, as wine flowed like water. Mirel, the glowing *kallah,* basked in the admiration of her neighbors and friends.

And in Rimanov, Benzion, the *chassan*, also made a *seudah* to celebrate the occasion, a simple repast thanking the *Ribono shel Olam* that he had found his destined match. The *bachur's* friends congratulated him, sang songs, and then went back to the *bais medrash* to learn.

Nearly two months after the *shidduch* was finalized, Moshe was finally able to tear himself away from his business to go meet the *chassan*, his future son-in-law, in person.

Filled with rosy dreams and excited expectations, Moshe set out from his home in a magnificent coach pulled by four white steeds. All the way to Rimanov, he dreamed of the noble, brilliant *chassan* and envisioned the joyous meeting.

He arrived in Rimanov and headed straight for the yeshiva. It was the middle of *seder*, and the sound of hundreds of *bachurim* learning together made a powerful impression on Moshe. He motioned to a *bachur* sitting at the edge of the *bais medrash* and asked him to summon Benzion Shein, the *bachur* who had recently become a *chassan,*

The *bachur* was happy to oblige. He slipped away and returned a few minutes later with another *bachur,* a tall, skinny boy in patched trousers, whose eyeglasses were held together with string. His shirt was threadbare and missing a button and his shoes had split at the sole a long time ago. The *bachur's* kaftan had been sewn from a discarded remnant, and the front and back were different shades of black.

Moshe stared at the *bachur* and sighed. *Nebach, such a poor bachur, obviously without a penny to his name.* But he had no patience to wait longer.

"Nu, can you bring me Benzion Shein, please?" he demanded. "I've come a long way to see him."

The *bachur* with the tattered clothes smiled and said, "I am Benzion Shein."

Moshe gasped. He held onto the wall for support as his head began to spin and he sank to the floor. There was an instant commotion in the *bais medrash.* "Water! Bring water! A man has fainted!"

But Moshe waved them away. He gestured to Benzion to come closer and said to him, "I am, or was going to be, your future father-in-law. However, that is a thing of the past. I see I have been terribly misled. I trusted the messenger, but he fooled me. You can rip up the *tena'im* we signed. The *shidduch* is now over."

"B-but you have barely met me!" said Benzion, shocked and humiliated.

"Just looking at you is enough," said Moshe, his voice dripping with poison. "You are obviously unsuitable for my Mirel. She is a noble girl, born and raised in a wealthy family. This would never do."

Benzion recovered his wits quickly and said to Moshe, "If you want to cancel the *shidduch,* that's your choice. However, I refuse to rip up the *tena'im* until we meet with the Rimanover Rav."

Moshe had no choice but to agree. The two of them marched to the Rav's home and were immediately allowed to meet with the Rav. The Rav regarded his star pupil lovingly, with an approving gaze.

Moshe was the first to speak. "I made a long-distance *shidduch* several months ago and now I have come to see my *chassan* firsthand." He gestured to Benzion, who cringed. "As soon as I saw the *bachur,* I realized the *shidduch* is obviously a mistake. This ragged young man would never fit into my family!"

The Rav waited until he had finished and said, "Do you know who this *bachur* is? Benzion Shein is the star of the yeshiva. He has a brilliant future awaiting him."

"Let him find his brilliant future elsewhere," said Moshe shortly. "I'm canceling the *shidduch* and going back home."

Benzion's face reddened with humiliation. The Rav thought quickly.

"I think you are making a big mistake, which you will come to regret," he said. "Be that as it may, I ask one thing of you. It is only proper that you pay Benzion the sum of ten gold rubles for his shame and humiliation."

Though ten rubles was a large sum, Moshe did not hesitate, eager to calm his conscience. He immediately opened his pouch, counted out the money and gave it to Benzion.

Reb Moshe was eager to leave, but the Rav had other plans.

"It is not fitting for such an important visitor to leave Rimanov without having a meal in my home," said the Rav to Moshe. "I would like to invite you to join me for supper in an hour."

Though he was itching to go home, Moshe readily agreed. He grabbed the opportunity to "break bread" with the illustrious Rav. He decided to take a walk at the edge of town while he waited to clear his head and organize his churning thoughts.

As soon as Moshe left, the Rav accompanied Benzion to the home of Reb Menachem, a wealthy and generous *baalebos*. The Rav quickly apprised Menachem of the situation and advised him on how to proceed.

The hour passed quickly. Soon Moshe was back at the Rav's home to join him in a simple, home-cooked repast. The Rav and the arrogant businessmen dined together, talking about everything but the *shidduch*.

Suddenly, the Rebbitzen sent the Rav a pre-arranged signal as she banged the pots in the kitchen. The Rav then turned to

Reb Moshe and said, "I have a *bachur* who would be perfect for your daughter. He is well-dressed, well-groomed and also a great learner."

Moshe perked up his ears. "Nu?" he asked eagerly.

"I have actually summoned him here to meet with us," said the Rav. "See him and judge for yourself."

At that moment, there was a knock on the door. The Rav bade the visitor enter.

A tall, aristocratic young man stood in the threshold. He was wearing a becoming, velvet-trimmed overcoat, shiny black shoes and a starched white shirt. His beard was neatly combed and his *payos* were trimmed, and he wore an elegant black hat on his head. Moshe, who was well aware of the latest fashion in dress, smiled in appreciation.

"What do you say to this *bachur*?" asked the Rav. "He is a real *lamdan*, an *iluy*, a genius, a *masmid*, *alleh maylos*. He has every good quality. And to top it all off, he also has a handsome dowry of ten gold rubles."

Moshe could barely contain his joy. "I am willing to close the *shidduch* right now!" he crowed with excitement.

The Rav chuckled and said, "Look carefully, Reb Moshe. Perhaps you may have met this young man before?"

"I have never seen him in my life," said Moshe boldly.

"Are you certain?" asked the Rav.

Moshe walked up to the *bachur* and scrutinized him closely. He paled when he recognized Benzion, the *bachur* he had spurned a short while ago.

"B-but you look so different!" he stammered. "I would never have believed that it is the same *bachur*."

"It is the same *bachur*," said the Rav, "Benzion Shein, the genius of Rimanov. All we did was change his external shell. His internal qualities are shining forth in all their glory."

Moshe was quiet for a few moments collecting his thoughts, but the Rav didn't give him too much time to reconsider.

"So now that Benzion's apparel meets your expectations, you are willing to take him for a son-in-law, correct?"

But Moshe still had reservations.

"But where will he take the dowry from? He is an impoverished *bachur* from a poor family!"

The Rav was quick to retort. "A short while ago, he received ten gold rubles, which will be his dowry."

The Rav, Moshe and the *chassan* drank *l'chaim*, and everyone's happiness was complete.

Young Benzion married Mirel, the wealthy man's daughter, and they raised a fine Jewish family. Benzion became a great *talmid chacham* and brought much *nachas* to his father-in-law. Thanks to the Rav's keen insight and wisdom, and a fresh, elegant set of clothes, a wonderful *shidduch* was saved.

The BEAR DANCE

Rav Yehudah Leib of Shpolah, known as the Shpoler Zeide, was an exceptional dancer. Every Friday night at the Shabbos *tisch*, the Zeide would break into rapturous song and dance, singing praises to the *Ribono shel Olam*.

When Reb Avraham HaMalach, son of the Mezritcher Maggid, heard what a tumult and commotion the Zeide's dancing caused in *Shamayim,* how the angels would gather to watch the scene, he was determined to meet the Zeide and see him dance. He resolved to spend Shabbos in Shpolah as a guest of the Zeide.

The Shpoler Zeide welcomed him warmly, and on Friday night, they sat together at the *tisch* surrounded by the *chassidim.* Suddenly, the Zeide stood up and began to dance. What a dance! The angels must have been dancing along with him. The Zeide's feet were possessed of a life of their own as he nimbly executed complicated steps with grace. For a full hour the Zeide danced, his holy face shining with exaltation.

Finally, the Zeide sat down, exhausted, whereupon Reb Avraham HaMalach said to him, "Shpoler Zeide, until now I had not realized what true dancing means. I sense that you have caused a great pleasure for the *Shechinah*. I beg of you, tell me where you learned to dance this way."

The Shpoler Zeide smiled and said, "The holy Baal Shem Tov blessed me with the gift of dance. When I was a *yungerman,* the Besht looked at me and said to his *talmidim,* 'See now, *chevrah,* this *yungerman* will be able to set his feet down on this earth.' The *brachah* was indeed fulfilled."

"But how did you learn such complicated dance steps?" wondered the Malach.

The Shpoler Zeide smiled. "I had an excellent Rebbe," he said. "Would you like to hear the story?"

The Malach sat back in his chair and listened. The *chassidim* crowded around, enraptured. They sensed that an extraordinary tale was about to be told.

"When I found out that I was destined to become a Rebbe," said the Zeide, "and my job would be to heal the spiritual defects of my fellow Jew, I insisted that I first be given the opportunity to heal my brothers physically. Only after I had exerted myself to save my brothers from danger would I feel ready to care for their spiritual welfare. This request was granted me from *Shamayim*.

"I became a *melamed tinokos*, a teacher of small children. I traveled from village to village until I found a position as a *melamed* in one of the towns. I gathered the small children and taught them the Aleph Bais. When they became proficient in the letters, I taught them to read, and so on.

"One afternoon, I heard several townspeople discussing the frightful news. In a neighboring village lived a poor, simple Jew who leased the local tavern from a feared and hated *poritz,* lord of the entire region. This Yid lived in a small cottage with his family and eked out a meager living selling vodka and whiskey to the peasants. He had fallen on hard times. Business was slow and he was unable to pay the rent. The *poritz* threw him into a deep dungeon, bound in chains. His fate was to be decided three days hence, on the *poritz*'s birthday.

"The news spread a pall of sadness over the village. I had never met this unfortunate Yid, but my heart felt his pain. The night before the *poritz*'s birthday, we heard from several peasants that the *poritz* was planning a great ball in honor of the occasion. Dukes and noblemen from the outlying areas were expected to take part, to eat, drink and make merry.

"The *poritz*'s faithful servant Ivan, a vile anti-Semite, had a brilliant idea. The *poritz* owned a bearskin, a trophy from his hunting conquests. Every year, one of his servants would be forced to don this costume and dance before the inebriated crowd.

" 'So, who shall we choose this year?' asked the *poritz*.

"Ivan cackled with fiendish enthusiasm. 'Let us take the miserable Jew out of the dungeon and force him to dance for us.'

" 'An excellent idea!' said the *poritz*, rubbing his hands with glee. He walked over to the edge of his property, where the dungeon was located. It was merely a deep hole dug in the ground, accessible through a trapdoor. The *poritz* bent over the black hole and called out, 'Moshke, can you hear me?'

"A weak and trembling voice replied, 'Yes, my master.'

" 'Tomorrow will be my birthday,' said the *poritz*. 'I am hosting a grand ball in my dining room. I want to invite you to the feast, to make my guests merry. I have prepared a special bearskin for you to wear. You will dance, and Ivan here will lead you.'

"Moshke trembled. He hadn't eaten in two days and his strength was rapidly waning. How could he ever dance before a jeering crowd? As if reading his thoughts, the *poritz* continued, 'Make sure you do a good job. Because if you don't, I will throw you to the dogs!'

"Moshke burst into piteous tears. 'Have mercy on my wife and children,' he cried. 'Please give me another chance. I promise I will pay the rent.'

" 'Quiet, *Zhid*!' roared the *poritz*. 'Have I not treated you fairly? All you do is complain. Nothing is ever good enough for you. You will dance with Ivan tomorrow, and make me proud. If you fail, you can say good-bye to your family before my dogs are let loose. But if you succeed, you will be freed, and I will give you the tavern rent-free for three years. Understood?'

"With those words, the *poritz* and Ivan walked off, chortling at their brainstorm. And poor Moshke began to say *viduy*, certain his end was near.

"Later that night," continued the Shpoler Zeide, "I quietly slipped out of my village and walked toward the *poritz*'s mansion.

In my hand I held a thick rope. When I reached the dungeon at the edge of the property I tied the rope to a tree and lowered myself down.

Moshke was shocked to see me standing there.

"'What … what are you doing here?' he asked. 'Did the *poritz* throw you in as well?'

"'I came to save you,' I whispered, '*b'ezras Hashem*. Let us change clothes, and you climb up to safety. Then remove the rope and run away. I will take your place.'

"'*Chalila!*' said Moshe. 'I won't allow another Yid to be killed instead of me.'

"But I insisted. 'Don't worry,' I assured him. 'The *Ribono shel Olam* will help me. I am an excellent dancer and I will make the *poritz* happy.'

"Thus assured, Moshe changed into my clothes and scaled the rope to safety. When he finally climbed out of the deep hole, he removed the rope, thanked me emotionally and ran off into the night. That same night, Moshe, his wife and children escaped to a nearby village to wait until the danger had passed.

"I spent a sleepless night in the dungeon, davening to *Hakadosh Baruch Hu*. I knew I would need a miracle to save me. Suddenly, Eliyahu Hanavi appeared in the dungeon beside me. 'I will teach you how to dance,' he said.

"For the next several hours, Eliyahu Hanavi taught me complicated dance steps, one after the other. I followed his lead, and soon I was proficient in all manner of dance. Daylight dawned. I bid good-bye to Eliyahu and waited for the *poritz* to summon me.

"The day passed slowly. I could hear the sounds of visitors arriving at the castle and the clatter of horses' hooves. The hullabaloo intensified toward evening when the actual drinking and merriment began. The *poritz* hosted dozens of illustrious guests and provided them with a sumptuous meal. Wine and spirits flowed freely. The servants scurried to and fro to accommodate everyone's demand. I sat holed up in the dungeon, listening to the sounds and waiting for my turn to come.

"Toward midnight, the drunken sounds of laughter began echoing through the palace grounds. Most of the guests had imbibed the excellent alcohol and were already quite inebriated. It was time for the action to begin.

" 'Dear guests,' said the *poritz,* his speech slurred, 'I would like to present you with superb entertainment. My Moshke is sitting in the dungeon, waiting to come before you. He will dance like a trained bear. Ivan here will lead him and the orchestra shall play.'

"The audience clapped and cheered. Ivan was dispatched to the dungeon. He opened an underground trapdoor and pulled me out.

" 'Nu, Moshke, ready for the action?' he asked. I smelled alcohol on his breath.

" 'Put on this bear skin,' continued Ivan, 'and follow me.'

"I meekly slipped into the bulky costume, and allowed Ivan to lead me to the ballroom. We entered the enormous room filled with costly furnishings and tables loaded with food and drink. Ivan introduced me to the crowd. 'This is Moshke, the trained bear!' he jeered. 'I will lead him in dance. If he succeeds in following me, he will receive a special prize. But if he fails, I personally will throw him to the dogs!'

"The orchestra struck up a tune, and the dancing began. Ivan chose a complicated dance and signaled for me to follow him. To the audience's surprise, I began to dance, possessed with supernatural strength. I danced gracefully, first following Ivan and then continuing with my own steps. The lords and noblemen gasped in surprise, and then began to applaud.

" 'Bravo! Moshke! Bravo!'

"Ivan didn't know what hit him. He struggled to keep up with my dance, but kept on stumbling. His drunken legs couldn't keep up with my dance steps. I kicked him aside and began dancing on my own. Soon Ivan was lolling on the floor, helpless. In true bear fashion, I walked over him and continued dancing. The noblemen roared with laughter. At last, the dancing was over. The *poritz* walked over to me and shook my hand.

" 'Bravo, Moshke. You've done a good job. You deserve a reward. Three years free rent for you and your family!'

"The audience cheered. And Ivan? He slowly roused from his drunken stupor and limped off, nursing his wounds. I was released and went back to my village to share the good news with Moshke. Moshke returned to the tavern with his family and enjoyed the good graces of the *poritz* from that day on."

The Shpoler Zeide ended his tale with a smile. "So now you understand how I can dance so well."

"I envy you," said the Malach. "Your dancing is truly worthy because it saved a Yid and his family from certain death."

The
G'VIR
and the
AVREICH

sher Trachtenberg. The name was well-known in the streets of Yerushalayim during the early 1900s. Trachtenberg was a wealthy tycoon from Elizabeth, New Jersey, who lived in a splendid mansion and was on friendly terms with many important personalities. Yet despite his fame and affluence, he didn't forget about his suffering brothers in Eretz Yisrael and generously supported the struggling *yeshivos* and *kollel yungeleit*. He often visited Eretz Yisrael and was given the "grand tour" by his grateful beneficiaries, who thanked him again and again for his kindness.

There was ample reason for them to be grateful. A generous *g'vir* like Trachtenberg was hard to come by. Although far from a *ben Torah*, Trachtenberg respected and appreciated those who dedicated their lives to learning. In fact, he enjoyed meeting and conversing with the pure, single-minded *b'nei Torah* who crowded in the Old City and Meah Shearim.

One bright and sunny Elul morning, Asher Trachtenberg, who had recently arrived in Eretz Yisrael for a two-week visit, was strolling along the narrow side streets and crowded markets in Meah Shearim breathing in the holy air of Yerushalayim, reveling in every moment. He had managed to take some time off from his pressing business affairs to visit the Holy Land and perhaps receive a *brachah* from the great *tzaddikim* and *gedolim* who resided there.

Having no pressing business to take care of, the *g'vir* strolled up and down the streets, regarding the passersby and wondering if any of them recognized him from his last visit. He smiled as he saw young, pure *cheder* children rushing to the Etz Chaim yeshiva, their brown paper bags containing lunch and a snack to give them strength for their long day of learning.

Asher thought back to his previous visit when he had stopped a young boy on the street and spontaneously asked to see what he had in his bag. How horrified was he to find that the child's lunch, the main meal of the day, consisted of a chunk of black bread smeared with oil and a small piece of herring! The *g'vir* had led the child to the local vegetable market and bought him a few tomatoes, a luxury in those days.

The little boy had thanked the wealthy man, then turned and gave away two ripe tomatoes to the old beggar who sat at the market gate, keeping only one for himself. In reply to Trachtenberg's surprise, the child explained, "Tatteh taught us never to eat luxuries on a weekday."

Asher had been moved by the child's faith and simplicity. His children back in New Jersey were spoiled and indolent, spending their days playing games and trying to get out of doing their schoolwork. But these young *cheder* boys — there was something about them — a special glow reflected in their innocent eyes. Today, the *g'vir* knew better than to offer a little boy some tomatoes. The simple, coarse food they ate seemed to satisfy these children more than the fine rich meals his cook served at home satisfied his children.

As Trachtenberg walked down the street absorbed in his musings, he suddenly felt a tap on his shoulder. "*Shalom aleichem*," said a hearty, familiar voice. "What brings such a worthy guest to our shores?"

"I came to the Holy Land for a brief vacation," said the *g'vir*, instantly identifying the stranger as the secretary of the Etz Chaim yeshiva. "Business is not so hectic these days and I haven't been to Eretz Yisrael for over a year."

"We're really glad you came," said Reb Sender, the secretary, warmly. "Why don't you follow me to the *cheder* and I'll give you a tour?"

"Perhaps a little later," said Trachtenberg. "I was actually thinking of paying a visit to the Rav of Yerushalayim."

"To Rav Shmuel Salant?" asked Reb Sender. "But, of course. I'll take you there right now." And he began walking purposefully toward Rav Shmuel's humble home, the *g'vir* at his heels.

In order to see Rav Shmuel, then chief Rav of Yerushalayim, one didn't need an advance appointment. Rav Shmuel's home was open at all hours of the day or night, and there was usually a crowd of people in the humble waiting room.

Now, since it was early morning, the waiting room was deserted. The secretary knocked on the door and then quickly ushered the *g'vir* into the Rav's private study.

"*Shalom aleichem*, Reb Yid," said Rav Shmuel warmly. "Where are you from?"

"From Elizabeth, New Jersey," Asher explained. He mentioned that he was a well-known businessman back home and frequently supported the fine Torah institutions of the Old City, including the Etz Chaim yeshiva. The secretary enthusiastically volunteered that Trachtenberg's constant support helped the yeshiva continue to function and pay their *melamdim* on time.

Rav Shmuel listened carefully, nodding warmly and encouraging the *g'vir* to continue his charitable activities. Trachtenberg beamed with pride as he accepted the blessings from the great Rav of Yerushalayim.

Then, in the midst of their conversation, there was a faint tap at the door. Rav Shmuel asked his secretary to invite the visitor into the waiting room and casually asked who it was.

"The young Polish *avreich*," answered the secretary.

As soon as Rav Shmuel heard the visitor's identity, he said to Mr. Trachtenberg, "Please excuse me. I'm sorry our conversation must wait, but speaking with this Torah scholar must take priority." Rav Shmuel enthusiastically got up from his seat and rushed out to the waiting room. He personally ushered the *yungerman* into his private study and embraced him, pulling out a chair and asking him to sit down.

Mr. Trachtenberg remained in Rav Shmuel's study, staring at the new visitor. And indeed, it was nearly impossible to ignore the strange guest, or his attire. It was clear that he was desperately poor; his thin, threadbare shirt was patched in several places and his pants were held up by a rope of twine. The soles of his shoes were flapping and the upper part of the right shoe sported two large holes. His misshapen hat covered the top part of his face and his eyes were sunk deeply into their sockets, apparently from strain. When the *avreich* opened his mouth to speak, he revealed a set of blackened teeth. Despite his physical appearance, or lack of it, the *yungerman*'s face shone with an inner glow.

Asher Trachtenberg compared the *yungerman*'s desperate appearance to his own classy attire: smart top hat, exquisite Italian suit and new crocodile shoes. His shirt was custom-made, as was the belt that held his crisply pressed pants in place. Each article of his clothing probably cost more than this man had seen in his lifetime! And yet, Rav Shmuel seemed to treat this beggar as if he were a millionaire!

"How can I help you, my dear Reb Hirshele?" asked the Rav of Yerushalayim with affection and warmth. "Do you need anything?"

"Nothing special, Rebbe," replied the *yungerman* in a soft voice. "I came to suggest an answer for the difficulty that Rav Akiva Eiger poses in his *gilyon* on Mishnayos. The answer struck me this morning while I was waiting at the eye clinic."

"Well," Rav Shmuel joked, "a *chiddush* that was developed at the eye clinic should be quite enlightening. Let's hear the answer."

As Asher Trachtenberg sat there impatiently, the *yungerman* opened his mouth and let the words flow. A steady stream of *chiddushei Torah* poured from his lips while Rav Shmuel listened raptly. One *chiddush* led to another, and soon the Rav of

Yerushalayim was deeply involved in the exchange with Reb Hirshele.

As the conversation continued, Trachtenberg's irritation eventually got the better of him. The wealthy and powerful businessman was not used to being ignored, and this insult to his honor was more than he could bear. During a break in the flow of words, he said caustically, "I doubt if in America a similar incident would happen. I doubt if an important Rav would make such a to-do over a miserable beggar."

After a moment of stunned silence, Rav Shmuel responded forcefully. Striking his fist on the table, he turned to the *g'vir* and shouted, "How dare you express yourself in such a manner about a brilliant *talmid chacham*, an *avreich* of our yeshiva? How dare you humiliate a *ben Torah* to his face!"

The secretary, as well as Rav Shmuel's household members, were paralyzed. It was rare to see the Rav so angry. After his outburst, the Rav remained silent for several moments, composing himself with great effort. Asher Trachtenberg had turned pale and was staring at the floor.

Finally, Rav Shmuel turned to the secretary and said in a quiet voice, "Why do we honor wealthy people? Is it not so that they can help us cultivate *b'nei Torah* such as Reb Hirshele? For they are the ones who uphold the entire world! But if the wealthy humiliate and abuse the *b'nei Torah*, do we really need them?" Turning to Mr. Trachtenberg, the Rav said, "Do you think it is a small thing to publicly humiliate a *ben Torah*? And in front of the Rav, no less?"

Asher Trachtenberg did not wait to hear more. He abruptly got up and stalked out of the Rav's home, leaving Reb Sender to bemoan the great loss to the yeshiva. For all intents and purposes, Trachtenberg's support was likely lost forever to the Yidden of Yerushalayim.

Let us interrupt our story for a moment to supply some background about the ragged stranger who had been publicly humiliated at the Rav's home.

Reb Hirshele was a young man in his early thirties, but already the father of a large, growing family. Born in Poland, he had been a *talmid* of the Chiddushei Harim and learned in the Rebbe's yeshiva with single-minded devotion. Though blessed with a brilliant mind and keen insight, Reb Hirshele was doubly afflicted with poverty and physical ailments, including failing eyesight and blackened teeth. Yet he bore his lot with serenity and fortitude.

When his only brother had passed away in Yerushalayim several years earlier leaving a childless widow, Reb Hirshele and his family packed their meager bags and headed for Eretz Yisrael to give his sister-in-law *chalitzah.* He was eager to take advantage of this opportunity and settle in the Holy Land, whose streets were saturated with holiness.

Before he left, the Chiddushei Harim had given Reb Hirshele a letter of recommendation to Rav Shmuel Salant. The contents of the letter were brief, but powerful:

"I hereby testify that this yungerman, known as Reb Hirshele, has been studying Torah in a state of desperate poverty ever since his youth. He blackens his face in the toil of Torah for its own sake. Please befriend him and help him."

The Chiddushei Harim handed the letter to his beloved *talmid,* unsealed, and bade him an emotional good-bye. Two days later, Reb Hirshele and his family boarded the ship that would take them to the shores of Eretz Yisrael.

The journey was long and exhausting. The children were seasick and spent most of their time in the cabin. Reb Hirshele tried to learn during the long and arduous weeks on board, but he was kept busy caring for his family.

At last, a few days before they docked, the stormy seas calmed down and Reb Hirshele's children began to recover. Feeling calm and optimistic, Reb Hirshele took a stroll on deck, immersed in his Torah thoughts. Suddenly, he remembered the letter given to him by his Rebbe, the Chiddushei Harim. Reb Hirshele was seized by a yearning to read his Rebbe's Torah thoughts. It didn't occur to him that the letter would be about him.

"The letter is not private," he rationalized. "Why else would the Rebbe have given me an unsealed envelope if it did not contain Torah thoughts?"

The *avreich* reached into his pocket for the letter and opened it eagerly. Yet his eagerness lasted only as long as it took him to read the contents. Reb Hirshele, who was exceedingly humble, felt ashamed to be the object of Rav Shmuel's pity. He began to experience an intense inner conflict. Should he destroy the letter or deliver it to Rav Shmuel as instructed?

Back and forth the arguments raged in his mind.

"If I destroy the letter, I will be disobeying my Rebbe's instructions. Yet if I hand the letter to Rav Shmuel, I will be using my Torah learning as an 'axe' with which to earn a living."

Reb Hirshele's mind was ablaze with the warnings from the *chachamim* not to use one's Torah knowledge for personal gain. He remembered the story about Rabbi Tarfon who was grabbed off the street and almost killed by a kidnapper. Rabbi Tarfon pleaded with the murderer to save him, but the criminal was unmoved. Out of desperation, Rabbi Tarfon finally revealed his identity, that he was one of the *gedolei hador,* and he was released. However, he mourned and regretted this action for the rest of his life; he had used the crown of Torah for personal reasons.

The tormented young man now recalled the *Chazal* in *Pirkei*

Avos, "He who uses the crown of Torah for personal reasons shall die." Yet he was still in doubt. How dare he transgress his Rebbe's explicit order to deliver the letter?

The ship was sailing rapidly across the ocean waves, spraying a fine, salty mist over the deck. Reb Hirshele breathed deeply, taking in great draughts of refreshing air. His wife, who had been busy caring for the children in their cramped cabin, came up to join him. In a few succinct sentences, she was apprised of his moral dilemma.

"I beg of you to put off your decision for a few days until the boat docks," she pleaded, knowing full well that without the letter, they were condemned to a life of penury. However, her heartfelt pleas only spurred him to act now before he weakened.

Reb Hirshele begged his wife not to interfere, and in an instant, seized the paper, tore it to shreds and let it fly over the vast ocean, lost forever.

His wife bravely watched her last chance at a respectable life in the Holy City disappear, yet she did not say a word. If it was meant to be that her husband should not be recognized among the respected *b'nei Torah* in Yerushalayim, if it was destined for them to suffer penury and deprivation, so be it.

Several days later, the ship docked at the port of Yaffo and the passengers disembarked. Reb Hirshele, his wife and six children boarded a rickety cart along with their meager possessions for their long and bumpy journey to Yerushalayim. They arrived in the Holy City, alone and friendless, and quickly found lodgings — a ramshackle, moldy apartment in one of the endless courtyards that dotted the narrow streets of the Old City.

The day after their arrival, Reb Hirshele arranged for the *chalitzah* ceremony with his sister-in-law, thus freeing her to remarry. Then he headed to the nearest *bais medrash* and began to learn with devotion.

For the first several weeks, until the money they had brought with them was used up, all was fine. The boys were enrolled in the Etz Chaim yeshiva and the girls remained home, helping their mother keep house. The family was content with the meager possessions they had brought and the rickety furnishings that were supplied with the apartment. They bought bread, herring and olive oil from the local grocer, and an occasional vegetable for Shabbos. Such was the life of penury that the Yerushalmi *talmidei chachamim* of old were accustomed to.

However, soon their meager savings had disappeared and there was no food in the house. The children began to feel the meaning of hunger. Reb Hirshele's wife pressured him to go to Rav Shmuel Salant, Rosh Yeshiva of the Etz Chaim yeshiva and *kollel*, and ask to be admitted into the *kollel*. The meager stipend he would receive would suffice to buy some bread and herring for the children.

As the *yungerman* walked out the door, trying valiantly to straighten his crooked hat, his wife sighed. It was a sigh filled with meaning, a sigh that spoke volumes of the opportunity he could have had if he had not destroyed the letter.

The humble *avreich* walked into Rav Shmuel's study a short while later, presenting himself as a newcomer from Poland. With eyes downcast and head bowed, he silently inquired whether it would be possible for him to be accepted in the yeshiva.

"I have no source of income," he quietly explained.

Rav Shmuel was shocked. "Since when does one enter yeshiva in order to make a living? Isn't the sole purpose of going to yeshiva to study and teach Torah, to immerse oneself in the sea of Torah? Once that purpose is clear, the bread won't be lacking."

Reb Hirshele remained standing silently, ashamed to respond. Rav Shmuel continued. "In any case, do you have a letter of recommendation from abroad stating that you are a *ben Torah*?"

Reb Hirshele winced as he recalled the letter that would have opened many doors for him, but was now lost, forever. Even now, as he stood before the Rav of Yerushalayim, in shame he refused to mention the letter.

Several uncomfortable minutes passed. Neither Rav Shmuel nor Reb Hirshele had anything to say, each sunk in his own thoughts. Rav Shmuel, who was then an elderly *gadol*, momentarily dozed off, exhausted from the heavy burden of the *kehillah* that he shouldered all day long. Reb Hirshele's mind was far, far away, in the middle of the ocean.

Suddenly, heavy footsteps were heard in the courtyard. It was the postman carrying a huge pile of mail that had come from abroad, all directed to the Rav. Reb Hirshele moved back a bit so as not to disturb Rav Shmuel, who shook himself awake and began to peruse the letters.

Suddenly, the Rav took one letter out of the pile and opened it with eager interest. It was a letter from the Chiddushei Harim, postmarked Poland. Instead of the customary *chiddushei Torah* or complicated *shailos*, the note contained a message for the Rav of Yerushalayim.

"*My* talmid, *Reb Hirshele of Tomashov, has immigrated to Yerush-alayim, and is unknown there. Although I have given him a letter of recommendation, I am afraid that due to his humility, he will not deliver it. Therefore, I have rewritten the contents of that letter.*

"*I hereby testify that this* yungerman, *known as Reb Hirshele, has been studying Torah in a state of desperate poverty ever since his youth. He blackens his face in the toil of Torah for its own sake. Please befriend him and help him.*"

Rav Shmuel looked at the letter, then at the *yungerman*, and back at the letter again. Now all was clear to him; he realized that the *avreich* who stood before him was a true gem.

"Amazing," said Rav Shmuel. "What amazing *hashgacha pratis!*"

Reb Hirshele could not understand why Rav Shmuel stood up, hugged and embraced him and tearfully announced, "You are one of ours. You are one of ours."

From that day onward, Reb Hirshele became one of the honored *b'nei Torah* in the Etz Chaim yeshiva and occupied a special place in Rav Shmuel's heart.

Thus, it was no surprise that Rav Shmuel reacted so angrily when Asher Trachtenberg publicly humiliated this humble *avreich*.

When Reb Sender recovered from the shock of seeing Asher Trachtenberg storm out of the Rav's study, he immediately swung into action. He could not bear to lose such a valuable supporter who had contributed so generously in the past to the Etz Chaim yeshiva and to the Yerushalmi Torah institutions. Thus, he thought long and hard about a plan of action.

Swallowing his pride, he paid a visit to Trachtenberg's hotel that evening to talk to him. The *g'vir*, his pride wounded, was brusque and uninterested in seeing him.

"I want no more of you and your yeshiva," he said. "I'm leaving for New Jersey tomorrow. I'm finished with giving my hard-earned money to beggars."

In vain did the secretary beg and plead with Mr. Trachtenberg to come and visit the yeshiva and be impressed — as he was each time anew — with the commitment of the *b'nei Torah*. But the humiliation he had suffered that day in Rav Shmuel's office was still fresh in Asher Trachtenberg's memory, and his ears still buzzed with the rebuke he had received.

"Be off with you," said Trachtenberg gruffly. "I have work to do."

Reb Sender sighed. "I'll be on my way soon," he said, "and I won't bother you again. But before we part ways, perhaps forever, won't you accompany me on an eavesdropping mission?"

"An eavesdropping mission?" The *g'vir* was intrigued. "What's this all about?" he asked as Reb Sender urgently gestured him to follow. But the secretary did not elaborate. His curiosity piqued, Trachtenberg followed the secretary down the narrow streets of Meah Shearim until they arrived at the Old City. His amazement increased as they went down a narrow alleyway, stopping in a ramshackle courtyard surrounded by rickety apartments.

"Come with me," gestured Reb Sender as he tiptoed toward a window, illuminated by a pale glow from within. Asher Trachtenberg, the wealthy, self-important tycoon, bent down near the secretary and peered inside.

The sight almost made him gasp out loud.

Reb Hirshele, the beggar he had shamed that morning, was sitting at the head of a long, rickety table wearing his shredded kaftan over a yellowed shirt that was patched in two places. His bare feet were immersed in a pail of cold water to keep him awake. Around him sat his four sons, eating supper. Trachtenberg watched as Reb Hirshele's wife doled out thick slices of black bread, smeared with olive oil, to each of her sons, and a slice of bread with tea for her husband. The children ate heartily, their faces shining with joy.

When they had finished eating, they said the Grace after Meals aloud along with their father and the table was cleared. One of the sons brought a pile of *sefarim* to the table and the learning session began.

Soon the room was abuzz with the singsong *ay-ay-ay* chant of Torah learning as the children hunched over their *gemaras*, reviewing the day's lessons with their father. The dim light of a kerosene lamp in the center of the table illuminated the dingy room, and the sweet, satisfied faces of the cherubic children shone with an otherworldly light.

Mr. Trachtenberg bent down near the window, crouching next to Reb Sender, oblivious to the ache in his back and the lateness of the hour. The two eavesdroppers were hidden in the shadows of the home and watched the entire scene, unobserved. As the melodious voices of the *kinderlach* learning with their father wafted out of the decrepit home, Asher Trachtenberg's eyes filled with tears. He stood, transfixed, staring at the scene, pinching himself to make sure it was real.

An hour passed, then another. The strong, vibrant voice of Reb Hirshele and the thin, clear voices of his children never wavered. In an age-old *gemara niggun* they continued reviewing the *sugya*, while their mother sat nearby *kvelling*.

Finally, one by one, the eyelids of the exhausted children began to droop. In a short while, they had all dropped off into a blissful slumber at the table. Yet Reb Hirshele continued learning with enthusiasm.

Reb Sender rose to his feet. It was time to go. He gestured to Trachtenberg, who impatiently waved him away. The *g'vir* was glued to the window, unable to tear himself away from the riveting scene.

Soon Reb Hirshele also dozed off in front of his open *gemara*, but only for a few moments. He shook himself awake, gently woke his children and brought them water to wash their hands. Then they said *Kriyas Shema* together, before being led off to the lumpy mattresses in the corner of the room that served as their beds.

Finally, when the kerosene lamp had been extinguished, an exhausted Mr. Trachtenberg allowed his guide to lead him back to his luxurious hotel room. He sank into bed, his mind abuzz with the otherworldly scene he had observed. "This must be what the Heavenly Angels look like in Heaven," he mused.

Though exhausted from his late adventure, the *g'vir* tossed and turned all night, unable to fall asleep. The melody of the children and their father still reverberated in his ears. Each time he closed his eyes, the image of Reb Hirshele, his feet immersed in freezing water, and the children eating bread dipped in oil, appeared before his vision.

The memory of his callous and selfish remarks in Rav Shmuel's study made him shudder. How had he dared to humiliate and insult a holy man of such caliber? *The Rav was so right when he censured me,* Trachtenberg realized.

Finally, after hours of recriminations and painful soul searching, he saw the first rays of dawn on the horizon. At the first sign of daylight, Trachtenberg was already dressed and on his way to the home of Rav Shmuel Salant. Crying bitterly, the *g'vir* apologized for the way he had humiliated Reb Hirshele, unaware of his true worth.

"I cannot forgive you until you ask Reb Hirshele for forgiveness," said Rav Shmuel. The *g'vir* immediately headed for the Etz Chaim yeshiva where Reb Hirshele was already sitting over his *gemara*. With copious tears, he begged the *yungerman* to forgive him.

Reb Hirshele forgave him with a full heart. "What is there to forgive?" he asked. He had not felt slighted in the least! But Trachtenberg still wanted to make amends. He offered the Torah scholar a long-term learning partnership whereby the *g'vir* would support Reb Hirshele's family and receive a share in his Torah learning.

"I must first discuss it with my Rebbe, the Chiddushei Harim," said Reb Hirshele, and the matter was temporarily put aside.

Trachtenberg sailed back to America the next week filled with inspiration and idealism, resolving to triple his support of the Torah institutions where "Reb Hirsheles" were cultivated. Indeed, Reb Sender's "eavesdropping" brainstorm was a worthwhile investment, which reaped dividends for many years to come.

VIDUY
for the
CONDEMNED MAN

t was Rosh Hashanah in Brisk. The entire community, men, women, and children, were assembled in the Great Shul. The fear and trembling upon the Holy Day of Judgment, when the books of life and death were open, was palpable. All were cognizant of the words of *Unesaneh Tokef,* "Who shall live and who shall die?"

Suddenly, the silence of the Mussaf *tefillah* was shattered. The sound of wagon wheels and horses' hooves clattered down the street. Who could be driving a horse and buggy on such a holy day? Certainly, not a Jew. The Yidden of Brisk looked nervously at each other. The horse and buggy certainly spelled trouble, probably a new edict from the authorities who always sought new ways to vent their hatred of the Jews.

They did not have long to wait. Within moments, heavy footfalls echoed through the courtyard as an armed soldier entered the *bais medrash.* Striding straight to the podium, he unfurled a scroll and read:

"Attention, Brisker Rabiner: A Jewish peddler who lives in a neighboring village has been condemned to death by firing squad for thievery. He is accused of stealing from our Church, a crime punishable by death."

The congregants gasped. What could have possessed a Jew to commit such a foolish act? Or was it perhaps staged by the gentiles who wanted to spill his blood for sport?

The soldier cleared his throat and pompously continued:

"As is the law, the Jew has the privilege of saying his final prayers with the pastor of his choice, and only then shall he be put to death. Thus, I command the Grand Brisker Rabiner to come with me to the jailhouse and say the final prayers with the condemned man."

The Jews listened fearfully to hear what penalty was to be meted out to the entire community, but the soldier had finished and was rolling up his scroll. An uneasy sigh of relief spread through the shul. So "only" the poor Jew was condemned to death! The rest of them were given a reprieve. Of course, the congregants felt sorry for the probably innocent soul who awaited his fate, but they were grateful that no new decree was hanging over the entire community.

All looked expectantly at the great Rav Velvel Brisker who stood at the *amud* like an angel bedecked in white, leading the *tefillos*. The Brisker Rav made no response to show that he had heard the edict at all.

The soldier waited, tapping his boots impatiently. Several moments passed.

Finally, the furious messenger loudly called to the *gabbai* and asked him to repeat the request to the Brisker Rav.

The *gabbai* apologetically went over to the Rav and, in a hushed whisper, began to repeat the soldier's words. The Rav gestured that he could not be interrupted and resumed the *tefillah*.

The soldier waited, his anger mounting, yet the Rav showed no sign of complying. Instead, Rav Velvel calmly continued leading the Mussaf *tefillos*, with the nervous congregation singing along.

As the minutes turned to hours, the soldier finally snapped. His voice tinged with fury, he burst out, "I shall not wait any longer! If the Rav will not come willingly, I will arrest him by force!"

Murmurs of consternation rose and fell among the congregants. All wondered why the Rav was so firmly refusing to go fulfill a dying Jew's last request. After all, it was a true act of kindness, a real mitzvah on the Day of Judgment! But apparently, the Rav thought otherwise.

As Mussaf wound to a close with *Birkas Kohanim* and the *shofar*'s final blow, the Brisker Rav, bedecked with a *tallis*, turned to face the messenger. His holy eyes shone with purity and determination.

"I refuse to accompany you to the jailhouse," the Rav said firmly.

"The command must be carried out," growled the soldier. "You will pay a heavy price for refusing."

"I obey a Higher Command that forbids me to hasten the death of a fellow Jew," the Rav explained. "Since you have declared that the condemned cannot be put to death until I come, the very act of my following you to the jail will hasten his demise. I want no part of it!"

The soldier was impressed with the Rav's bravery and reasoning, but he had a task to fulfill. "Very well," he intoned. "Know, then, that you are playing with fire. I will report to my superiors that you refused to come and you will be imprisoned. In addition, the entire Jewish community will have to pay a heavy tax."

The Jews gasped in horror and dismay. Another tax? They had already been taxed to the limit. Several congregants began to murmur that perhaps the great Rav was going too far. But Rav Velvel refused to discuss the issue and gave the signal for Mincha to begin. The soldier turned on his heel and left.

Another half hour passed, during which the *kehillah* grew edgy, waiting for further developments. Finally, when Mincha was over and the congregation prepared to go home, a group of soldiers stormed into the shul. One of them walked up to the *bimah* and began to read: "In the name of the Governor, I hereby decree that the Rabiner of Brisk must immediately come to the jailhouse to fulfill the last request of the condemned man. If the Rabiner refuses to comply, the entire community will be severely punished."

Silence. The Rav did not deign to reply. The congregants were frantic. What new decrees were awaiting them? How high a price would they pay for the Rav's obstinacy?

Suddenly, one of the *baalebatim*, a local troublemaker, came up with a brilliant plan.

"Soldiers!" he said with a pleading tone. "True, our main rabbi refuses to come, but we also have another rabbi for when the first rabbi is out of town."

All gasped at this ludicrous charge, but the troublemaker did not waver. He pointed to Reb Getzel, an ignorant man with a snow-white beard who sat in the *bais medrash* most of the day saying *Tehillim*. "The substitute rabbi will oblige your request."

The soldiers mulled this over for several moments and decided to accept the offer. After all, several precious hours had already been wasted and the executioner was eager to finish his job. The condemned man was desperate to say *viduy* with the rabbi and the commander of the jail was furious. It was high time that someone broke the impasse.

"Very well. I'll take the old Rabiner," the head of the delegation said carelessly. "If he's good enough for you Jews, he's good enough for me."

Quaking with fear, the simple Reb Getzel slowly followed the soldier out the door. The Brisker Rav gave him a look filled with pain and anguish, but said nothing. The congregants went home to their Yom Tov meals in relief. A catastrophe had been averted. Only the Rav was too disturbed to enjoy the *seudah*.

A short time later, Reb Getzel arrived at the jailhouse where he was taken to the terrified Yid who was bound in chains, awaiting his fate.

"Dirty Jew, I brought your rabbi!" the guard growled. "Now you can say your final prayers and go to the Next World."

"But this isn't the Rabbi," the Yid cried. "I wanted the great Brisker Rav to say *viduy* with me."

"The main rabbi refused to come," snapped the guard. "We waited many hours for him, but then we became impatient. So we sent you a substitute rabbi. Too bad."

Having no choice, the quivering Yid slowly said *viduy* with

Reb Getzel, sobbing and wailing bitterly. As soon as he had finished, he was roughly grabbed by two soldiers and taken to face the firing squad. Reb Getzel was forced to wait in the police station until the order was carried out.

As the soldiers trained their guns on him, the condemned cried, "Know that I am innocent! My enemies who want to take revenge upon me concocted the entire story! But Heaven will avenge my blood!"

A few seconds later, the shots rang out. It was over.

A quarter of an hour passed. Suddenly, a horse appeared, foaming at the mouth. The agitated rider shouted breathlessly, "A message from the government headquarters! The true robber has confessed! The Jew is innocent!"

"What?" shouted the local police chief. "He was just shot!"

"Oh, no!" cried the messenger. "I was hoping I would arrive in time!"

The rider handed the police officers an official document declaring that the Jew was innocent of the charges, which were trumped up by his enemies who had suddenly confessed to the crime.

The executioners didn't feel too sorry that they had killed a *Zhid*, but Reb Getzel felt sick to his stomach. He knew that he was indirectly guilty of murder. Because of his cooperation, an innocent Jew had been killed! Had he not agreed to follow the commandant, the poor Jew's life would have been spared!

As if pouring salt into his wounds, the police chief sarcastically said, "What a shame, Rabbi, that you were so eager to comply! The other rabbi didn't want to come. Maybe he knew something you didn't ...."

On *motzaei* Yom Tov, the sad news was spread in Brisk. A tragedy had occurred because of one hothead who refused to follow the Rav's guidance.

Now, instead of the anger they felt at the Rav for endangering them, all of the congregants were in awe of the Rav's wisdom and courage. Rav Velvel had been prepared to flout an official order and put his life in danger in order to fulfill the *pasuk,* "Even if a sharp sword rests upon one's neck, he should not despair of Hashem's mercy."

Hashem had extended His mercy to spare the Yid, yet it was not meant to be. All because of those who second-guessed the great Brisker Rav.

REPAID *in* FULL

*T*he *Baal* Hatanya was a great *chassidic* leader who drew thousands of his brethren close to *chassidus*, warming their frozen hearts with the life-giving wellsprings of Torah. He was highly regarded by the great disciples of the Baal Shem Tov and was an important force in the revival of Yiddishkeit in Russia.

However, his "counter-revolutionary" activities did not sit well with the Czar who sought many opportunities to punish the Baal Hatanya for spreading Hashem's word among the masses.

Sadly, even among the Jews, the Baal Hatanya had many enemies who fought for "liberty" and "equality," and wanted the Jews to assimilate into Russian culture. These enemies followed the Baal Hatanya everywhere he went and reported his every move to the authorities. The Czar gritted his teeth in anger as he heard about the glorious *chassidic tischen* and of the thousands who thronged to the Rebbe to drink from the wellsprings of Torah and *kedushah*. He bided his time, waiting to punish the Rebbe when the opportunity would arise.

The opportunity arose soon enough when the Baal Hatanya's enemies rose up to slander him for taking sides in a specific issue. To the shock and distress of the *chassidim*, a group of soldiers arrived at the Rebbe's home, shackled the great leader and dragged him off to jail in St. Petersburg.

The Rebbe languished in sub-human conditions, sitting on the cold, wet ground with only a few hard crumbs of bread to eat. Yet the Baal Hatanya did not despair, continuing to learn Torah from memory, sending messages of hope and faith to his *chassidim*.

The *chassidim* of the Baal Hatanya did not sit idly by while their Rebbe languished in jail. Many prominent *shtadlanim* rallied and met in secret to plot for the Rebbe's release. They tried to bribe important government officials and prove the Rebbe's innocence. These *shtadlanim* sent each other regular "update letters" discussing their progress in securing the Baal Hatanya's freedom. At the very least, they hoped that the Rebbe's situation would improve and that he would be given a chair, a small table and *sefarim* to learn from. These improvements would mean a great deal to the frail and elderly Rebbe who was suffering greatly from the miserable conditions. The *chassidim* had great hopes of accomplishing their goal.

However, after a while, they realized that all their planning was futile. The Baal Hatanya's enemies, who campaigned for liberty and assimilation, had bribed an official at the post office who forwarded all the letters to them. Thus, they were kept up-to-date about plans for the Rebbe's release and were able to stay one step ahead of the *chassidim*. Whenever they found out about a new development in the Rebbe's forthcoming trial, they used this information to work against the Rebbe's release and malign him to the authorities.

The desperate *chassidim* were at the end of their rope. Without a reliable method of delivering mail, they were unable to communicate with each other, and the campaign for release fell apart. The distraught *askanim* met in secret to discuss the turn of events. How would they secure the Rebbe's release? Thousands of the Baal Hatanya's *chassidim* flocked to the *bais medrash* to daven, while a core group of *askanim* tried every diplomatic channel possible. Finally, someone suggested contacting Bronya.

Who was Bronya? And how could she help them?

Bronya Wislovsky was a religious girl in her late twenties employed at the local postal station. She worked from early morning until late afternoon sorting the mail and preparing it for delivery to the main post office in St. Petersburg. Bronya's father, a simple man named Shmuel, was sympathetic toward the *chassidim* and occasionally had attended the Rebbe's *tischen*.

As soon as the *chassidim* discovered what was happening to

their mail, they approached Shmuel and begged him to ask his daughter Bronya to help them save the Baal Hatanya. The simple girl was not familiar with the Rebbe or his *chassidim*, yet she was goodhearted and greatly distressed to hear of the Rebbe's situation. "I'll do whatever I can to help you," she promised.

The *chassidim* met with her in secret and explained their plan. They would mark all their correspondence with a special, secret sign that nobody but Bronya would notice. It would be Bronya's job to carefully scan the envelopes and put aside correspondence regarding the Rebbe. These envelopes would be delivered to the main post office separately, so the Rebbe's enemies would be unable to get hold of them.

In addition, Bronya was asked to monitor the correspondence between the Rebbe's enemies and report if there was an unusual volume of mail. Bronya agreed to the top-secret mission, recognizing that if she was caught, her life was in danger. Yet she promised to do everything in her power to help the Rebbe.

The devoted young girl was true to her word. Every day, as she sat and sorted mail into piles, she scanned each envelope carefully, waiting to see the specific sign the *chassidim* had agreed upon. Within a short while, the mail was getting delivered to its rightful addresses and the *chassidim* breathed more easily. The *shtadlanim* redoubled their efforts, raising large sums of money and buying expensive "gifts" for the right party officials.

After a few painful months, the Rebbe's situation slowly improved. Now the Rebbe was able to receive visitors and was allowed the luxury of his precious *sefarim*. The Rebbe's prison rations also improved and his cell was exchanged for another, more spacious one. But the *chassidim* still did not rest, determined to secure their beloved Rebbe's release.

Finally, after intense negotiations and bribery, the Rebbe was released, sending waves of joy throughout the Torah world. The

Baal Hatanya, who had become pale and emaciated from his months of pain and suffering, rejoined his family and thousands of *chassidim*, continuing to spread Torah with self-sacrifice.

And what happened to Bronya who had been so instrumental in the Rebbe's release? She became engaged to Kalman, a refined young man, and moved to the town of Tultchin to begin her new life. Her elderly parents remained in the Baal Hatanya's hometown and Bronya would visit them from time to time.

Bronya's husband Kalman slowly became attracted to *chassidus* and was especially drawn to the great Rav Baruch of Medzibuzh. Following the advice of Rav Baruch, Kalman earned a fine living as an oxen merchant, trading in strong oxen on the local market. Business was booming and the young family was blessed with *parnassah*.

A year after their wedding, Kalman and Bronya were blessed with a little girl whom they named Chana. Chanale was a beautiful, precocious child who brought her parents great *nachas*. Their joy and satisfaction was complete.

Yet the wheel of *mazel* and *nachas* that had accompanied the young family was about to turn. As the months went by, the family was hit by one disaster after another. It started innocuously when Kalman invested in a large shipment of healthy, strong oxen that would fetch a good price on the market. Suddenly, from one day to the next, the healthy oxen became infected with a severe epidemic and began dying. Every single day the disease spread until Kalman's entire flock was ill and dying. Within a short while, the family was virtually penniless.

As if that weren't enough, the epidemic that had brought bad luck to their flock now entered their home as well. One fine afternoon, little Chanale, who had just begun to take her first steps, was outside with her mother playing in the front yard of their spacious home. Bronya went inside for a moment to check on the bread in the oven. She was gone for a few seconds, but it was long enough for the tragedy to occur.

One-year-old Chanale was attracted by the sound of a passing wagon and toddled outside the courtyard to have a better look. As the wagon lumbered down the road, the driver did not notice the toddler who had stepped into its path. Little Chanale was trampled by the horses' hooves and thrown to the side of the road, bleeding and unconscious.

The distraught mother ran into the street yelling "Chanale!" When she saw what had occurred, she collapsed. The neighbors, who had heard the commotion, ran outside to help her. Some kind-hearted women picked up the unconscious child and took her to the local village doctor, while others tended to the hysterical mother.

The doctor carefully checked the little girl's vital signs and ascertained that she was alive, though badly hurt. The doctor tried to stem the flow of blood and stitch up the wound, yet it was impossible to determine the extent of her internal injuries. It was clear that her windpipe was damaged and she was only able to breathe in short, shallow gasps of air. In those days, before the advent of modern surgery and X rays, the most the doctors could do was treat the external symptoms.

Kalman and Bronya hovered over their unconscious daughter's bedside, tears streaming down their cheeks. They davened and said *Tehillim* ceaselessly, imploring their Heavenly Father to save the child's life. They took the comatose child to many doctors, but none were able to help her. All the professionals they consulted sadly agreed that the child was dying.

When Kalman heard this, he rushed to his Rebbe, Rav Baruch of Medzibuzh, and cried bitter tears over his situation. The Rebbe listened, his heart filled with sorrow.

"Rebbe, please have mercy!" Kalman cried. "She is my only child!"

The Rebbe sighed along with his brokenhearted *chassid* and reminded Kalman to have *emunah* and *bitachon*. Yet he could not promise Kalman a *yeshuah*. "That is only in the hands of the *Ribono shel Olam*."

Having exhausted all their options, Kalman and his wife sat by their daughter's bedside, crying and davening. In the meantime, Kalman's business with the oxen went from bad to worse. Nearly his entire flock was decimated and the creditors were already pounding on his door. The beautiful life the young couple had built was disintegrating before their eyes.

A short while later, good news spread to Tultchin: The great Baal Hatanya had arrived in a neighboring village and was receiving his *chassidim*. When Bronya heard the news, she didn't hesitate for a moment. Leaving her little girl in her husband's care, she set off for the Baal Hatanya's lodgings, hoping that she could secure an audience. She knew it was her only chance to save her daughter.

When Bronya arrived in the village, the streets were in turmoil. Hundreds of *chassidim* thronged around the Rebbe's inn hoping for the opportunity to meet with him in person.

Bronya soon realized she would accomplish nothing by waiting patiently since it would be several days before the Rebbe would see her, perhaps too late to save her dying daughter. So, with a plan born of desperation, she stood outside the Rebbe's window and shouted, "Holy Rebbe! Please help your maidservant who has helped you in so many ways!"

The Rebbe heard the cries and commanded his *gabbaim* to let the distraught woman enter. Bronya was escorted into the Rebbe's study and handed the Rebbe a *kvittel*, shedding bitter tears. She told the Rebbe that she had worked in the post office during the Rebbe's imprisonment and her cooperation had been instrumental in his release. "I am asking the Rebbe to show his gratitude and help me in this desperate situation."

The *kvittel* that Bronya had given the Rebbe contained descriptions of both tragedies. The Rebbe asked her to rewrite the *kvittel*, putting each of the tragedies — her daughter's illness and the epidemic with the oxen — into its own *kvittel*.

Bronya went into the waiting room, where she rewrote the *kvittlech*, and then came back to the Rebbe's study, putting the first *kvittel* about her sick daughter on the table. The Rebbe read it carefully and said to the *gabbai*, "Please bring me the Shulchan Aruch Yorah Deah."

The *gabbai* brought him an old, weathered volume of Yorah Deah, and he began leafing through it until he arrived at Hilchos Treifos. The Rebbe began to argue fiercely with himself, quoting numerous sources as if debating the fate of an animal that had recently been slaughtered. Finally, with a smile of triumph, the Rebbe announced, "Kosher!"

Then he turned to Bronya and said, "The doctors are making a great mistake. Your daughter will not die of her injuries. Her wound will heal and she will live to a ripe old age. Her wound is not a *treifah*, one that renders an animal non-kosher, and she will recover."

Next, the elated woman delivered the second *kvittel* to the Rebbe. The Baal Hatanya read it carefully and advised, "Tell your husband not to deal with oxen any longer. Let him sell the rest of his stock and go into a different line of business."

The thankful woman blessed the Rebbe and left the city, her heart brimming with hope. When she arrived in Tultchin, her husband greeted her with wondrous news: Little Chanale had opened her eyes! From one day to the next, she slowly regained her strength. Her breathing became steady as her wound slowly healed. Soon the child was smiling at her parents and toddling around the house.

The young couple took Chanale back to the doctors who had

despaired of her life. They were unable to believe that this was the same child who had lain comatose, hovering between life and death! All agreed that it was a miracle, creating a great *kiddush Hashem.*

Kalman soon found a buyer for the few remaining oxen that had survived the epidemic and began to deal in furs. His new business proved successful, and he became a wealthy man.

Kalman and Bronya used their wealth to do many *mitzvos,* feeding the poor, healing the sick and opening their home to wayfarers. They became known as *baalei tzedakah* and *baalei chesed,* raising a beautiful family that followed in their lofty example.

The
SATAN'S
PLOT

n his early years, the renowned Shach, Rav Shabsai Cohen, sat and learned, supported by his wealthy father-in-law. One year, the annual fair was taking place in the marketplace and his father-in-law was too busy to attend. Having no choice, he called his young son-in-law and handed him a bundle of bank notes, saying, "Please go to the fair and see if you can buy a *metziah*, some merchandise on the cheap, and sell it for a profit."

The Shach took the money and went to the market. Within a short while, he was offered a vast quantity of merchandise at a bargain price. The Shach accepted the offer and bought the entire lot. A few hours later, he found a buyer who paid far more than he had invested. At the end of the day, the young *talmid chacham* had earned a small fortune.

He went back to his father-in-law who warmly praised him for his efforts and business acumen. The Shach went back to his *gemara* and continued learning intently.

The following year, the annual fair once again came to town, and his father-in-law encouraged him to go and try his *mazel* once more. With a sinking heart, the Shach realized where this would lead, that slowly he would be forced to abandon his *gemara* and become a businessman.

Thus, with the utmost respect, he told his father-in-law, "I cannot go because of a *pasuk* in *Az Yashir*."

"Which *pasuk*?" asked his father-in-law, surprised.

To which the son-in-law replied: "'*Amar Oyeiv*,' the enemy, the *yetzer hara*, said, '*Erdof*,' I will run after my customers. How? '*Achalek shalal*,' I will allow them to earn a large profit and they will slowly be lured away from the *gemara*. And finally, when they have already abandoned their learning, '*Torisheimo yadi*,' I will take away their fortune, and they will remain a pauper, both spiritually and financially."

With those words, the Shach returned to his *gemara*, vowing never to forsake it for the business world. Thus, *Klal Yisrael* gained a tremendous *gadol* who illuminated the world with his Torah insights.

A Burning Midnight Thirst

*T*he *renowned tzaddik* Rav Shmuel Abba of Zychlin, known as the Zychliner Rebbe, once had occasion to travel to a small Polish *shtetl* where he was honored with being *sandek* at a *bris*. The *bris* ended at a late hour and Rav Shmuel Abba decided to remain in the village overnight, returning to Zychlin the following morning.

Though it was past midnight, the Zychliner Rebbe was still awake, learning in his private room, at the inn where he was staying with his *chassidim*. Suddenly, the Rebbe opened the door of his room and stood at the threshold.

"I am suffering from a terrible thirst," the Rebbe called out to his *chassidim*. "Please go out immediately and bring me some beer." Then he went back into his room and shut the door.

The Rebbe's assistants looked at each other, startled. This request was definitely unusual for the Rebbe who was completely divorced from worldly pleasures. There definitely was a hidden meaning in the Rebbe's urgent need for beer. Yet how could they accommodate him at such a late hour? Where would they find beer in such a small *shtetl* so late at night?

But Rav Shmuel Abba's devoted *chassidim* would not leave a stone unturned to do their great Rebbe's bidding. After much discussion, two young and energetic chassidim were chosen for the mission. Despite the late hour, they were instructed to head for the nearest train station in a neighboring village where they might find some beer in the small shop that sold drinks to the train passengers. Immediately, the two *chassidim* headed out in the darkened streets to buy the Rebbe some beer.

After a long, dangerous walk through a thick, forbidding forest, they arrived in the neighboring village and headed for the train station. When they arrived, exhausted and frozen to the bone, they found, to their intense disappointment, that the station was already closed.

In desperation, they began to bang on the door of the enclosed waiting area, hoping that the manager of the depot was still awake and would hear them. However, no one heard their frantic banging. After several minutes, they gave up and decided to head back to the inn.

The two *chassidim* began walking back to the small village, empty-handed and intensely disappointed. How could they disappoint the Rebbe who was waiting to quench his thirst? They were embarrassed to show their faces in the inn without having accomplished their mission. They decided to return to the train depot and try banging on the door once more.

With a sense of renewed resolve, the two strong young men banged and kicked at the door with all their strength until, suddenly, the door gave way and they stood inside the darkened depot.

The *chassidim* looked at each other, frightened, sure they would get into trouble. Perhaps they would be arrested for daring to break into the train station! But their anxiety was soon replaced by a deeper fear. Suddenly, they smelled the sharp odor of burning coals. Something was terribly wrong!

A layer of heavy smoke blanketed the room, nearly blinding them. Thick vapors choked their nostrils, making them dizzy and nauseated. The smoke entered their lungs and they began to gag.

In the thick blackness, it was impossible to see anything, but it was clear that they were in terrible danger. They began to yell, "Help! Help!"

Hearing their screams and shouts, the night warden finally awoke from his sleep and stumbled over to the train depot. Sizing up the situation, he quickly lit a candle, whose feeble glow illuminated the area. To their horror, the *chassidim* saw several Jews lying on the floor, unconscious and near-death. Apparently, the passengers had decided to wait indoors for the early morning train and were locked inside, trapped in the heavy smoke.

The two men valiantly tried to wake up the unconscious victims, to no avail. With the help of the warden, they quickly dragged the victims outside into the crisp, fresh air and poured water on them. In the meantime, rescue personnel arrived and took over the effort while employees extinguished the smoking stove that was emitting such a terrible odor.

It took a long while for the victims of the choking gas to awaken and come to their senses. They sat up slowly, rubbing their eyes, not realizing where they were and what had happened to them.

"W-where are we?" asked one of the victims, his face a sickly gray. "What has happened?"

The two *chassidim* filled him in on the details and emphasized that they had come especially to the train depot on the request of their Rebbe. "Apparently, we were the messengers to save your life."

"How can we thank you?" cried another. "If you hadn't pulled us out, we would have perished from the smoke."

"Don't thank us," said the *chassidim*. "Thank our Rebbe who sent us to buy some beer."

At that moment, they recalled that they had not yet fulfilled the Rebbe's mission and immediately purchased several bottles of beer. Then, satisfied that the victims were in stable condition, they headed back to the small village where their Rebbe was staying.

The journey back home went by speedily. They hurried along, eager to share the news of the rescue they had merited being part of. However, when they finally arrived at the inn with the beer, the Rebbe's door was tightly shut and there was no sign that he was awake and waiting for them.

The next morning, the Rebbe came to Shacharis acting as if nothing was amiss. The *chassidim* noticed that he made no mention of his "sudden thirst" and the errand to bring him beer. Rav

Shmuel Abba did not even ask whether the *chassidim* had been successful in their mission. It was as if the entire incident had never occurred.

Only then did the *chassidim* realize that the Rebbe had never really needed beer. He thirsted only to save the endangered lives of his fellow Yidden.

ANOTHER CHANCE
for
AVREMEL

*R*av *Moshe* Sofer, known as the great Chasam Sofer, Rav of Pressburg, spent his early years attached to his holy Rebbe, Rav Nasan Adler. For a time, young Moshe lived in Rav Nasan's home in Frankfurt, where he grew in Torah and piety.

In Frankfurt, there lived a wealthy Jew who owned many mansions, acres of land and a stable with the finest steeds. He hired a staff of stable boys to care for the horses, to see to their grooming, feeding and exercise. The stable boys were among the lower class elements of society, both in behavior and education.

Among the stable boys was a Jewish lad, sadly alienated from Yiddishkeit, who had sunk so low that he was soon indistinguishable from the others. Rav Moshe Sofer, who, though young, was already a renowned *talmid chacham*, was told about Avremel, whose refined Jewish traits had been coarsened by his lifestyle. Rav Moshe was determined to rescue this precious soul before it was too late.

Thus, overlooking his stature and image among the townspeople, Rav Moshe made it his business to visit the stables and have a talk with the youth. With great concern and warmth, the young prodigy asked Avremel about his job, and the boy self-importantly explained about his various responsibilities. Then Rav Moshe deftly led the conversation into spiritual matters and began talking to the ignorant lad about the meaning and purpose of life. The uncouth boy merely laughed and shrugged off these ideas.

Seeing that he was getting nowhere, the *yungerman* bid farewell to the stable boy and went back to his *gemara* with a heavy heart. However, he didn't give up for long, and several days later, paid the boy another visit. This time, Avremel was even more antagonistic and sneered as Rav Moshe spoke about *Olam Habah*, about the purpose of every Yid and the concept of reward and punishment.

Due to the *talmid chacham*'s stature and the high regard in which he was held, the youth did not walk off, but merely listened impatiently and waited for Rav Moshe to stop. When Rav Moshe paused for breath, Avremel said, "I am truly sorry, honored Rabiner, but your 'merchandise' does not interest me. You are wasting your time." Then he mounted his master's steed and rode off into the gloomy dusk.

The Rav's heart fell as he bade the youth farewell. Would he ever succeed in penetrating the iron defenses of the lost Jewish lad? It seemed as if Avremel had a heart of stone.

However, unbeknownst to Rav Moshe, his impassioned words had set Avremel thinking. "The young Rabiner with the piercing eyes and polished manner may be saying the truth," he mused. "Perhaps I have come down to this world for a more important purpose than grooming horses! Maybe it is time for me to do something for my soul, which I have neglected for so many years! After all, a person is not an animal!"

The more he thought about these ideas that had never occurred to him, the more confused the lad became. Soon he felt that his head was spinning and he was losing his equilibrium. Then and there, he decided to dispense with this "nonsense" and never to think about religious matters again.

But Rav Moshe did not give up. Day after day, he searched for an opportunity to bring the youth back into the fold.

Late one afternoon, Rav Moshe met Avremel riding on a horse in the street. Rav Moshe greeted him warmly, but Avremel only nodded coldly in reply, preparing to ride on. Rav Moshe signaled for him to stop, just for a moment or two. But Avremel, who was fed up already with hearing about the purpose of life, arrogantly snapped, "Make it quick, Rabiner! I am in a very great rush!"

Rav Moshe realized that all his words of *chizuk* were not accomplishing anything. It was time to switch tactics. Thus, he declared loudly in fluent German, "My dear friend! You must return to your heritage! You possess a lofty soul! If you won't return with friendliness and warmth, then you will be forced to do so! And who knows how much pain and bodily harm it will cost you?"

The youth did not want to listen to another word. Furious, he nodded, whipped his horse and rode off into the gathering dusk. "What nerve!" he muttered. "So the rabbi is threatening me? I'm not afraid of him! One sneeze can blow the frail man away! What will he do to me? Will a hand come down from heaven and hit me? I am a boxing champion. Nobody can touch me."

However, despite his arrogant words, deep down the youth was afraid. Rav Moshe's warnings still rang in his ears. He knew that the young Torah scholar was a spiritual man who did not make idle threats. As he rode off to the stables, the warning kept on reverberating in his mind, filling him with anxiety.

For his part, Rav Moshe was not slighted or discouraged at the arrogant behavior of the youth. His mission was to save this Jewish soul, no matter what it took. He did not desist and continued thinking of ways to reach out to Avremel and shake him out of his stupor.

Several days passed. Once more, Rav Moshe stood at the side of the road waiting for Avremel to ride down the street. He had learned Avremel's schedule and intentionally took precious time from his lofty pursuits to try to convince him to do *teshuvah*.

This time, when the arrogant stable boy saw Rav Moshe waiting for him, he didn't slow down or even utter a greeting. Instead, he whipped his horse and spurred it onward at a fast trot, passing the Rav without taking notice of him. Rav Moshe stood shaking his head sadly as Avremel's horse galloped off into the distance.

Suddenly, Avremel's horse began to neigh with fear, and it reared its front legs. Terrified, Avremel tried to hold onto the reigns, but it was no use. The frightened horse bucked up and down, throwing Avremel onto the road with a terrifying crash.

As the youth lay there, unconscious, the horse trampled over him several times before galloping away. After finding the horse, it took several strong men to subdue him and lead him back to his stable.

In the meantime, Avremel lay in the street with serious injuries. Rav Moshe, who had witnessed the sorry incident from afar, was the first to reach the youth. He called for water, to bathe the unconscious patient's face. With great difficulty, the stable boy opened his eyes and began to moan in pain. Rav Moshe spoke to him softly, with warmth and love.

"It pains me terribly, my dear friend, to see you in such a state. I warned you that you were in danger, though I never believed that something so terrible would happen. However, thank Hashem you are alive. Don't give up hope. Trust in our Merciful Father and He will heal your wounds."

As he spoke, the first aid wagon drew up and a team of young men lifted Avremel gently. He screamed with pain, as many of his bones were broken from the fall and from the trampling by the horse.

He was taken to the hospital, where the doctors ascertained that he had a cracked skull, as well as broken bones in his arms and legs. However, with good medical care and numerous surgeries, he would recover.

Rav Moshe did not leave the patient's bedside, tending to him as a mother tends her sick child. He kept encouraging Avremel, telling him that Hashem would heal him in due time.

"Does Hashem even heal sinful people like myself?" said Avremel in a barely audible voice.

"Of course," said Rav Moshe Sofer. "The *Ribono shel Olam* is a merciful Father. He helps any Jew who turns to Him and begs Him for assistance."

Avremel's eyes filled with tears. He could have spared himself so much pain and suffering had he listened to the Rav's warning. But he was greatly heartened by Rav Moshe's assurances that it still was not too late.

A long road to recovery lay ahead for Avremel. He remained in the hospital for nearly a year, undergoing numerous surgeries to straighten out his limbs. During this entire time, Rav Moshe visited him on a regular basis and bolstered him with words of *chizuk*.

During this period, while at the mercy of the doctors, Avremel became humbled and contrite, eager to listen to words of *chizuk*. His pain and suffering transformed him from an ignorant stable boy into an avid disciple of the future Chasam Sofer. He anxiously awaited Rav Moshe's visits and thirstily drank from the knowledge and ideas the Rav shared with him.

"I am grateful for all my suffering and pain," he once expressed to Rav Moshe, "because that is how I merited doing *teshuvah* and recognizing the emptiness of my former life. Were it not for my fall, I would have spent the rest of my days in darkness, an unrepentant sinner until the end. Yet I am still so ashamed! I have sinned so much during my twenty-six years on this world. How can I ever cleanse my soul?"

Rav Moshe comforted him, assuring him that he was a true *baal teshuvah*, greatly beloved by Hashem. He promised Avremel that he wouldn't abandon him and would teach him everything about Yiddishkeit. When Avremel was finally released from the hospital, he became Rav Moshe's ardent disciple. Rav Moshe began teaching him Aleph Bais, then progressed to *Chumash*, *Rashi* and finally *gemara*. For two years, Rav Moshe, the future Torah giant, learned for Avremel for several hours each day!

After two years, Rav Moshe left Frankfurt and followed his great teacher Rav Nasan Adler to Boskowitz. By that time, the *baal teshuvah* was already a budding *talmid chacham* in his own right and continued learning with the *baalebatim* of the city. Gone were his days as a stable boy, and his former lowly lifestyle. Avremel had undergone a transformation.

A SANDEK at the BRIS

Reb Asher Reuven, a well-off merchant, was an ardent *chassid* of the Tzemach Tzedek of Lubavitch. His wealth and social status made him unwilling to endure the hardships of travel to his Rebbe with the other *chassidim* in a rickety wagon. Instead, he hired Yerucham, a simple coachman, to take him to Lubavitch in a well-padded coach, wait for him several days and drive him home.

On one of Reb Asher Reuven's visits, the Tzemach Tzedek expressed an interest in Yerucham and his *parnassah*. The merchant was surprised at the *tzaddik*'s interest in a simple wagon driver, but he related that Yerucham was an upright, though illiterate, fellow. And another thing. He was also a certified *mohel*.

"The next time you come to Lubavitch, I want to meet Yerucham," the Tzemach Tzedek declared. Reb Asher Reuven was eager to do his Rebbe's bidding. Several months later, when he again planned to spend Shabbos with the Rebbe, he made sure to hire Yerucham to drive him. When they arrived in Lubavitch, Reb Asher Reuven immediately rushed to the Rebbe to tell him that Yerucham was in town. The Rebbe's face lit up with joy.

"Please invite him to my home, as I want to meet him," the Rebbe commanded. Reb Asher Reuven, ever the faithful *chassid*, hurried to do the Rebbe's bidding. He rushed to the inn where his wagon driver was staying and informed him that he was wanted at the Rebbe's home.

But Reb Asher Reuven was in for a surprise. The simple wagon driver categorically refused to go to the Rebbe.

"I don't have any connection with your Rebbe!" he snapped. "Just leave me to my own devices."

Reb Asher Reuven did not give up so easily, however. The Rebbe's request was his command.

"Well, then, you can go back home and I will find another driver to take me back," he declared.

Now, Yerucham had no choice but to comply. After all, a large sum of money was at stake. Grudgingly, he followed Reb Asher Reuven to the Rebbe's home. The Rebbe greeted him warmly, as if he had been a distinguished Rav.

"*Shalom aleichem*, Reb Yerucham," said the Tzemach Tzedek. "I would like to have the honor of dining with you tomorrow evening."

Instead of being delighted at the invitation, Yerucham turned his head away, clearly unwilling. Using his powers of persuasion, Reb Asher Reuven again reminded him that he would send for another coachman, if necessary. Finally, Yerucham agreed to come.

The Tzemach Tzedek instructed his *gabbaim* to prepare a festive *seudah* for the following evening when all the *chassidim* would attend. The guest of honor, of course, would be Yerucham.

The *chassidim* were puzzled. No one could understand why he merited such an honor. Many of them flocked to the inn where Yerucham was staying, trying to ask him questions and determine why he had found favor with the Rebbe. Perhaps he was one of the thirty-six hidden *tzaddikim*? Or maybe he was a distant relative of the Rebbe? But the more they prodded the brusque, boorish man, the more they saw he was simply a coarse peasant, undeserving of the Rebbe's attention.

There must be a hidden meaning to the Rebbe's intent, they decided. In the meantime, they observed Yerucham closely as he went about his business, drinking in the tavern with the other wagon drivers and acting as ordinary as could be.

Finally, the following evening, everyone gathered in the Rebbe's home. The tables were bedecked with snow-white tablecloths, and candles were lit, adding a Yom Tov-like aura. The Rebbitzen had prepared a feast fit for a king: fresh challah, sweet carp fish, pungent chicken soup with *kneidlach* and roast meat.

The Rebbe sat at the head of the table, beaming with joy, and Yerucham, dressed in a spotless white shirt and black kaftan, sat at his right side. Though at first he was morose and sullen, as the meal wore on, the wine loosened his tongue until he began to smile and feel at ease.

During the meal, the *chassidim* began to sing spirited *niggunim*, and then the Rebbe related *divrei Torah*. It was an elevating, spiritual *farbreng*, though no one was aware of any *yahrtzeit* or special occasion that would warrant such a festive meal. They all sensed, however, that it was somehow related to their guest, whose ruddy face and wild gestures made it obvious that he had downed one drink too many. Soon, his head began to drop and he dozed off, his snores echoing across the room. The *chassidim* shook their heads in puzzlement, unable to understand what the great Rebbe had seen in this simple man.

Finally, towards the end of the *seudah*, one of the closest *chassidim* dared to ask the Rebbe what the special occasion was. "Is it, perhaps, a *yahrtzeit* of an unknown Chassidic Rebbe?" he ventured.

The Rebbe shook his head, smiling. "I simply wanted to have the pleasure of eating with a Yid who merited to share a meal with Avraham Avinu!"

The Rebbe's words hit the *chassidim* like a thunderbolt. That simple coachman had once shared a meal with Avraham Avinu? Impossible! But if the Rebbe said so, it had to be true.

Soon the Rebbe bentched over a *becher* of wine and the meal was over. The Rebbe entered his private study and the *gabbaim* began clearing the tables. The *chassidim* remained, still puzzling over the mystery.

After a while, Yerucham awoke, rubbed his eyes sleepily and tried to stand up, unsure of where he was. "W-where am I?" he asked groggily.

"You are in the Rebbe's home, at a special *seudah* in your honor," several *chassidim* replied. "In fact, we are trying to figure out the mystery. Perhaps you can help us?"

Yerucham sleepily shook his head. "Me? Help you?" he asked. "I don't understand it, either. I am just a simple man, a coachman, and I never had the opportunity to learn more than a little *Mishnayos.*"

"Is there anything special you did recently?" the *chassidim* pressed on. "Did you see a *tzaddik* with a long, white beard? Did he come to your home to eat with you?"

"What are you talking about?" Yerucham snapped. "Stop bothering me with your questions. I am not in the habit of receiving visitors to my one-room hovel, certainly not men with long white beards."

But the *chassidim* would not relent. They held onto him tightly, steadying him as they walked him to the inn where he was staying.

"You must tell us why the Rebbe invited you to eat with him," they persisted.

"How can I tell you something I don't know myself?"

Seeing that they were getting nowhere, the *chassidim* decided to reveal the Rebbe's words. "The Rebbe told us that you merited to share a meal with Avraham Avinu."

Hearing these words, Yerucham blanched. "That tall man in the woods was Avraham Avinu?" he asked. "Woe is me that I didn't honor him properly. But how could I have known?"

Seeing that they were stumbling on a remarkable story, the *chassidim* gestured to each other to stay until the end of the tale. They arrived at the inn and sat around the table, signaling to the innkeeper to bring Yerucham a hot glass of tea. Yerucham sipped slowly, sucking on a cube of sugar. The *chassidim* sat impatiently, waiting for him to begin his tale.

"Nu?" one *chassid* prompted. "What happened to you in the woods?"

Seeing that he had no choice, Yerucham launched into his tale.

As you know, I am a wagon driver, and my main specialty is driving wealthy merchants to distant towns. In addition to Reb Asher Reuven, I have several other steady customers whom I often take on business trips. Often these trips take me to distant villages where only a handful of Yidden live without a shul or *minyan*. I feel sorry for these abandoned Jews, living so far away from their Source.

In addition to their daily difficulties of finding *melamdim* for the children, arranging for a *shochet* to slaughter their meat and having a *minyan* for the Yamim Tovim, one of their most pressing problems is making a *bris* for their newborn sons. Often, weeks and months go by without a single certified *mohel* appearing in their forsaken *shtetl*; so innocent Jewish newborns often have to wait a long time to receive their *brissin*.

The *chassidim* nodded knowingly, aware of the problem. *Nebach*, for *parnassah* or other reasons, some Yidden lived so far away from the centers of Yiddishkeit that they slowly lost contact with their Source and slowly abandoned tenets of Yiddishkeit, such as *bris milah*.

Anyhow, continued Yerucham, after a while, I began to pity these innocent babies who are deprived of their *bris milah*, and I decided to rectify matters of my own accord. Thus, I begged one of the professional *mohalim* in my hometown to teach me how to become a *mohel* and he agreed.

After attending many *brissin* as his assistant and doing several *brissin* on my own, I was confident that I knew how to perform *bris milah* according to halacha. Thus, along with my personal belongings, I always kept the tools of my trade: a sharp knife, bandages and other necessities. It didn't take long for my expertise in this area to become known, and soon I was performing *brissin* in distant villages on a steady basis. In fact, the Jewish villagers in these far-flung *shtetls* eagerly awaited my arrival and sent me messages whenever a baby boy was born. I was able to perform many *brissin* on children who might otherwise have waited several months for their *bris*.

Just several weeks ago, Yerucham continued, unaware of the looks of admiration he was receiving from the *chassidim,* I was hired by a wealthy timber merchant to travel to a distant *shtetl* on the Ukrainian border where he wanted to conclude a business deal. He would remain there for a while and I would go back home, coming back to pick him up a week later.

We set out on our journey before dawn on a blustery, windy day, when only the hardiest of souls dared to venture outdoors. After several hours of riding through a dense forest, we arrived at the village, a tiny appendage to a larger, gentile town some kilometers away. As usual, I had taken my *mohel* implements along, though I was convinced that no Yidden lived in that forsaken *shtetl*.

I dropped off the businessman at the local tavern and stopped for a while to rest and eat the simple meal I had taken along, washed down by a glass of tea. The stable boy fed my horses, and I waited for them to rest and recoup their strength. Finally, toward late afternoon as the sun was beginning to set, I prepared the horse and buggy and made my way home.

I had only been traveling through the forest for several moments when a light snow began to fall. Within a short while, my path was completely obstructed and I began driving blindly, not knowing where to turn. Soon I realized that I was lost, and would have to find some shelter for the night.

I continued down a small dirt trail in the woods hoping I

would see a light shining in the distance. And then I heard it — a small, faint cry of a newborn infant.

"Somewhere, there is a home among the trees," I realized, and spurred my horse toward that direction. Before long, I noticed a tiny hovel standing in the middle of nowhere, surrounded by a thick copse of trees.

I dismounted, tied my horse and knocked on the door, my body soaked from the snow, my hands nearly frostbitten. It was opened by a gaunt, sickly young woman, who held a well-wrapped newborn baby.

"Who are you?" she asked suspiciously. "What brings you here?"

I explained that I was a Jewish wagon driver who had lost my bearings and I was looking for a place to spend the night.

Hearing the word Jewish, her face lit up and she ushered me inside. "I am so glad you came," she said. "My husband is dying and I was afraid there would be nobody to say *viduy* with him. I sent a gentile neighbor to get the Jews in the next village, but nobody was able to come back in this weather."

She gestured to a rickety bed in the corner of the room where a young man was dying, his face white as the sheet that covered him. "He has been coughing for a long time, but we could not afford money for the doctor," she said. "A few days ago, our first child, a boy, was born." She began to sob as she said, "The poor, innocent baby will never know his father. How will I raise him on my own?"

"When was he born?" I asked, noticing that the baby appeared healthy and hale despite his impoverished surroundings.

"Exactly a week ago to this day," said the poor woman.

"Then he needs a *bris milah* today," I said, realizing that Hashem had brought me to that forsaken hovel.

"*Bris milah?*" she stared at me as if I were hallucinating. "Who can think about a *bris milah* when my husband is dying? And besides, where would I find a *mohel* in this tiny village, with the nearest Jewish community so far away!"

"Do not worry," I reassured her. "The *Ribono shel Olam* has sent me here to help you. I am a certified *mohel* and I will perform the *bris* on your son. It is nearly dark so we have only a short time. Is your husband able to be the *sandek*?"

"My husband?" she echoed. "Go and see if there is any life in him. For three days now he has been hovering between life and death."

I walked over to the poor, dying man and realized that he only had a few more hours to live. According to halacha, it is forbidden to touch a *goseis*, someone close to death. But how could I perform the *bris* without a *sandek* to hold the baby?

In desperation, I went outside, hoping against hope that someone would pass by. But it was a futile dream. The weather was worsening, with heavy snow falling, blocking the roadway. My poor horse was nearly frozen; I led him to a small shelter under the trees where he would be protected from the elements. I realized that I would have to remain in that small hovel overnight because I would not survive a snowy night in the woods.

I waited for several moments, but no one showed up. Desperation took hold of me as I whispered a fervent *tefillah* to the *Ribono shel Olam*. "*Hakadosh Baruch Hu, please send me a Jewish man so that I can perform the bris on this innocent baby before the day has passed.*"

Suddenly, as I finished my *tefillah*, I noticed the outline of a tall man in the distance. He walked through the snowstorm as if the weather did not affect him at all. I ran toward him, suffused with excitement. I noticed that he had a snow-white beard and an otherworldly expression. *Perhaps he was an apparition?* I wondered. But my desperation forced me to try.

"Reb Yid, please come with me!" I begged. "I need a *sandek* so I can perform a *bris* on a Jewish baby."

But the man continued walking as if he had not heard me.

"Reb Yid!" I begged again. "Please, it is very important that you come with me to be a *sandek* for a little baby boy."

But the elderly man with the snow-white beard continued walking right past me. In desperation, I ran after him and grabbed him by his coattails. He pushed me aside with remarkable strength.

"You must come with me, do you hear?" I cried, tears choking my voice. "For Hashem's sake, please help me! A baby boy needs a *bris* and there is no more time!"

The elderly man stopped and stared at me, a look that pierced me to my soul. Then he turned and followed me into the hut. There was no time to spare. It was nearly dark. I quickly prepared my implements, gave the baby to the *sandek* and performed the *bris*. The overjoyed mother thanked me profusely.

I took care of the baby and bandaged his wound, then turned to the *sandek*. "You are free to go now," I said. "Thank you very much for your help. You had a great merit today."

The elderly man then spoke up for the first time. "Now that the child had a *bris,* we must make a *seudah*, as is the custom by Yidden."

I stared at him, surprised. "What do you want, some cake and *schnapps*? Don't you see there is not a morsel of food in the house?"

But the elder was not deterred. "We must make a *seudas mitzvah*," he said. Then I remembered that I had some bread in my sack, still inside the wagon. I braved the weather and went to get my food sack, where I found some dry bread and a small bottle of *schnapps*. I put the "meal" on the table and invited the elderly *sandek* to take part in the *seudah*.

But the mysterious guest was still not happy. "How can we

make a *seudah* without the father of the baby?" he asked.

"Don't you see the father is dying?" I retorted.

But the elderly man made believe he didn't hear me. With incredible strength, he walked over to the sickbed, took the dying man by the hand and pulled him out of bed. Wonder of wonders! The dying man stood up, and slowly the color returned to his face. Supported by the *sandek,* he made his way to the table and feebly took part in the meal. By the time we had finished eating the bread and drinking the *schnapps,* the father of the baby looked completely healthy, as if he had never been ill!

His wife, who had given him up for dead, began to shout with excitement. "It's a miracle!" she cried. "Blessed is Hashem Who has brought the dead back to life!"

I don't know how it happened, but in the ensuing commotion, the old man quietly disappeared. I tried to run after him, but it was as if the earth had swallowed him up.

The *chassidim* looked at each other, in awe at the greatness of this "simple" Jew.

"Do you realize with whom you had the merit of sharing a meal?" they inquired. "Your guest that day at the *seudas bris* was none other than Avraham Avinu."

The Tzemach Tzedek, with his *ruach hakodesh,* had sensed the great *zechus* of Yerucham and thus was eager to invite him to a special *seudah.*

SAVED
by the
SHABBOS QUEEN

It was 1831, the notorious year of the Polish Uprising, when the long-suffering Polish Patriots organized a rebellion against their Russian overlords, successfully driving them out of Warsaw in January. However, later that year, the Russians managed to regroup and capture Warsaw, wreaking havoc in their thirst for vengeance.

Yossel was a pious Yid who managed an inn in a little *shtetl* near Kovno. His inn was well-known in the entire vicinity as the best place to get a good meal and a warm drink of vodka, along with a comfortable bed to stay the night. Yossel's wife cooked hearty dinners to feed their steady guests, who swarmed to the inn from the entire vicinity. In fact, members of the Polish nobility frequented his inn, where wine flowed like water and the meals were plentiful.

Late one Friday afternoon, shortly after the Russians had recaptured Warsaw, a Russian general and his entire regiment arrived in the *shtetl*. They were weary and exhausted after a skirmish with the Polish Patriots near Warsaw. By the time the noisy soldiers set up their camp, it was already past sunset, and they were bone-tired and in a restless mood. The general wisely realized that the best recourse was to ply them with wine so they would become drunk and sleep soundly.

"Where can I get some good ale and wine for my men?" the general asked the locals.

"The best place is Yossel's inn," the townspeople were quick to oblige.

The general wasted no time in sending some of his men over to the inn to buy as much wine as they could carry.

The noisy soldiers marched through the darkened streets singing rowdy tunes. The streets were deserted at that hour and mostly dark. But in the Jewish section of the village, the modest Jewish homes were aglow with the light of candles reflecting into the street. As the soldiers passed the homes, they smelled the heavenly aroma of freshly baked challah and chicken soup. The strains of happy *zemiros* wafted out of the open windows as families sat around the Shabbos table, savoring the contentment and bliss.

Soon the soldiers had reached Yossel's inn at the edge of town, which was identified by the large sign upon his door. However, to their surprise, the door to the tavern was tightly bolted and the tavern itself was dark. In the back was the family living quarters, where the candlesticks glowed softly.

The men knocked loudly at the back door. The door swung open, and the soldiers stood facing the master of the house who was dressed in his Shabbos *kapoteh*, his face aglow with the serenity of the holy day.

"Yes, may I help you?" Yossel asked courteously.

"We are soldiers in the Russian army. We've come to buy wine for our troops," the eldest of the soldiers explained.

Yossel didn't flinch or quaver as he replied, "I am sorry, but I cannot sell you any wine tonight. It is our holy Sabbath and my tavern is closed."

The soldiers were surprised, to put it mildly. They thought that the *Zhid* would have been thrilled to make some money. They tried to reason with him, but Yossel would not budge. "I am sorry, but I do not do business on Shabbos."

The soldiers trooped back to their general and reported on the strange Jew. When he heard the tale, the general flew into a rage.

"Tell that *Zhid* he had better sell us some wine or he will pay dearly for his arrogance!" the general snapped. "Perhaps he is a Polish sympathizer. He ought to be hanged for treason! He had better cooperate with us or his life is not worth a rubbed-out *kopek*!"

The emboldened soldiers marched back to Yossel's home, and knocked on the door once again. When Yossel opened, they repeated the general's threat.

Yossel listened calmly and replied, "You can tell your honored general that I am not a Polish sympathizer and do not want to give him a hard time. However, I cannot do business on the Sabbath. Yet I am prepared to give him the keys to my wine cellar so that he can come and help himself to as much wine as he needs, on the house."

The soldiers were shocked at these words. They rushed back to the general and repeated Yossel's offer. Now it was the general's turn to be surprised. "The Jew is bolder than I thought," he decided, "and also very brave."

The general resolved to go to Yossel's home and meet the brave Jew in the flesh. He joined the delegation that went to Yossel's home for the third time that night.

The general knocked softly and the door opened almost immediately. Yossel had been expecting his guests.

"Come in, honored guests!" he said warmly.

The general, though, was reluctant to enter. He remained standing at the door, mesmerized, absorbing the powerful scene.

Yossel's wife and children were sitting around a table decked with a bright white tablecloth and piled with Shabbos foods. The candles burned brightly, reflecting the eager faces of the children as they sat respectfully around the table dressed in their Shabbos best.

The general finally allowed himself to be persuaded to sit down at the table and take a glass of hot tea.

As he sipped the beverage, the general's anger and hurt at Yossel's behavior began to evaporate. In a voice that was almost human, he asked, "Why did you refuse to sell wine to my men? Do you know that during wartime such an act is tantamount to treason?"

"I do," replied Yossel. "However, I still cannot sell you wine on my Sabbath because it is against my religion. We are forbidden to do business on the seventh day of the week. The King of all kings, our holy Creator, has forbidden us to do so. However, we'd like to invite you to join our festive meal. It will be our honor to host you. By doing so, we will be fulfilling our Torah's commandment to be hospitable to guests."

The general and his men sat down at Yossel's urging and were treated to a plentiful meal. Gefilte fish, hot chicken soup with dumplings, roast chicken … all the trimmings. They ate their fill, and when they were done, Yossel escorted them to the wine cellar and told them to take as much wine as they needed. The general took several gold coins out of his pocket and offered them to Yossel. Though the coins were worth a small fortune, Yossel did not even glance at them. "I cannot handle money on my Sabbath," he said.

"So I will send you the money on Sunday," the general said.

Yossel shook his head. "I don't want to accept money for my hospitality," he explained. "This is my special gift to you."

"I will never forget you," vowed the general as he left, soldiers in tow.

The general's men lugged several barrels of wine to the rest of the regiment, and the atmosphere became merry and joyous. The soldiers soon drowned their exhaustion in drink, but the general could not allow himself to join in their revelry. He was still in awe of his visit to the tavern on Yossel's holy day. A few days later, the regiment left town and was never seen or heard from again.

Many years passed. The crisis of 1831 was, by now, a distant memory. Yossel's elder children were grown and some of them had married and lived in other cities. Yossel's tavern continued to flourish as he attracted customers by virtue of his gentle personality and his wife's good cooking.

One spring, the inn began to be frequented by high-ranking Polish generals who sat for hours sipping ale and talking about secret matters. After a week or so, Yossel grew uneasy and hinted for them to leave. However, the damage was done.

Several days later, Jan Piotrokowski, one of the noblemen, was arrested and charged with plotting to overthrow the Russian leadership. In the incriminating documents found on his person, the name "Yossel's Inn" was mentioned several times as a central meeting place and a cover for spying activity.

The Russians wasted no time. They burst into Yossel's tavern the next day and, ignoring the cries of his family, carted him away in chains. Yossel was dragged to the local dungeon where he was fettered with an iron ball to prevent his escape.

For several weeks, Yossel wasted away in prison while his frantic family and friends rallied for his release. *Tehillim* was recited, fasts were proclaimed and attempts were made to bribe the local Russian authorities to win Yossel's release. However, as the weeks went by without success, his concerned friends began to despair.

Though Yossel knew he was innocent, he realized that his situation was grim, indeed. He knew the Russians did not take charges of spying lightly and the best he could hope for was deportation to Siberia where he would die of frostbite, starvation or exhaustion. Either that, or he would face a quick and merciful death by firing squad.

Yossel also realized that a guilty verdict would not only seal his own doom, but it would mean trouble for all the Jews in the vicinity. No Jew would be above suspicion.

Thus, he spent his days davening and crying to the Father of all prisoners to redeem him and prove his innocence.

The day of his trial loomed closer. Early one morning, Yossel sat on the floor of his cell, davening with all his heart, when suddenly the door burst open and a high-ranking official strutted in. The official, who had come all the way from Moscow, was checking up on prisoners accused of spying. Yossel squinted in the pale morning light, certain that the man was familiar. However, try as he might, he could not place him.

Emaciated and weak, Yossel was but a shadow of his former self. During the weeks of his imprisonment, he had lost a great deal of weight and was now bent and stooped. However, the high-ranking visitor had no trouble identifying him.

"Yossel!" the general exclaimed in astonishment. "What are you doing here?"

Instantly, Yossel realized who his illustrious visitor was. He was none other than the former general who had been stationed in his hometown some years ago.

Yossel related the entire story of his capture. The general listened intently and said, "Your trial is scheduled for two days hence. I plan to attend." After he left, Yossel continued to daven and beg *Hakadosh Baruch Hu* for a miracle.

The day of Yossel's trial arrived. He was dragged to the courthouse in chains and shoved onto a bench. When his name came up, the high-ranking general who had been in his home vouched for his generosity and goodness. "It is impossible to believe that this man would be capable of spying," he said to the judge, describing Yossel's strength of character.

On the basis of the general's testimony, Yossel was set free. He went home joyfully to his family. When his wife later asked how he was saved, Yossel replied, "Why, the queen herself personally interceded on my behalf."

"The queen? Which queen?"

"Oh ... the Shabbos queen, of course," replied Yossel.

GLOSSARY

Agunah — a woman whose husband is missing and who cannot remarry because her husband might still be alive

Aleichem Shalom –

Aleph Bais — the Hebrew alphabet

Aliyah — being called up to make a blessing on the public Torah reading

Alleh maylos (Yidd.) — every good quality

Almanah — widow

Amein — Amen

Amud — podium from where the prayers in the synagogue are led

Askan, askanim — those involved in community affairs

Avodah zarah — idolatry

Avraham Avinu — Abraham our forefather

Avreich — a man learning in kollel

Az Yashir — the Song at the Sea, recited by the Jewish people after the Splitting of the Sea

B'ezras Hashem — with the Almighty's help

B'nei Torah — Torah students

Baal bitachon — one who trusts in Hashem

Baal chessed, baalei chessed — those who regularly perform acts of kindness

Baal emunah — one who has faith in Hashem

Baal habayis — householder

Baal teshuvah — one who returns to Torah observance

Baal tzedakah — charitable person

Baalebatishe (Yidd.) — characteristic of a householder

Baalebos, baalebatim (Yidd.) — householder(s)

Baalebuste (Yidd.) — housewife

Bachur, bachurim — young, single Jewish male(s)

Bais Hamikdash — the Holy Temple

Bais Medrash — house of Torah study

Bar Mitzvah — the age of thirteen, at which a Jewish male becomes obligated to follow the Torah's commandments

Bareich Aleinu — the blessing for livelihood

Baruch Hashem — thank Hashem

Becher (Yidd.) — valuable drinking cup

Bentching — reciting the Grace after Meals

Ben Torah — a student of Torah

Besht — acronym for the Baal Shem Tov, founder of Chassidus

Bimah — platform in the synagogue from where the Torah scroll is read publicly

Birkas Kohanim — blessing delivered by the Kohanim, the Jewish priestly class, to their fellow Jews

Bitachon — trust in the Almighty

Borei p'ri hagafen — blessing over wine

Brachah/Brachos — blessing(s)

Brachah l'vatalah — a blessing made in vain

Bris milah — circumcision

Bris, brissin — circumcision(s)

Bubbe (Yidd.) — grandmother

Chacham, chachamim — Torah sage(s)

Chalila — Heaven forbid

Chalitzah — ceremony that releases a childless man's widow from the obligation to marry her husband's brother

Challah — special braided bread eaten on the Sabbath and holidays

Chanukah — holiday that commemorates the victory of the Jews over the Seleucid Greek armies

Chas v'shalom — Heaven forbid

Chasdei Hashem — (thanks to) the kindnesses of the Almighty

Chassan — groom

Chassid, chassidim — devoted follower(s) of a Rebbe

Chassidus — lit., "piety"; a movement that began in Eastern Europe in the eighteenth century in response to what some felt was the dry academicism of Jewish life. Chassidus stressed the spiritual and joyful elements of Jewish life.

Chazal — acronym for "our Sages, of blessed memory"

Chazzan — cantor

Cheder — Jewish primary school

Cheirem — excommunication

Chesed — kindness

Chevrah — fellows

Chiddush — original insight

Chiddushei Torah — original Torah-related insight

Chizuk — emotional support

Chodesh — month

Cholent — traditional Sabbath stew

Chometz — leavened bread, which is forbidden on Passover

Chumash — the Five Books of Moses

Chutzpah — brazenness

D'var Mitzvah — a matter relating to a Torah commandment

D'var Torah, divrei Torah — Torah thought(s)

D'veikus — close attachment to the Almighty

Daven (Yidd.) — pray

Davening (Yidd.) — praying, prayer

David Hamelech — David, King of Israel

Din Torah — a judicial case brought before a Jewish court

Eibeshter (Yidd.) — the Almighty

Eliyahu Hanavi — Elijah the Prophet

Elul — the last month of the Jewish year

Emunah — faith

Emunas chachamim — faith in our Sages

Eretz Yisrael — the Land of Israel

Erev Pesach — the day before Passover

Erev Shabbos — Friday

Essen teg (Yidd.) — a rotation system in which Torah students were hosted for meals by members of the local Jewish community

Farbreng (Yidd.) — joyous gathering

Farfel (Yidd.) — cooked barley

Frum (Yidd.) — religiously observant

G'vir — a wealthy supporter of the Jewish community

Gabbai, gabbaim — synagogue manager(s) or charity collector(s)

Gabbai tzedakah — agent appointed to collect and distribute charity funds

Gadol, gedolim — Torah giant(s)

Galus HaShechinah — the exile of the Almighty's Presence

Gan Eden — the Garden of Eden

Gadol hador / Gedolei hador — Torah leaders of a generation

Galus — exile

Gemara (Aram.) — Talmud

Gemara kup (Yidd.) — a mind well attuned to studying Talmud

Get — divorce document

Gevald (Yidd.) — help!

Gezeira — decree

Gilyon (Aram.) — notebook

Haggadah — the guide and prayer book for the Passover Seder

Hakadosh Baruch Hu — the Holy One, Blessed be He

Halacha — Torah law

Ha Lachma Anya — lit., "this is the bread of affliction"; words recited at the beginning of the Passover Seder

Hallel — psalms of praise, specifically Psalms 113–118, recited on certain holidays

Hashem — the Almighty

Hashgacha pratis — Divine providence

Hatzlachah — success

Hekdesh — poorhouse

Heter — permission based on Torah law

Hilchos Treifos — the laws of physical defects that render an animal not kosher

Hishtadlus — effort

Iluy — genius

Im yirtzeh Hashem — if the Almighty desires it

K'zaysim — olive-size portions

Kabbalas Shabbos — psalms recited to usher in the Sabbath

Kaddish — prayer for the exaltation of the Almighty's name, often recited by mourners

Kadesh — the first part of the Passover Seder, a blessing on the sanctity of the day

Kaftan — a man's cloak buttoned down the front, with full sleeves, and worn with a sash

Kallah — bride

Kapoteh (Yidd.) — long men's dress coat

Kapparah — atonement

Kashrus — kosher status

Kavanah — intent

Kedushah — holiness

Kehillah — congregation

Kibud eim — respect for one's mother

Kichel (Yidd.) — type of cookie

Kiddush — blessing that sanctifies the Sabbath or Yom Tov

Kiddush Hashem — sanctification of Hashem's name

Kinderlach (Yidd.) — children

Kislev — third month of the Jewish year

Kittel (Yidd.) — a white robe that serves as a burial shroud for male Jews and is worn by adult Jewish males on Yom Kippur and, according to many, at the Passover Seder

Klal Yisrael — the nation of Israel

Kneidlach (Yidd.) — dumplings

Kollel — full-time program of study for married Jewish men

Kopek — a monetary unit of Russia

Kosel — the Western Wall

Krechz (Yidd.) — groan

Kriyas haTorah — public reading from the Torah scroll in the synagogue

Kriyas Shema — recital of the Shema, the fundamental Jewish prayer that proclaims the unity of the Almighty

Kreutzer — a silver coin and currency unit in the Southern German states prior to the unification of Germany, and in Austria

Kugel (Yidd.) — baked puddings, usually of noodles or potatoes; a traditional Sabbath and holiday food

Kvelling (Yidd.) — smiling radiantly

Kvittel, Kvittlech (Yidd.) — note(s)

L'chaim — to life

Lamdan — learner

Lishmah — for its own sake

Maariv — evening prayer

Machnis orach — one who is hospitable to guests

Maggid — the part of the Passover Seder in which the story of the Exodus is retold

Mah Nishtana — the Four Questions that the youngest child asks at the Passover Seder

Makom kavua — established seat in the synagogue

Malach — angel

Maror — bitter herbs

Masmid — studious person

Matzah/Matzos — unleavened bread eaten on Passover

Matzliach — successful

Mazel — fortune

Mazel tov — good luck

Medrash — part of the Oral Torah

Melamed, melamdim — teacher(s)

Melavah malkah — meal eaten on Saturday night to escort away the Sabbath

Meshumad — one who converts from Judaism to another religion

Middos — character traits

Midrashim — homiletic teachings of the Bible

Mikvah — ritual bath

Mincha — afternoon prayer

Minyan — quorum of ten adult Jewish males necessary for public prayer

Mishnayos — the Oral Torah as codified by Rabbi Yehuda Hanasi

Mitzvah, mitzvos — Torah commandment(s)

Mizrach — the eastern wall in the synagogue, traditionally a place of honor

Mofes, mofsim — miracle(s)

Mohel, mohalim — those trained to perform circumcision

Motzaei Yom Tov — the night after a holiday

Mussaf — the additional prayer recited on Sabbath and holidays

Nachas — pleasure

Nebach (Yidd.) — a pity

Ner tamid — the eternal light

Neshamah, neshamos — soul(s)

Niggun, niggunim — Jewish melody(ies)

Nisayon — spiritual trial

Olam Habah — the World to Come

Oveid Hashem — servant of the Almighty

Parnas — supporter

Parnassah — livelihood

Parshas — the weekly Torah portion of

Pasuk — verse

Payos — sidelocks

Pesach — Passover

Pidyon — redemption

Pidyon shevuyim — redemption of captives

Poolish (Yidd.) — antechamber of a synagogue

Poritz, p'ritzim (Yidd.) — wealthy landowner(s)

Rabbanim — rabbis

Rabiner — rabbi

Rashi — acronym for Rabbi Shlomo Yitzchaki (1040–1105), famous for his classic commentaries on the Bible and Talmud

Rav — rabbi

Reb — honorable title, like "sir"

Rebbe — Chassidic leader; Torah teacher

Rebbitzen (Yidd.) — rabbi's wife

Refael — the angel of healing

Refuah — healing

Ribono shel Olam — Master of the Universe

Rosh Chodesh — the beginning of a new month in the Jewish calendar

Rosh Hashanah — the Jewish New Year

Rosh Yeshiva / Roshei Yeshiva — head of a yeshiva / heads of yeshivas

Ruach hakodesh — holy spirit, Divine guidance

Sandek — one who holds a baby boy during his circumcision

Satan — the angel appointed by Hashem to entice people to sin, to accuse them after they sin, and to execute judgement

Schnapps (Yidd.) — whisky

Seder — 1. Traditional meal on the first night (or two nights outside of the Land of Israel) of Passover; 2. a Torah learning regimen

Sefer, sefarim — Torah book(s)

Seudah — festive meal

Seudas — festive meal of

Shaatnez — mixture of wool and linen, forbidden by the Torah

Shabbos — the Sabbath

Shabbos Mevarchim — the Sabbath on which a blessing is recited for the upcoming month

Shacharis — morning prayer

Shadchanim — matchmakers

Shailos — questions of Torah law

Shalom aleichem — lit., "peace be upon you"; traditional Jewish greeting

Shamayim — Heaven

Shammas — assistant

Shechinah — the Divine Presence

Shema — prayer that proclaims the unity of the Almighty

Shemos — Exodus

Sheva brachos — festive meal during the seven days following a wedding

Shidduch, shidduchim — marriage match(es)

Shishi — the sixth portion of the public Torah reading on the Sabbath, a mark of honor, but secondary in importance relative to the third portion

Shiur — Torah lecture

Shivah — seven days of mourning for an immediate family member

Shlemazel (Yidd.) — loser

Shliach — messenger

Shlishi — the third portion of the public Torah reading on the Sabbath, a mark of honor

Shmad — decree of forced conversion

Shnorrer (Yidd.) — beggar

Shochet — ritual animal slaughterer

Shofar — ram's horn blown during the prayer service on Rosh Hashanah

Shtadlanim — negotiators

Shteibel, shteiblach (Yidd.) — small, homey synagogue(s)

Shtetl (Yidd.) — village

Shul (Yidd.) — synagogue

Shulchan Aruch — classic work of Torah law

Shulchan Oraich — part of the Passover Seder, the festive meal

Siddurim — prayer books

Simanim — distinguishing signs

Simcha, simchos — joyous occasion(s)

Siyata d'Shmaya (Aram.) — Divine assistance

Sukkos — the festival of Booths, which commemorates how Hashem sheltered the Jewish people during their forty-year stay in the desert

Sugya (Aram.) — topic

Tallis — prayer shawl

Talmid, talmidim — student(s)

Talmidei — students of

Talmid chacham/ Talmidei Chachamim — Torah scholar(s)

Tatteh (Yidd.) — father

Tefillah, tefillos — prayer(s)

Tefillin — phylacteries; black leather boxes containing scrolls with certain Torah portions, worn by adult Jewish men during prayer

Tehillim — Psalms

Tena'im — marriage agreement

Teshuvah — repentance

Teves — the fourth month of the Jewish year, counting from Rosh Hashanah

Tikkun — lit., "repair"; food supplied by the child of a deceased person on the anniversary of the deceased person's death. It is believed that the blessings made over the food act to elevate the soul of the deceased.

Tisch, tischen (Yidd.) — lit. "table"; a gathering of chassidim around their Rebbe

Treif (Yidd.) — not kosher

Tzaar — pain

Tzaddik, tzaddikim — righteous one(s)

Tzarah, tzaros — difficulty(ies)

Tzedakah — charity

Tzenter (Yidd.) — the tenth man needed to complete a *minyan*

Tzimmes (Yidd.) — a traditional Jewish dish in which the main ingredient is diced or sliced carrots

Tzitzis — fringes attached to the corners of a four-cornered garment, as mandated by the Torah for Jewish males

Viduy — confession of sin

Y'rei Shamayim — one who fears and respects the Almighty

Yagon va-anacha — sighing and groaning

Yahrtzeit (Yidd.) — anniversary of someone's death

Yenta — blabbermouth

Yerushalayim — Jerusalem

Yerushalmi — of Jerusalem

Yeshiva, yeshivos — Torah school(s)

Yeshuah, yeshuos — salvation(s)

Yetzer hara — the evil inclination

Yid / Yidden (Yidd.) — Jew / Jews

Yiddishe (Yidd.) — Jewish

Yiddishkeit (Yidd.) — Judaism

Yishuv — the period of initial resettlement by Jews in the land of Israel in the nineteenth and early twentieth centuries

Yom Tov, Yamim Tovim — holiday(s)

Yungeleit (Yidd.) — young men studying in kollel

Yungerman — young man

Z'man — term

Zemiros — Jewish songs

Zaidy, Zeide (Yidd.) — grandfather

Zechus — merit

Zhid — insulting term for "Jew"